THE
MADSTONE

THE
MADSTONE

A Novel

ELIZABETH CROOK

LITTLE, BROWN AND COMPANY
New York Boston London

Little, Brown and Company
Hachette Book Group
1290 Avenue of the Americas, New York, NY 10104
littlebrown.com

First Edition: November 2023

Little, Brown and Company is a division of Hachette Book Group, Inc. The Little, Brown name and logo are trademarks of Hachette Book Group, Inc.

The publisher is not responsible for websites (or their content) that are not owned by the publisher.

The Hachette Speakers Bureau provides a wide range of authors for speaking events. To find out more, go to hachettespeakersbureau.com or email HachetteSpeakers@hbgusa.com.

Little, Brown and Company books may be purchased in bulk for business, educational, or promotional use. For information, please contact your local bookseller or the Hachette Book Group Special Markets Department at special.markets@hbgusa.com.

ISBN 9780316564342
LCCN 2023934038

Printing 1, 2023

LSC-C

Printed in the United States of America

For Charles Butt

THE
MADSTONE

Comfort, Texas
November 1868

Dear Small Tot,

I hope to lay down these events in a manner helpful to you, concerning some days you will probably not fully remember when you get older. I think you will want a clear idea of what occurred. It is plain to me I should do this, as otherwise you might worry over too many hard questions you can't ever answer.

I will arrange for this account to come to you when you are nineteen years of age or greater, not sooner, there being sundry adult matters involved in it.

Currently I am nineteen years of age myself and think it a suitable age for you to read this. That should give you time to of done a few things and known people and figured some of them out. Also to of read books. Amongst the books given or borrowed to me is a autobiography of Benjamin Franklin about his quest at the age of twenty to improve on his morals and scruples. I figure he must of had worthy ideas by the age of nineteen to of even embarked on such a notion, and from what I have seen of you, Tot, I believe you might grow to be equally wise and nineteen would do to read this.

As well, don't read it if you don't want to, on account of you didn't ask for it.

Another point made by Benjamin Franklin was how the best method to live your life over again, if a person might want to, is to put down tracks to recall it even whilst it takes place. He advised noting events on paper. I can't do that on your behalf, as you are but four years old currently and no doubt seen different things from what I did, and seen some of the same things in different lights as well. But I will do what I can to that end.

For myself, I am bound to remember these days I write about until the reaper should come fetch me.

It is not the best paper and my grammar is not perfect but I intend to be truthful and keep to the point and not go on about other things. To get to it, here is how I come to be mixed up in the matter of your life.

I first laid eyes on you earlier in this year, in the town of Comfort, where I live and now am. You will probably not remember the place. It sits just south of the center of Texas if maps is correct in their scale. Folks who live here is mostly Germans who built the town some fifteen years back. There is a few hundred citizens all told. I settled in here a year ago when I give up on some things in my life and a German widow allowed me use of a shed for my carpentry. I make chairs and coffins and tables and such items that might be called for. My specialty is chairs. I lodge in the woman's house, pay board, and work in her shed.

I was stationed out in the yard on a morning in May, six months back from now, shaping the legs of a rocker, when I seen across the street our sheriff enter the privy alongside the livery stable. He had papers for reading and shut hisself in. It is a two seater privy intended for stage travelers, but the sheriff is in the habit of latching the door and keeping the place to hisself whenever he wants, no matter if there is travelers who need in it or not.

Whilst he was shut in the privy a coach of the Ficklin line rolled in and drew up at the livery. It was a mere mud coach, worse for wear, not the Ficklin's best, coming south from Fredericksburg twenty miles off. The mules was jaded. A door of the coach swung open even before the mules come to a halt, whereupon a man sprang out in haste and headed direct to the privy, as a issue must of come over him. His shirt had a ratty aspect, his trousers was shabby, his hair called for a cut and his beard was untidy. He was a stout man. I had not seen him before. He attempted to open the privy door and was shouted at from within by the sheriff. I could not make out the exact words of the sheriff.

The traveler answered back, It's urgent! I need in!

The sheriff denied him again.

The traveler shouted, It's a two seater size! Is there two of you in there! Unlatch the door! He cursed to express he was in a hurry. He said, God damn, can you not understand the bad straights I am in.

He then commenced to pound at the door. A person or two who was passing seen the fuss but did not tarry. I wished I might offer the use of the privy back of the house where I live, but I required the right to do that.

I should tell you our sheriff is not a person to suffer nonsense nor rudeness, nor even excuses from others, no matter his own bad habit to hog the stage privy. He was brought down here from up north by the U.S. army that has took over to see folks abide by the laws and won't go about cheating and mistreating Negroes and local folks who was true to the Union in the war, as that time is meant to be over. He gets along fine with the Germans here, as they had nothing to do with the fight between Yankees and rebel Confederate sesesh. Mostly the Germans tried to escape that, down to Mexico. They are fond of the sheriff and give him all manner of treats and strudel. He wears his Yankee uniform and is friendly with them but not with folks passing through, such as the traveler, as they are often a bad lot and cause strife and yell at the Germans to go back where they come from. The sheriff affords such travelers no second chances, and rightly not, mostly, although on this occasion I thought he might of been nicer, given the man's trouble.

Therefore I tried to warn the traveler of who it was in the privy. I whistled to get his attention but he did not hear me nor turn.

He shouted such things as, I'll kick this door down!

You might think the Ficklin driver would act on the issue, but he did not. The traveler appealed to him, yelling, There's somebody hogging both shitholes! Is there another privy!

The driver paid him no mind. I suppose he had seen worse quarrels. He was old for a driver and missing a ear. He got down from the box in a weary manner, called for the stable boy, hauled a mail sack out of the boot and started across the livery yard to the store with the postal office. He appeared as spent as the mules. It was a warm day, although early.

The stable boy commenced to exchange the mules in harness with a team eager to cut loose. The fresh ones caused a fuss, and he jerked them about and hollered at them in German and put on their blindfolds to get them settled. The fracas jolted the coach and swung the door open. The traveler must of not properly closed it, being in haste to bust out.

That was the moment I seen your mother seated within, and you there alongside her. You was both mostly hid by heaps of parcels and bags of mail piled up around you, however I made out one of you was a child, the other being a woman. I wondered why neither of you had got out to visit the privy nor walk about for a respite, as most people do. Your mother then pulled the door closed. I did not see more after that, on account of the window flaps was all down.

Whilst this happened the traveler give up the shouting, looked about him and seen nobody passing at that moment, it being early, as I have stated. He then jabbed a hole with his boot in the dirt close alongside the privy and squatted and done as he needed.

It was not lucky for him the sheriff come out at that time. The sheriff give him a look of disgust.

The traveler got hisself up and arranged his clothes. I figured he might be sorry to learn how it was a sheriff he had been hollering at. This was not the case, however. He told the sheriff, You son of a bitch. Look what I had to do.

The sheriff said, That is publicly lewd behavior. You'll have to clean that up. You'll need to be fined. I'm charging you with crimes against public morals and decency.

The traveler spat to express he was not sorry.

The sheriff said, There is a steep fine for public indecency.

If this is public indecency, where is the public, the traveler said. There is no public about. I see no public just now. I see a coach with the shades down. I see a store with nobody at the windows. Where is the public. Nobody seen me but you.

The sheriff looked about, and spied me, and called out, Young man! Come over here!

What else could I do but go. I crossed the street to him.

He said, What is your name.

Benjamin Shreve, I told him.

You witnessed what happened here at the privy, did you not, he said.

I owned as I had.

Well then, here is your public, he said to the traveler, and told me to state the particulars of what I had seen occur.

I related the traveler had undertaken to enter the privy, had been denied, had appeared in discomfort, and then had done what he did.

The traveler become heated at hearing events of the wrong inflicted on him recounted. He cursed the sheriff a great deal, to which the sheriff replied there was now two charges, those of public indecency and public profanity. Raise your hands, sir, he said, I need your piece.

The traveler scoffed but done as ordered, and the sheriff disarmed him of a pistol. The sheriff then got fetters out of his belt pouch and said, I am taking you to my office to decide what penalty should incur and collect the charges.

On seeing the fetters, the traveler commenced to beg. He said, I got to get back in the coach. I got business. I got important matters! The coach is fixing to leave soon and I got to be on it!

The sheriff granted no hint he might yield.

I have a through ticket to San Antonio! the traveler said. Name me a fine and I'll pay it, but I got to get back on the coach!

He drew a large money pouch out of his coat to show he could make the payment, but the sheriff ordered he put it away, as papers would have to be signed in his office for proof of the charge and imbursement.

Tot, if I had behaved in a different manner from what I did in that moment, I would now be telling a different account, or none at all. Moments have either a short bend or a long bend in the way they turn how things go, and this one had a long bend to it.

There stood the traveler and sheriff, face to face. And there stood I, called to the situation for being the only public. It was a unlikely pair of men I stood alongside. The traveler was husky and shabby, whilst the sheriff was tidy. The sheriff had made a name for hisself as a Yankee soldier, which I believe was the best side to of been on. But he was mistaken in this occasion.

I thought I might speak up for the traveler and felt a urgent need to do so, and yet my better angel did not advise me of it. And whilst I stood quiet and considered what I might do, I caught sight of you, Tot, looking direct at me from under a window flap in the coach. I seen only your eyes and a small share of your face, but you looked eye to eye with me, and I felt you evaluating my actions. I felt the weight of your expectation, and words was urged to my lips. And yet the voice that come in my ear was my worse angel's. It whispered at me to stay quiet, as who wants to be on the wrong side of the law. I had lived in Comfort but one year, having moved from my home near Camp Verde, and my carpentry business was on the rise. I had nobody but myself to depend on, and I did not want to bring any trouble upon my standing. On that account, I said nothing. I seen your eyes witness my silence from under the flap in the Ficklin, and I felt shame, and yet my mouth remained shut.

The next I seen was the hand of your mother draw you away from the window, and the window flap fall shut. Your judgment of me, whatever it might of been, was not to be seen anymore. This left me to bear the weight of my own judgment of myself, the sort that's hardest to shoulder.

The sheriff then called to the stable boy to bring over a shovel, and he come running with one.

The traveler had a forlorn look whilst he shoveled a hole and buried his shat. He piled the dirt neater than called for, yet the courtesy gained him no favor. When he was done, his wrists was placed in the fetters, even whilst he continued to make his case and ask, in desperate terms, if he might be turned loose. He showed distress at the risk of his rifle and bags going off on the coach without him and repeated a number of times, I need my bags! There's one in the coach and one in the boot. I need to be on the coach. My hat is in there! I got to get to San Antonio and catch a stage out!

The sheriff give me permission to take my leave. Whilst I crossed back over the street I heard him charge the stable boy to let the driver know the traveler was apprehended. He further told the boy to check the waybill and remove the traveler's bags and rifle and hat before the coach should depart. The boy answered in English so I supposed he knew enough of the language to work out the instructions.

I retired into the shed to get tools and my water jug, it being a warm day, although early, as I have aforesaid. Whilst in there, I heard the coach depart. When I come out, the sheriff and traveler was nowhere in sight neither, as they was off to the sheriff's office to settle claims which was, to my thinking, trumped charges.

* * *

For a half a hour or so after this event, I seen nothing unexpected, just folks starting about their morning routines. I returned to my work on the rocker. It was a nice piece in my opinion and better than what the cabinet maker in town turns out, and that is saying a lot. He studied back in the old country of Bohemia and learned his trade in a place called Prog. He turns out good looking furniture named Beedamiyer and does scroll-back in walnut with a cross splat carved like they do it on islands in Greece. I have not been to Greece, nor anywhere else, but that is what he told me. He has asked me to work for him, but I work best on my own. My customers is loyal on account of the fact I am cheaper and my work is just as good. Also I will make a hide seat if requested. The folks here generally do not want hide, but some lack funds for the Beedamiyer and look to the new ways here, not the old ones back there.

I don't know if any of that is of any interest to you.

So for a short time I worked on my rocker. I was powering the lathe and getting warm, as it was hard foot work. The spindles was looking nice, and I was thinking of taking a rest when a rider come charging down the street from the same direction the coach come before, dodging folks and carts and aggravating people. He reined in hard at the livery. His horse was a fine looking roan but must of been rode some distance at a reckless pace, as it was badly lathered and winded.

The rider was dressed in a frock coat and bowler hat and appeared to be greatly agitated. He had a shotgun strapped to his saddle. He alighted and run into the livery calling for assistance. However, he found none to his satisfaction. I heard him exchange but a few words with the stable boy before he come back out in a hurry, seen me across the street working my lathe, and headed my way whilst hollering about there being no mount to be had at the livery.

He said, Do you know of a horse I can let! Mine is played out. I'll pay good money!

I did not care to offer the use of my mare, as she is a good mare, if past her prime, and by the lathered look of his roan I knew the man was a hard rider.

I said, If the livery don't have one, I know of none.

In the whole town, he asked. Not one horse to let.

I said, There might be. I don't know of it.

I did not like the way he seemed to blame me for the fact. He appeared about ten years my senior, perhaps thirty years of age, and his features was decent but there was a meanness about him. His whiskers was dark and thick, not mutton chop but almost. His shirt was nicely pleated, however I noted the buttons was loose. His frock coat was frayed and looked to be made for a man bigger around, like maybe he'd lost some heft of recent. Whereas mostly a belt or suspenders will do on their own, his pants was held up by both. His shoes was fine but appeared to of spent time roaming on soggy ground. He carried a sidearm as well as the shotgun. It was a Colt's revolving belt pistol such as was used in the war.

He bore down a hard look on me, saying, You must know of a person to ask for a horse.

It's not my business to find you a horse, I told him. I got my business here with this rocking chair.

He give me a long stare and I give him one back. He had already made it such that even had I known of a horse, I would not of told him of it, but I knew of none. Comanches was coming through town at nights and helping theirselves to horses.

The man turned about and hollered at folks that was going into the store, Do you know of any mounts to let, buy or trade in this town!

Two men give him a look but declined to answer and went on into the store. They was Germans, and Germans is not by habit the friendliest people.

The man crossed back over the street and went into the store hisself. He must of found no satisfaction by way of a horse for offer, as he come back out in a huff, stomped to the livery, mounted his spent roan, set spurs to it and rode off.

I sat in my yard to rest my foot from the pedal and drink water, and to reflect on the man and to further consider the question of if I might be a coward not to of spoke up to the sheriff on behalf of the traveler at the privy earlier in the morning. I could not get that issue out of my head.

About then, here come the traveler hisself, freed of the fetters and wearing his pistol again, tramping back down the street from the direction the sheriff had took him off in. He went direct into the livery, from where I heard him engage with the stable boy within and commence to argue.

The stable boy shouted in English, despite it sounded like German. He yelled, I do not have blame of your baggage!

The traveler replied, Then where is it! There was two bags! There was one in the coach and one in the boot. The one in the coach was small. Did you not get it out! The sheriff told you to hold two! You was told to check the waybill!

The stable boy answered he did not have the waybill, it was the driver that had it. He maintained he had told the driver to check it, and the driver only give him the rifle and one bag. He yelled at the traveler to take them and go, and commenced to shout what likely was curses in German. The traveler demanded a horse, and the stable boy yelled, I have none horse!

The traveler come out red in the face, hauling his rifle and one bag. It was a sizable bag. I could not see why he would need another.

He spied me and come over, saying, The driver took off with one of my bags! Do you know of a horse for sale or let! I need to catch up with the coach!

He appeared beside hisself and breathed hard. I figured the gone bag must hold money or some other valuable item. Yet how a traveler as grubby as him might come by a bag of money was hard to fathom. If I was to judge by his ratty attire, I would say he had not spent much in a while.

I asked what the bag might hold that was crucial, but he did not say.

He said, I appeal to your earnest nature, which I see that you've got. The coach is headed to San Antonio. I need a horse to catch up.

I said, I have only my mare and she's not for let.

The traveler tossed down the bag he carried, opened his coat and seized from a inside pocket his money pouch, it being large and leather and tied with a hide string. He took from the pouch a coin the likes of which I had not seen before.

He said, Help me get hold of a horse in decent shape and I'll give you this piece. It's a twenty peso piece from Mexico worth a dollar. It's gold. I got more of these in here. I'll hand over your asking price, just ask it. You look like a fair man to me. I appeal to your tenets.

I will tell you, small Tot, I was not prone to let him take off with my mare, but there was that in his eyes which I somewhat trusted, and that in his speech which struck me as genuine and which I liked. Also I felt I owed him, as I had not spoke up for him to the sheriff, so my tenets was smart to appeal to. As well, the desperation he showed is hardly that which a man will pretend at. He might claim he is doing just fine, and that things is all to his liking, and to his own devising, but a man is not apt to pretend despair. I believed the fellow. His teeth was bad, his attire was seedy, and he wore no socks. But he did not seem a swindler by trade, as his eyes was accordant with his words, and his consternation appeared true.

He give me the coin to study, and it decidedly looked to be gold. It was the size of a silver dollar and but two years old, dated 1866. One side had a man's head and said Maximiliano Emperador. The other side said Imperio Mexicano, 20 pesos, and had on it a crown and a eagle and dragons alongside the date I already said. The pouch appeared like it might hold nearly a hundred such coins of that size.

I said, Here's the problem I've got. I won't chance my mare.

There might be a person in town with a horse to sell you, but I don't know who that might be. Comanches was through here a night last week and taken four horses I know of. If there's none for let at the stable, then you're unlikely to find one. Horses that folks has hired out don't always come back, so folks here in town won't chance letting.

That was the truth of the matter. There was thieves attacking travelers in every direction. Out west was bands of Comanches and Mescaleros and others not fun to meet up with. Roads north and east was preyed on by low life robbers. South was plenty of Mexican bandits. The bandits was primarily known to be friendly and not harm and kill folks like Comanches done on the roads, but nevertheless they was thorough in what they took. This traveler wanted to head southeast on roads that was pretty well used, but who could say what danger might arise out of the brush.

I offered, I won't put my mare at risk without me along to see to her, but I could take you myself in my wagon as far as Boerne. You might find you a horse for let there. If you tell me a price you think is fair I'll see how it strikes me.

Is your mare fit, he asked me.

She's old but she pulls a wagon, I told him.

He said, I got fleeced on the Ficklin but I'll raise that if she'll pull in a hurry. I'll pay you four dollars to get me to Boerne. That's better than first class wet rates, and we got good weather.

No thank you, I told him. Boerne's fifteen miles off. We'd not get there much before dark. I'd have to pay board tonight and travel back home tomorrow. I can make upwards of five dollars a day, staying here. What did you pay by the mile on the Ficklin.

Short of twenty cents by the mile, he said.

Well I guess I cost more, I told him. First you was begging, and then you was bargaining. Name me a fair price.

He consulted a watch he got from his trouser pocket. It was a scratched up stemwinder with a cracked face, but appeared to tell time, as he cursed how the time was passing.

All right then, he said. I'll pay you a generous two days of work, at more than your price by the day, plus another half dollar. Twelve of these gold ones and fifty cents. Plus your board for the night.

And feed for the mare, said I.

He argued my mare would need feed regardless of if she went or stayed here.

She'll need more if she's drawing a wagon all day, I told him.

He thought on it, and agreed fair is fair.

Do I have your word it's genuine coins, I asked him.

I seen counterfeit all my life, and this ain't any of that, he swore. This come out of a hole in the ground. Who buries counterfeit. Nobody. I found this. It's honest coins. The sheriff had no problem taking these coins just now. He took plenty. How quick can you hitch up the mare.

He did appear honest and short on time. He commenced to stomp and fidget.

I told him I had to talk to the lady that owns the house about putting her chickens up for the night, as that was a task I usually done and she would need to see to it.

He said, Show me the mare and the wagon and I'll get her hitched.

I put my work away in the shed and took the man around back to the pen.

He seen my mare in full light and lost heart in the situation, and said, If that's her, she won't do! She'll drop in the traces! She's too old! She'll die on the road!

Then find you another, I told him.

He agreed he could likely not find one in time.

Tot, that is the conversation we had, to the best of my recollection. I aim to be thorough.

I then went into the house and took care of things with the woman who owns it. She's young for a widow. Her husband was with a assemblage all slain by the rebel Confederate sesesh whilst trying to travel to Mexico. He was a socialist free thinker and she is likeminded, the best I can tell. I said to her I would be off to convey a man to Boerne in my wagon and would be gone for the night but back by the next. It took me a while to make myself clear, on account of I don't speak German.

She give me a bag of dinner to have on the way. It was nearly enough to feed the traveler as well as myself, although she was short on items, the varmints having plundered more than their share of her garden.

I retrieved my spectacles from my room, as they help me see down the road. The traveler and myself then buckled my mare in the traces, loaded his rifle and bag along with my rifle and satchel and what might be needed, and pulled for Boerne.

It was half past nine, by the traveler's watch, at that time.

* * *

We went at the usual pace for my mare, which is not a fast one.

The traveler pestered me over it, saying, Can you not even give her a tap on the rump.

I told him she had come by her age the hard way and should not be bothered. She appeared to of had a rough youth. Comanches had used her up and left her for spent until my father found her, and claimed her by law, and patched her up and left her for me when he passed, of a fever.

The traveler give up pestering but continued to lean frontward and bounce his weight on the seat as if to thrust us forward. He offered his name was Richard Dean Bell and I was to call him Dickie. He said he had made a arduous journey from El Paso, long portions of which he traveled afoot for days. He'd taken a stage part of the way but got delayed on account of Indians struck a station and took off with stock that then had to be replenished. He'd finally arrived in Fredericksburg and stayed the night and boarded the coach at sunrise, the only other passengers being a lady in the domestic manner, that being your mother, and her son, who was you. Your mother had shown a ticket and told the driver on boarding that she would be traveling to San Antonio and from there to the port of Indianola, which lies down the coast from Galveston. This was Dickie's destination as well.

I asked what business he had at Indianola.

A ship to New Orleans to get on, he told me.

What's your business in New Orleans, I asked, and he said there was things entailed which he would be poorly advised to speak of.

I asked what he might of been up to out in El Paso, and he begun to talk a great deal about hunting gold in Arizona, which he swore had promise to it. He said he had strayed from that enterprise due to rumors of silver down in El Paso, which turned out false. There being no silver, crowds of upset seekers was stranded without fare to leave, and those who had fare was all taking off in a sorry mood. It was a bust, he said. He had lit out from there in the company of three seekers he'd met up with, but they had got disgruntled with one another and split up and left him. He was making his way through Castle Gap on a mule by hisself, keeping a lookout for Apaches and Kickapoos and Comanches and Mescaleros and whatnot, and feeling concerned about his prospects, when his life took a harsh unforeseen turn. This happened nearby the Horsehead Crossing on the Pecos river.

Upward or downward turn, I asked.

Upward, he said in a solemn manner. But how far upward is yet to be seen. It entails what's in my bag that's gone with the stage, and why I have to retrieve it, and why I'm headed to Indianola. I should never of left that bag when I got out for the privy. It's small, but it holds my future.

His urgency to press forward come to a brief halt when he stated these words, and a stillness settled on him. I wanted to prod him further, as he had presented a mystery and his manner give me a sense he would like to speak more of the situation. Yet it also give me pause to pry, and I decided to keep my questions to myself.

The road we traveled was rocky, with difficult inclines, but it was familiar to me and well trod. We come on sundry carts and folks afoot and was hindered skirting a cattle outfit that hogged a portion of road. I wished I might be going along on horseback with the cowhands, not making my way by wagon to Boerne, someplace

I had already been and nothing to it I hadn't seen. There's plenty of cattle need to go north, now that the war is over, and I dream often of striking out and seeing a piece of the world. If I was to make enough money at that, then things might play out in such a way I could purchase cows of my own, and someday buy a good patch of land in south Texas, or maybe out west. I believe I'd do well in the business.

But that is off the point of what I mean to tell you.

We ate our meal of jerked beef and carrots, and Dickie told more of his hunt for treasures. It was a lifetime hunt, he said, embarked upon when he was a boy and his father taught him to pan for gold in a stream in Arkansas nearby their house. The stream was no more than a gully and oftentimes dry, and this give him the gift of eternal hope, he declared, as there was no gold in the waters he learned to pan in, and none was ever found there, and the task was only a trick to get him out of the house, as otherwise he was a pest to the family, being the youngest. But he was good at the work, he said, such that he come into a notable talent. He could pan mud if he had to. He could pan dust.

How did that make you a optimist, I asked, as it seemed a sensible question.

He scoffed that I should ask it. If you find nothing, you hold the eternal hope of coming across it, he claimed.

A point or two against such thinking come to my mind, but I did not see any purpose in making any of them, and kept my mouth shut whilst he carried on with his talk of treasures and being hopeful and such. It was primarily hogwash. The day become hot, in spite of it wasn't June yet, and after some time Dickie dozed off and I lost myself in easy thoughts, as I had a open view and heard none but accustomed sounds of birds and crickets, and the creak of a wheel I aught to of oiled, and the tread of my mare. I had my rifle along, and Dickie had his, and also his Whitney pistol returned by the sheriff, and a knife as big as a Bowie tucked in his boot. Therefore we was prepared in case of trouble, although it seemed unlikely.

I halted at the Big Joshua to await a boy with a haul of lumber crossing the bridge from the far side, and Dickie woke from his snooze and hailed the boy to ask if by chance he'd come head on with a Ficklin at any point in the day.

I come on one stopped with wheel troubles this side of Boerne, not too far from here, but they'd got the rim back on and was heading on to Boerne, the boy recounted.

Dickie become excited on hearing the coach was close ahead, thinking how if we hurried we might catch up sooner than he had figured.

We crossed the creek and pulled on down the road. The heat and doggedness of the work commenced to trouble my mare and she grew damp beneath the harness. I rested her at the Small Joshua whilst Dickie complained of the resting, and then we continued, and was keeping a steady pace on a desolate spell when I spied a person afoot ahead.

Is that a lone figure up there, I asked Dickie.

He give it a squint, and replied, A lone figure indeed.

The figure was far enough off I could not make out which way it was moving. However, on dusting my spectacles, I seen it to be a man, viewed from the back, traveling the same direction as us.

There was a oddness to how he walked, and a strangeness to him being there in a lonely patch of the stretch, with neither a mount nor conveyance. He did not appear to of heard our approach, and did not turn to take note of us.

He ain't out taking a stroll here in the midst of nowhere, Dickie noted. I'm thinking he's trouble. Let's halt and let him move on out of our sight.

Out of our sight is exactly where I don't want him, I said.

You got a point about that, Dickie granted.

My thought was to hail the man, as what was our options. We had either to speak to the fellow and take his measure, or follow along at a walking pace to keep him in sight, or allow him to vanish into the brush, that being the worst idea of the three, as folks that go into the brush tend to come back out with their friends.

Therefore we halted to make ourselves ready for a encounter. Dickie crawled to the back for his bag. He brought it up front and secured it under his feet, unholstered his Whitney and placed it in hand, and loaded his rifle. It was a foreign type muzzleloader called a Lorenz, and nice looking. I checked my rifle was ready across my lap, then encouraged my mare to pick up time.

One thing I noted as we come closer upon the figure, although he was yet far off, was the odd and rather wobbly hitch to his walk, as if he was taking his steps with some care whilst still trying to move at a pace. His arms was thrust out from his sides and moved up and down, as if working to keep his balance, and he appeared to be gazing down at his feet rather than out before him or side to side in the normal way of a walker.

Might he be barefoot, I said.

Dickie concurred as he might.

We pulled a bit closer and seen that this was the fact of the matter. The man had no shoes. He was picking his way on sharp rocks. He appeared to have no shirt, neither. Trousers was all that he wore. He heard our approach and turned and stared at us, standing his ground.

His whiskers is what give away who he was. They was nearly mutton chop whiskers, as I before stated, he being the character who had rode through Comfort a few hours prior in haste on a badly spent roan. Whatever become of the roan in the meantime was in question.

We hailed the man and pulled to a stop some distance off.

I know you! I called out. You was through Comfort early this morning requiring a horse to let! What might we do for you!

He looked on us, in not too friendly a fashion, and hollered at me in a hostile manner, Here you come in your wagon, driving the way I was going! I was in need of transportation hours ago and you offered me none!

You asked for a horse to ride! I answered. I have only my mare and she's not for let. If you are in need of some help I'm willing to help you! You seem to of lost your boots and your shirt, and not even to mention your horse!

It come to me I might add he had lost his hat and his pieces as well, but seeing his angry air I thought better about it.

He spat at the ground for a answer.

Are you wanting my help, or don't you, I said. I can take you as far as Boerne. You might find a horse there.

Tot, I will tell you what. I wished for him to forgo my offer. I had no doubt he was spiteful. He stood in that spot of the road, shed of his belt and suspenders as well as his shirt and frock coat, his pants sagging about his hips. The bowler hat he had wore was lacking, however it left its stamp on his head. One of his eyes appeared swelled and his face was beat up. He had certainly met with trouble. His arms was idle with nothing to hold, and he seemed like he might of been stripped of more than accouterments, and possibly long before now, as together with his look of being irate, he had a air of lost hopes. I believe there was something in him intended to drain the hopes of others as well, for despite my wish for him to decline my offer, he considered, and shrugged at me, and motioned me forward so he might climb into the wagon.

I drove up to where he stood and allowed him to do so. He settled hisself into the rear alongside my box of tools and looked on us with a sour face. Dickie remained at my side but turned halfway about and kept a good watch on him.

I'm headed to San Antonio, the man said. I'm in a hurry.

Boerne's as far as I'll take you, and that's at my own pace, I told him. I urged the mare forward whilst the man commenced to account for hisself.

Them goddamn imposter Indians robbed me! he proclaimed. A Mexican, two whites, and one goddamned nigger freedman, he said. Yankees turned them niggers loose and look what they make of theirselves. The saddle that's took was my grandpap's. All four was dressed up like chiefs. How many chiefs can there be. They appeared to be nearly kids. What kind of fool would mistake that sundry bunch for Comanches. Three of them talked plain English!

Plain, give me your horse, give me your shirt, give me every god-damned thing you got. The Mexican talked plain Mexican and called me Pendayho. Not a word of Indian jabber amongst the four. I think they broke one of my ribs.

It was a vulgar mouthful and enhanced my distaste for the man and regrets that we had come on him. However, the relevant question was if the kids who had robbed him might still be anywhere near.

I asked him as much, and he replied, No, they've took off into them hills behind.

Regardless that he was a sorry sight, he did not muster my pity. He had a right to complain of things, as he had been pretty well fleeced. I'll grant him that much. But there's times a man has to stand up in his own mind and appear sound and reasonable, even when things has not gone to his liking and he is picking his way barefoot on sharp rocks in the midst of no place, having been stripped down and socked about and had a time with. To the contrary, this man grumbled and griped. I disliked him.

Dickie disliked him too. I don't recall how the quarrel that followed between them two commenced, however I believe it pertained at first to the notion, held by Dickie, that the man was a ingrate and aught to thank me for stopping to help him out. The man refused to do so, given he held me at fault for not helping him out when he come through Comfort. And whilst I cared nothing about his thanks, or want of his thanks, it become a point with Dickie. As well, the man declined to tell us his name, saying he did not owe it to us.

A row sprung up and moved on to other matters, such as the

late war, the man stating he had joined up as a proper Confederate out of Grayson county up in the north part of east Texas in the ninth cavalry and seen a great amount of fighting in five different states, and got shot in the leg on a bridge, and what had Dickie done. Dickie owned as he had not fought, as he had not cared to. His brothers had got conscripted to the Confederate army when the sheriff come by their houses, which was in Arkansas and nearby each other, as they was a close tied family. But Dickie had disregarded the notice hisself, as he did not want to be bossed about. He said the ordeal was a rich man's war and a poor man's fight, on account of rich people was the only ones reliant on slaves, him and his family did not have any theirselves, and he did not care to take part and had gone down to Mexico to hunt treasure.

The man called him chicken hearted for going, whereupon Dickie called the man a loser for fighting, on account of his side lost. They yelled about which was worse to be.

My mare does not take to folks hollering at one another. She come to a standstill, set her ears back and would not budge. I give her a tap, and yet she refused. The man was so worked up I do not believe he noted the fact that we was no longer moving along. He snatched a hammer out of my toolbox, rose up in the back and hurled it in the direction of Dickie. It overshot Dickie and hit my mare on the back, and she let out a grunt and hove forward, upon which the man was toppled out. He fell in the road and Dickie commenced to shout at me to drive off in a hurry and leave him.

However, how could I leave a man nearly naked in the road, no matter we disliked him, and also how could I leave my hammer. It was a good horseshoe nailing hammer for which I had paid top price. Therefore I got down, got the hammer, settled my mare, and told the man to get back in the wagon. He done so peaceably, as I guess he had feared being left and also he looked woozy from the fall. He said he had hit his head and further injured his broke rib. I told him he better keep his mouth locked, and told Dickie to stay where he was on the seat, that I was doing them both favors to of put up with the ruckus they caused.

It ain't a favor to me, Dickie proclaimed. I paid you for the ride. This man paid you nothing.

He took aim on the man with his Whitney and claimed he would give the trigger a tug if the man made a move or even spoke one word. I was not sure if he meant it or didn't, and I suppose the man was not sure neither. He retired into a huff.

Dickie was not much for being quiet in general, and now he was stirred up besides. He commenced to regale me with tales of his hunts for treasure in Mexico whilst the war was on, as the afore conversation must of brought that subject to mind. He said there was gold down there to be had, and loads of silver. He told me of a time he spent on a journey with no company but his horse and a waterwise mule, in search of a lost town called Tayopa, in mountains in the west part of Chewawa, where there was rumored to be riches hid by priests under a church that was now gone. The riches was said to be jewels and candle holders and plates the likes of which is used in churches, as well as sixty-five pack loads of gold bars which was twenty-two carrots assay and wrapped up in cowhides. He had got hold of a chart, but did not find the town, or what might be left of it, having gone twenty or thirty miles in the wrong direction, on account of being misled by a old Mexican man he

come on in the early part of the journey who lied and told him der-
aycha meant left and izkeerda meant right, when it was the other
way around. He had got so lost in the mountains he ate horned
toads to survive and would of perished of thirst if not for his waterwise mule that found him a stream.

It was a long tale he told, with a side part concerning a wife,
of sorts, he once had. By the time he got finished the sun had sank
low in the sky behind us and the man in the back had complained
a time or two of the slow pace we was going, and of feeling like he
might retch on account of his head was injured, and had dozed off.
We was about three miles out from Boerne by then and nearing a
wash known to be tricky, one reason being that folks had, on occasions, been held up there by thieves, on account of the slopes was
steep enough to require passengers in coaches and such vehicles to
take the upward inclines by foot, with what baggage they might
carry, so as to lighten the load, and thus become targets.

I therefore felt uneasy on hearing shouts from down within.
Dickie heard them as well and ceased talking, that we might listen. Indeed, there was shouts. I pulled the wagon out of sight into
cedars, and Dickie and me left it there with the man in it, and set
out to scout the situation. We laid down on our bellies as we come
up to the edge of the wash.

It was a broad wash, maybe two or three hundred feet across,
with a steep grade on the far side. On looking down into it we seen
a peculiar picture that was at first hard to make sense of, other
than mischief was being done. Down in the shade at the base was
the Ficklin coach we was traveling after. It was not moving. The
driver sat on a rock alongside the road with his hands on top of his

head. The woman passenger, who was your mother, stood alongside him, and you alongside her. Four men was moving around and about the coach and hollering to one another and hollering at the driver to keep his hands on his head, although he did not seem to be doing otherwise.

On close study I inferred these to be the Comanche imposter kids that had robbed the man now snoozing in the back of our wagon, as two of them was white, one was darker, and one was black. Also they wore feathers. Also their faces was painted and they appeared to be young. The spent roan they had stole from the man was amongst their horses.

Dickie took in the spectacle and said, Ain't this unwelcome.

We returned to the wagon and stirred the passenger.

I told him, Wake up. We come on your imposters. You said they was behind us, going the other direction.

He roused hisself and said, They was.

Well they fooled you, I told him. They're down in the wash ahead, holding up a coach.

Dickie grabbed up his rifle and the Whitney, and I got hold of my rifle, and we found cover along the rim behind rocks where we was well stationed and took aim below. The traveler settled hisself in a similar manner, some ways from us, although he was no use to us without arms, nor did we want him to have any, as we did not trust him.

I admit I was jumpy, Tot. It is not every day one comes upon highway robbers. I had gone through all of my nineteen years without doing so. I had seen pickpockets and muggers and pinches and pilfers of other kinds, but not those of the highway breed, which is often known to be harsher. I could not figure how we might handle them, and Dickie did not seem to have ideas, neither. However, we was in solid agreement on one point, that being that we could not forsake a woman and child to their mercy. As well, Dickie wanted his bag.

He said, How true is your rifle.

I could see why he might ask. It is a patched piece that had a good many years of hard use already before my father traded for it. However, my father had it newly grooved and half stocked, swapped the flintlock to percussion and added a new lock and breech pin before it come down to me, when he passed, and it is a handy enough piece.

I said, It'll do.

We lay there looking into the wash and tried to sort out our options. The imposter thieves was not doing any harm to you and your mother at that time, and I figured if we opened on them, or was seen by them, we might stir up more trouble than we could take care of.

I said, Let's wait and see what they do. If we need to head down there we'll start.

We watched as the thieves made theirselves busy searching the contents of mail sacks and dumping letters and other matters on the ground. Three of them hauled parcels out of the coach and down from the roof and piled them into the road whilst the one that was a Mexican kept a watch on the driver and you and your mother. The last sharp light of the sun behind us laid hard on the far side of the wash but did not touch our side. You all was in shadows below, and I could not tell much of your mother except that she wore no bonnet and looked undoubtedly in a family way, as Dickie had stated. Her dress was blue. You and her stood side by side and did not appear to have much to say about what was going on, as what could you do about it. Your hat was big for your head and looked to belong to a grown man.

Whilst Dickie and myself lay there taking things in, the robbers tossed what looked to me like a ladies' handbag out of the boot and onto their pile. At that, Dickie commenced to breathe hard. He was on his belly, five or six feet from me, with a plain view into the wash, his barrel steadied upon a rock and his finger snug to the trigger.

That's it there, he said. That's my bag.

That's a ladies' purse, I said.

No, he said. It looks like one, but it's my bag.

Already he had avowed he would not say what it carried, so I did not ask again. However, I could not figure how a bag that size might hold much of importance, as I had pictured it bigger. It appeared no more than five inches wide by five tall, was cinched at the top with a drawstring of some kind, and was made of a old time tapestry of a dun color.

I warned that he would stir things to a bad end if he should fire, as we was outnumbered and they had folks to take for hostage. He allowed he did not plan to shoot anybody just yet.

The imposter thieves unhitched the mules and begun to pack them with items they had got from the coach. The one who was a Negro strapped Dickie's bag on top of a load and strove to tie the load with a shortage of rope. He hollered about how he needed more rope. One of the two white imposters said to make do, there being no more rope brought along. A argument commenced about who should of thought to bring it. This quarrel was undergoing when, of a sudden, a pack of mounted men come charging down into the wash from the far side, directly across the way from us, firing weapons and heading full tilt toward the coach. They was in bright sun that struck on that side. I counted five of them. They wore feed sacks over their heads and did not appear to of come for a good purpose. Some had feed sacks tied over their boots as well, the old trick to hide prints. They did not come down the road, but tore through the brush and cedars in a fluster of rocks knocked out of the way and birds taking off from their perches.

The imposter thieves seen them coming and taken cover in and about the coach. They drew their weapons. Your mother pulled you behind large rocks and laid down with you. The driver sought cover nearby. This all occurred in a jiffy. I did not have time to consult with Dickie nor even think what we might do but await more gunfire.

However, what come next was one of the riders heading downhill reined in and skidded down to a stop and hollered out to the others, Halt! Hold up! and such things as that, and they pulled rein of a sudden, halfway down the incline, in what appeared to be confusion. They shouted to one another about things I could not make out well on account of the feed sacks over their heads had eye holes but no mouth holes.

The one that had hollered the order to halt then drew off his feed sack and yelled down to the imposter thieves at the coach, saying, Maynard, I see that's you down there playing like you're a Indian! I see your horse, son! What in hell are you doing here!

A imposter that had took cover within the coach, one of the two that was white, put his head out the window, such that his head feathers was visible. He responded, What might it look like I'm doing!

Robbing a coach that's in my wash, that's what! the rider proclaimed. Get the hell out, and leave them mules and them bags. We're taking them over!

It was a holdup of a holdup. I had not thought there was such a thing.

We was here first and we taken the coach! the imposter, who was Maynard, asserted from within it. You don't own this wash! We done the work and got the bags. You might recall the tale Mama told me about the hen that done all the work. That hen gets the bread!

The rider said something akin to, Maynard, you're a grown man! I raised you better than to call on folk tales like that. I'll make you a deal. It's the best one you'll get. You load up half them bags and pick you two mules of the four, and you ride out and go play Indian west of here where it makes more sense to do so. Either that, or learn to work! This whole act is beneath what I would expect of you. You're too old to be up to nonsense like this, and too fresh to think you can beat me out of my wash. I didn't buy you that horse so you might use it to take my wash. And is that Josh you got with you down there! I seen his daddy in town. He's free of that son of a bitch what owned him and he's earning a good living. He won't like what his son is up to. Josh, is that you!

The Negro imposter come out from where he had taken cover. He replied, Yes sir, it's me! Don't tell my daddy! I'll give you my share of the bags! He then seized from off the mule the bag within reach, that by chance being Dickie's. I do not believe he had looked in it.

I don't want that bag you got there! the rider said. That's a purse! That likely belongs to that woman. You all know better than to take a woman's purse! You give that back to her.

Can we not see what's in it first, Maynard yelled.

No! shouted the rider. We do not rob women with children! You get out of that coach, Maynard! Help that woman up from them rocks and put her and her kid in the coach where it's safe. Lord! What have you turned out to be.

Maynard got out of the coach in a huff. He made plain by the way he moved he was mad. The feathers on his head was shaking with wrath. He went over to your mother and spoke to her, and you and her both got up. She had trouble doing so, on account of her family condition. It appeared far along. He give her a hand, then you and her went to the coach and got in it. I noted you was obedient under the circumstances, as I guess you was scared.

The rider hollered at the Negro imposter, Now you give her that purse!

The Negro taken Dickie's bag and passed it through the window to your mother. From what I made out of the situation, she took it and did not say boo about it not being hers. Dickie give me a grin upon seeing that happen, on account of his bag was now safe in the coach with the woman. I think he could not believe his good luck.

The rider yelled down at Maynard, saying, Now, son, take your playmates, take your spoils, and get moving!

The four imposters commenced to select bags in a hostile fashion. The five riders remained on the downward slope of the wash and kept watch through their eye holes. The shadows by then was crawling their way up that slope, as the sun was sinking behind us.

Whilst this went on, the traveler we had been hauling kept some distance from us, laying down on his belly like we was, although ours was not shirtless. He stared into the wash. I figured he might be doing some wishful thinking about his stole roan and his grandpap's saddle down there. It was a nice looking saddle. However, who ever knows a man's thoughts. Nobody. He did not twitch a muscle. His eyes was fixed on below.

Maynard hollered up to his father, We're keeping this roan horse we got, as we stole it fair and square! The saddle as well!

They took two of the four mules and cinched their packs. They strapped parcels onto the roan. Three of them mounted up but the Mexican did not, and commenced to argue with his companions. He appeared to hold the opinion they was all due more of the spoils and was being cheated by Maynard's father. He become worked up and begun shouting in Spanish whilst Maynard shouted a good many oaths in English. Things was considerably heated between them.

Those on the hillside must of been somewhat warm in the feed sacks, as it is not easy to get air through eye holes. They grumbled and taken to yelling, although it was not clear what they was saying. Shortly the imposters and the riders on the slope was all hollering at each other and at one another.

I am not sure who fired the first shot. However, one shot called for another. Soon there was a number of shots fired, although I think most was into the air and intended merely to put a halt to the rest, given how nobody fell. The men on the slope rode down in their feed sacks and there was a great deal of commotion and yelling about the mules and who might take which ones, and which parcels, and what was half, or not half. The driver stayed out of the way. I wondered how you and your mother was faring within the coach. Not a peep come from the two of you, whilst the turmoil went on without.

How long the affray lasted I can't say exactly. It seemed to go on for a time, although I think it was brief. To get to the point, it ended. The four imposter thieves come riding up the hill past us at a brisk gait with their haul, heading back in the direction of Comfort. We kept at our station, quite a few feet from the road and prone on the ground, and none of them seen us, nor seen my mare and the wagon, as those was well hid amongst cedars. Whilst this bunch was departing the one way, the other bunch rode back up the hill in the other direction, taking the sundry spoils left for them and yanking their feed sacks off for air. The stagecoach driver stood at the base and watched them all go. He now had his coach again, but no mules to pull it, no matter the load was lightened a great deal.

Dickie and myself arose from our stations and started down toward the coach, hallooing to say we was friendly and might we help out. The driver looked our way and appeared perplexed, given how I was a stranger to him and the last he had seen of Dickie was he was arrested in Comfort. Besides which, where had we come from.

Of a sudden, to our surprise, the disagreeable traveler we had fetched from the road come running afoot and skidding on rocks downward past us in haste, despite his broke rib and sundry pains and having nothing but trousers on him, not even shoes, and charged up to the door of the coach and drew it open. He then tumbled back out of it with the sound of a blast and dropped stone dead, shot in the face and instantly fallen. There he laid.

I was taken aback at how quick that happened. Here was Dickie and myself making our way downhill, and the driver looking at us, confounded at our unforeseen arrival, and the traveler prone alongside the coach and unexpectedly dead, shot from within.

I assure you I am no stranger to death, having seen it on many occasions. I once seen my own kin, of a sort, the woman who raised me, tore up by a panther and laying in shreds before me, a sight I try not to think on. I seen my own father breathe his last six years ago now, the hardest thing to make sense of. I seen eight hanged men dead on the ground and a passed man caught in the froth and churn of a current that carried him off downriver. I am accustomed to folks taking their leave of me and the world, in one way or another. Nevertheless, it startled me how sudden this man fell.

The sun was failed on the far slope by then, clear up to the rim, yet the man was plain to make out in the dusky light there at the base. He was shirtless and shoeless, wearing only the trousers, as I have before now mentioned, and he laid on his back in a weird way with one arm hung up in a patch of cactus. His face had a large hole in the forehead and was blackened by powder. It was strange to know how having his hand in the cactus would of been painful had he been vital, yet under the circumstances bothered him not at all. The reaper had come to fetch him without so much as a knock upon the door. I guess the blast was as much of a knock as the man was afforded, and whether or not he even had time to hear it I could not tell you. He was gone.

The driver looked on the body and looked on us, as if we might have a explanation about it. He seen in our faces we did not. He strode to the door of the coach and taken care about peering in, as who could say if he might likewise be hailed by a blast.

He said, Ma'am, are you all right.

I did not hear how your mother replied, or even if she did. The next I seen, Tot, was the door on the far side heave open and your mother come stumbling out, pulling you along with her. She had one hand to her face and held on to you with the other. She alighted on the ground and bent over and retched. Dickie and myself went over to see how we might help her, and the driver come around as well, but she did not want our help. She shoved her hand at us to keep away, and remained bent over and sick.

The driver inquired again if she was all right.

She whispered that she did not know the man and had not meant it to happen.

I remained nearby her and you, whilst Dickie and the driver went around the other side of the coach to look in on the body. I heard them speak on it being a grim business. Dickie told the driver how the man come to be traveling with us, and that my wagon was up the hill.

Your mother remained badly shaken. I asked how I might help her and she whispered at me, You can't.

She appeared young to be your mother. I guessed her around

my age of nineteen but figured she might be a year or so older, given as she had you.

You was perplexed. You asked her, What happen, Mama.

She come up with nothing to say.

Mama you shot somebody, you told her.

I didn't mean to, honey, she whispered at you.

You asked was the man dead, and she nodded to own that he was.

You said, You never done that before, Mama.

She agreed she had not.

How come you done it, you asked in a puzzled fashion, but she would not take up the matter.

Don't talk of it, honey, she said. She appeared to feel very sick.

You said, Mama, you shot his face.

Yes, honey, I know, she owned.

You said, You was quick. I didn't see him. Can I go see him.

She shook her head and drew you against her.

You inquired of the thieves and why grown boys was dressed up like Indians, and a number of other items that was making no sense to you.

She did not answer, being shook up. She held on to you like you was all she knew in the world.

I felt sorry for her. She looked undone. She was a fairly skinny woman but for the baby. I thought her pretty despite it.

When there was no answers coming from her you ceased your questions. I couldn't tell what you was thinking but felt I knew the manner in which you was thinking it. The forbearance in how you stood your confusion recalled me of times when I was a tot myself.

Dickie got in the coach and come out with the bag he had sought, and also the hat he had left in there on his jaunt to the privy in Comfort. It was a wool planter. He inspected the contents inside his bag and seemed to find things in order.

The driver retrieved your mother's pistol off the floor of the coach and showed it to me and Dickie. He said he had not known she had it, as it must of been hid in the pocket of her dress. It was a small, thick, strange looking derringer, a single shot with a fat four inch barrel and a spring loading breech. It had hard rubber grips. The stamp said it was made at Connecticut Arms with a patent of 1865. I had not seen such a pistol before.

The driver said, Goddamn, it's a Hammond Bulldog. I wonder where she got this. It's a powerful piece. Takes a .44 rimfire.

He went over and offered it back to your mother but she refused even to look at it. Therefore he kept it for the time being. He give her and you water from his canteen.

Are you sure you don't know the man, he pressed your mother.

She maintained she did not. The most the driver got out of her was she had not seen the man before in her life and had figured that he was one of the robbers come back to do harm. She said she had readied her pistol in case they might, and the man had then startled her.

She said, I fired without thinking.

She spoke like she was telling the truth, but I could not make sense of why she fired at all, as the man was plainly unarmed, being mostly unclothed.

It must of been nearly dark by that time, as I recall how the crickets was loud and a thread of red light laid on the west rim up top. The driver at last give up trying to get more information out of your mother, and him and me set about gathering mail strewn hither and yon. Dickie offered to bring down the wagon, and I told him all right, and he started up with his crucial bag tied at his belt. He was purely delighted to have it. He topped the road in what was left of the light up there, and soon was driving the wagon down. I found it a comfort seeing my mare coming in my direction, as she is familiar to me and things just then was hard to fathom, on grounds of knowing the body amongst us was that of a man I had spoke with, and argued with, and even conveyed along to his passing. There was no way around the plain fact that had I not come upon him, he would still of been walking the road some distance back.

On that account, as I stood there picking up mail scattered amongst the rocks, whilst dark sank on us, and death lay nearby, I felt very strange, and as I have mentioned was glad to be seeing my mare pulling my wagon down the hill and to hear the clomp of her hooves and the rattle of wagon wheels on the stony road as she come. She is a good mare and has been through a lot in my life with me.

* * *

Dickie halted the wagon behind the coach, then him and me and the driver walked out of earshot to talk things over in the near dark. The driver allowed as he did not believe your mother's story of the killing being a accident, and Dickie allowed as he did. Dickie said he had seen women do such rash things and thought it entirely bankable she tugged the trigger on account of being surprised and alarmed by the man running at her.

We then contemplated the question of why, as a point of fact, did the man run at her. We could not come up with a answer.

The driver and Dickie commenced to talk over what to do regarding the body.

The driver was of the opinion we might drag it off a ways and tuck it behind a rock, and go about our business, as that would offer less strife than hauling it into town and reporting the incident. He declared he would have to report the robbery but would rather not deal with a investigation into the man's death, as he was set back already on account of the coach being disabled, the thieves having taken the brake rods and other useful parts as well as the mules. He said he would be held to account for being late with the mail no matter the circumstances, and a inquiry would only prolong the issue.

He said, When I hired on with the company, Mr Ficklin give me twenty-five cents to buy myself a rope to hang myself with, should I ever be late with the mail.

Dickie then said, All right. I agree the body might be left behind, however I think we should dig it a grave.

The driver was tetchy to that idea and said, He's a naked son of a bitch we don't even know. Have you any notion how long it would take us to dig him a grave. This is rock under our feet. And unless there's tools in the back of the wagon, then we got only our hands.

I said, I got a spade in the toolbox, no shovel. However, we can't just go off and leave a body laying about.

Dickie then proposed we could leave it but report in town what had happened, and somebody there might come the next day and retrieve it.

It'll be ate before daylight, said the driver. There's creatures out there licking their chops right now. My job is ferrying folks and the mail, not taking on bodies stupid enough to get shot in the face. I got passengers with tickets, and mail that's tardy. I've dealt with that county marshal in Boerne on two occasions before. He's a deadly earnest son of a bitch. He'd have more questions about this mess even than we do.

Dickie took that in and give up his scruples. He agreed we might forsake the body, as a spade would not do to dig a grave, and let creatures devour it overnight and leave nothing more than the parts to identify who it might of been. He said if by chance remains was found, or the man was reported gone missing, it would likely be the imposter Indians who was caught and held liable, as they was the ones in possession of the man's boots and hat and other accouterments, not even to mention his horse and his grandpap's saddle.

The more I think on it, Dickie said, the more sound this plan appears to be. Or I got a even better lie to put forth if we care to. We could report he was one of them thieves hisself, harassing the woman, and we shot him in her defense.

I will tell you what, Tot. It was a quandary for me. I did not want your mother to have to account to the law for her act, yet a body has a right to be buried and folks should tell the truth about it. As well, I figured your mother should have a say in the matter.

I said, We should ask the woman how she wants to handle the situation. Maybe she wants to go to the law and confess to what happened. She's sick at what she done. If we leave the body, she might even state that we done so.

The driver and Dickie had not considered that thought, and suggested I talk things over with her. The driver declared he did not know her name for certain, as the waybill on which it was stated was stored in a satchel the robbers had taken, but he thought he recalled her sir name was Banes. He recalled her given name to be Nell. He recalled your name to be Henry.

Dickie said no matter your actual name, he had heard your mother call you Tot in the coach that morning.

When your mother spied me coming to talk with her she told you to stay where you was, and she come to meet me. We spoke in a quiet manner as she did not want you to hear. I noted as we talked that she was the same height as myself, being tall for a woman whilst I am a medium size for a man.

I told her we was trying to figure out what to do with the body, as we did not have much in the way of tools and a grave would be hard to dig. I said, If we convey him into town you'll have to talk to the marshal. I think it's the thing to do. How do you feel about it.

She was still badly shook up and said she was scared to talk to the marshal, as she did not want him asking questions of her boy, which was you, and might we see to a grave without that.

I said it was not likely we could see to a proper one.

Her hands kept on shaking. I told her the driver would have to go to the marshal to report on the robbery even if he did not mention a man being killed. If questions should be asked, then items might come to light and give the idea we was hiding things, and she could face worse trouble than telling the truth outright. I give her a chance to go back on what happened being a accident, but she would not say it was otherwise.

She said, I do want him to have a decent grave and be laid away right.

I told her it made sense to me, and we would load him up and take him along.

She said, I can't pay for a coffin. I have my handbag here in my pocket, but there's not much spare in it, mostly the ticket funds for our boat passage. Me and my son need to get to New Orleans.

I assured her the town of Boerne would likely provide a indigent coffin that I could shore up, if need be, as I was a carpenter and a cabinet maker. I asked did she have family we might alert of her being robbed of her things, and she replied that her family could not help her, and asked could we cover the body so you would not see it.

Yes ma'am, I told her. We can do that.

She appeared at a loss of hope, and said, What have I done.

I said, If you're asking me, I don't think the man was headed toward any end that would of been any kinder to him.

She took that in for a time, and said, He come out of nowhere.

He come out of the back of my wagon and down the hill, I replied, and told her how I was giving a ride to Dickie Bell when we encountered the man hobbling along afoot.

She seemed like she might have something to ask about that, but you come over to us, no matter that you'd been told not to, so we said no more at that time.

I returned to where Dickie and the driver was picking up mail in the dark and told them we was to haul the body.

They was sorry to hear that.

I got my lantern out of the wagon and it give us some light, although feeble, and we went at making things ready. There was empty mail sacks laying about, that was left by the thieves, so we got the man's feet and legs into one, and tugged one over his head, and heaved him into the wagon. It was none of it clean work. Even shot out of a pocket pistol a .44 cartridge can blast a sizeable hole. The lifeless aspect of the body was not new to me, as I have portioned coffins correct to bodies in my line of work, but it was not altogether familiar neither, death being the hardest thing to make sense of, no matter the form it takes.

After we got the body into the wagon we went about heaping cedar branches over the shirtless middle. When we was finished, it appeared like we was hauling no more than a pile of brush and a couple of mail sacks. We had a hard time shoving the stagecoach out of the road to drive the wagon past it, the road being narrow, with rocks either side that had to be moved or got around.

I alerted your mother we was ready to go, and she brought you over, and you climbed up on the seat, and the driver give her a hand up so she might sit beside you. You asked a good many questions about the man killed, and where we was taking him, and why. Your mother replied we was going to Boerne, where he would have a nice coffin and a proper grave. She told you not to look back on him nor remark on him further.

* * *

I should of mentioned before now that the driver went by the name Mr Pate. He was older even than Dickie, who looked to be forty at least, and he must of engaged in struggles, being scarred up and missing the ear I aforementioned. He wore spectacles like myself, though tied with a string over his head to keep them from falling, on account of the gone ear. He was a scraggy man. His hair was white and scanty. He expected I would take the reins of the wagon whilst him and Dickie would go afoot to spare the mare pulling the weight of us all. However, he appeared wore out by the ordeals of the day, and let on he had missed sleep on the previous night, having taken a extra leg of the route to stand in for a driver that went on a spree. As well, he lacked a conductor, who had been sick, and so had handled things on his own, hauling bags about and so forth. He was beat.

I therefore advised he might drive the wagon, my mare being easy to manage, and me and Dickie would go afoot. We was not more than three miles out from Boerne and it would be no hardship to us.

So Mr Pate climbed up and took the reins and we started for Boerne at a measured pace with Dickie and myself afoot alongside, or at times before and behind, depending on how tight the road was and if my mare needed me up front to talk her through the hardship, as she was played out.

You laid your head in your mother's lap and slept most of the way. I noted she did not once turn to look on the body, but appeared to of set her sights on the moon that come up left of the road ahead.

It was a uneasy journey. The moon was half full so we had some light, but clouds at times blocked it. The loud crickets and tread of my mare and scuff of our boots and creak of the wheel I aught to of oiled was mostly what we heard the whole way. Beyond that, it was just my thoughts that continued to yammer on and on. One particular thought lodged itself in my mind and become dogged.

Who ever shoots a man they just laid eyes on but half a second before, I asked myself. There was something about how that scene had played that did not appear like a accident. The aim was too dead to be wild. I have seen wild shots, and made my share as well, and none of them landed dead center of even a stump, much less of a stranger's face. But if the man was not a stranger, who was he. I wondered about all of this, and about your mother, and you, and what the marshal might say of things, and about Dickie's important bag and what was in it, and other questions I have had in my life and strived, to no purpose, to answer.

We traveled in this manner for some time and then come to fields at the edge of Boerne where Scotch dogs was guarding a great many sheep in the moonlight. Germans is partial to sheep, not being cattle people nor goat people, and on entering within the town we found things dark and quiet, as they tend toward being punctual people as well as sheep people, and it was late at night.

The marshal stationed in Boerne is a county marshal and not a German. His house sits next to his office and we went there. Me and Dickie and Mr Pate knocked at the door and roused him whilst your mother remained in the wagon with you, who was asleep. He was not happy to be roused, as he is not a young man, however he come fully awake at the door when Mr Pate related the stagecoach was held up back in the dry wash and we come along in a wagon bringing a dead man shot on a mishap by the woman now in the wagon. Dickie offered essentials of how the dead man run full speed at the coach in nothing but trousers, and snatched the door to gain entry, whilst your mother was within, and startled, and armed with a pistol we none of us knew she had.

The marshal then went for a lantern and come out to investigate the body. He give a nod to your mother. He took aside some of the brush and held his lantern to what there was of the man's face, which was not a great deal. Your mother sat still and did not turn to look.

The marshal said, I have no idea who this man is. He then ordered we come inside.

I asked could me and Dickie and Mr Pate make statements on your mother's behalf if she preferred to stay in the wagon, on account of her son, being you, Tot, was asleep. I said, We seen all that happened.

The marshal did not take to that idea. He said, I will need statements from all four of you. He inquired of your mother's name, and she replied, Nell Banes, and he assisted her down from the wagon and took us all inside, whilst you remained asleep on the wagon seat.

Dickie and me sat on a sofa and your mother sat in a chair near a window so she might keep a eye on you in the wagon, as she feared you might wake and not find her. The marshal set his lantern in the midst of us and took a hard look at our faces.

Mr Pate give a full description of the imposters and their attire. We stated that one of them went by the name Maynard and was quite young, one was a young Negro called Josh by Maynard's father who was likewise a thief but of a band of older men that come from another direction. We did not know the names of the other two imposters, nor anything about them, other than one was white and one was Mexican and both was dressed like they was trying to look like Indians. Nor could we give much information in the way of Maynard's father nor his cohorts, as we did not see much of them on account of their heads was in feed sacks.

The marshal asked to see the waybill and what parcels was listed, and Mr Pate stated the waybill remained in his satchel, which was stole, however he recalled one carton was labeled Comanche Skull and dispatched from a surgeon at Fort Concho to go to the United States Army Medical Museum in Washington, D.C.

It was a lot for the marshal to sort out. Your mother did not offer much in the way of statements, except to agree how what we had told of events was true and to say she was traveling to San Antonio in route to Indianola, and there she planned on boarding a steamer to New Orleans where she intended to live with her cousin.

The marshal asked where her husband might be. She said he had gone broke from the war and run off and left her to raise their son and the baby yet to be born, that being the reason she was leaving Texas. On further questions she maintained that she had not meant to shoot the man she had shot, and did not know who he was. She was plainly scared and badly troubled and mostly looked out the window to see you remained asleep on the wagon seat.

The marshal said he would take all matters in hand and send parties at daylight to hunt the thieves. He instructed we deliver the body to the undertaker in the morning, and pronounced he did not intend to charge Nell Banes with a crime. We was all of us eased to hear that, your mother especially.

We returned to the wagon and went to the Reed House for lodging. It is a stone house on the Cibolo with a nice porch and a wagon yard with holding pens for cattle headed for trails up north. I had laid eyes on it before but never been in it. We woke Mr Reed with the bell and he come out. He called Mr Pate by name, as they had spoke on other occasions, the yard being also the stage livery. He said two of the four rooms was taken and your mother might have the third free of charge on account of her condition. We would have to pay for the remaining room if we should want it.

Dickie claimed he wanted it and could pay. However, Mr Pate declared he would take it hisself, as Ficklin did daily business with Mr Reed and the charge could be billed.

The notion that Dickie would cheat me struck at my pride, and I maintained as the room should be mine, as I had drove a fair bargain with him to pay my room and board as well as my wages.

Therefore it was decided we would three of us share the room. Mr Reed disliked the idea and said wranglers and drovers would treat his rooms like a bunkhouse if he allowed more than two sharing. But he give in, seeing as we had gone through a hard day. He told us to wash up down at the creek, as he did not want to haul water so late in the night for any room but your mother's. As well, he did not want our wagon parked out front with a body in it, and did not want the body brought in, having no proper place for it but laid out on the dining table, where he did not care to put it, considering its condition of having been shot in the face and him having guests.

Mr Pate therefore agreed Ficklin would pay for the wagon's overnight stay in the wagon yard and assured Mr Reed the body was well covered and he figured would be all right until morning.

Dickie granted he would give over the charge for feed, as that was the deal he'd cut with me before starting out, and he was too tired to argue about it.

Mr Reed then pointed Dickie and Mr Pate to the creek and said he would put out food on the table inside for when they was back, as well as take food to your mother's room when she was settled. He and myself went to the wagon, and your mother give you into my arms, as you was asleep. She looked done in.

The event of her giving you down to me stuck in my mind, as I am not of a large family and there is no children much in my life these days. I liked how she trusted me to carry you.

*   *   *

I laid you on the bed in the room Mr Reed said your mother should stay in, went out and brought in the mail, as I had told Mr Pate I would do so, then drove the wagon around to the yard and turned my mare loose in the pen with feed and hay. There was no cattle there, only a couple of horses in need of shooing off whilst my mare ate her fill. I ensured the deceased body was well covered by brush and collected my satchel and rifle. By the time I got down to the creek to join Dickie and Mr Pate, they was already washed and gone to the house. The creek was narrow at the bend and the banks was crowded with large cypress, their knees three and four feet out of the water. After a good dunk I sat on the bank and listened to frogs having their say and owls hooting to one another.

When I got back to the house I ate and went to the room and found Dickie and Mr Pate hogging the bed. Mr Pate was sound out. Dickie looked improved from his time in the creek and had got his vital bag of the secret contents tied at his side for safe keeping. He was picking his nails with a folding knife and complaining he had a bad tooth. I laid on the floor with a quilt over my head so I would not have to listen. At some point Dickie ceased talking and I fell asleep.

Some while later I awoke to the noise of dogs in the wagon yard, and it come to me they would sniff out the body. I dressed in haste and went out and found a pack of three prowling about the wagon and run them off, then laid on the wagon seat, knowing they might be back. I could not sleep there, and after a while climbed down beneath to make myself as easy as possible on the ground.

I believe I might of slept longer than I thought, as I awoke from a dark dream overcome by a sense of deep dread. The dream was not of things I could name nor figure, and what I recalled of it on waking was a blackness that rolled about me and a anxious desperate need for air. It seemed as if the body laying above me had shed a portion of death upon me through the floor of the wagon. I had a powerful feeling of things being lost from me, and over with, as if all the scanty patches of wisdom I had gathered up in my life, and the scanty terms I had come to in my trials to feel peace about things in my past that was gone and things in my life that was missing, and the scanty portions of knowledge I had learned from within books, of how I might live and do right, was all just pennies put in a jar and spilled out and emptied, and what did I have to count on now.

And whilst these frightening feelings come from the dream, I perceived a change also in my surrounds. I was laying upon my side, my head upon my arm, my spectacles laid safe alongside me. Before me was the same items as when I closed my eyes, that being the wagon yard, mostly empty, and my mare in the fenced pen a few yards off from me. My vision was not entirely clear, on account of not wearing the spectacles, but I made out these things remained mostly as they was when I went to sleep.

The one difference I noted was that my mare no longer dozed, but rather had her head over the fence and appeared to be gazing in my direction. I figured she would not be regarding me in particular, as I would be hard to make out in the dark under the wagon, and therefore she must have her eyes on some other thing or person.

On that account, I took care whilst turning over to have a look. And when I turned, what I seen alongside the wagon, down at my level, was your mother's shoes from under the hem of her dress. It was plain from where they was lodged that your mother stood looking upon the body. I noted the dress was frayed and more faded than I had thought, or maybe the shine of the moon deadened the color. I awaited some movement of the shoes, and wondered if I might be dreaming, as who can ever stand that still, and make not a sound, and move not a inch, whilst beholding a dead body. And who would ever do so.

I can't figure how long your mother stood alongside the wagon in that manner, as I have no knowledge how long she might of stood there before I come up out of the dream, but there was a strangeness about the amount of time it went on, like she was keeping a vigil or awaiting something to happen.

A number of thoughts come to my mind, but they ended unfinished, given as all my attention was drawn to how still she was, and to how her shadow, laid by the moon, stretched out on the dirt alongside her. I will tell you, as I have vowed to tell you the truth in its full nature, that the manner in which her shadow appeared to lean on the shadow of the wagon revealed to me what her actual self had not yet, which I took to be a deep sadness and a profounder remorse even than I had noted before, and a number of other things I lack words to make clear.

It's hard to believe that a shadow might show what the person who casts it does not, but I seen in the one on the ground alongside the wagon more than I otherwise seen of your mother up to that time. It's a weird fact of the world how things can hide out in broad daylight, and then make theirselves plain in a patch of dark.

After a long while went by, your mother leaned closer against the wagon, and I heard her move the branches about or fix them in place, and then she left and walked to the gate and went through it, and closed it behind her, and started back to the house. I breathed again then, as I had not dared to take in, nor let out, a full breath the whole time she stood there.

I stayed awake under the wagon until the first light, then arose and went to the creek to wash off the dirt and the woeful sense of the dream, and to try to wash off the strangeness of what I had seen.

* * *

After a hasty dip I was getting my boots back on and spied you standing some paces off and eyeing me. You was barefoot and shirtless. I asked if your mother knew you was outside, and you replied that she did.

You was shy of me, but hung about, so I got my folding knife out and commenced whittling a bird from a stick for you to come look at. It was a small bird and did not take long. You asked if I might whittle a dog, so I had you hunt me a larger stick with good forks and no knots and made you a dog. You did not say anything whilst I was at it, but sat close and watched. When I give you the dog you asked might you keep him, and I said I'd made him for you.

After that, you stripped off and tromped out into the shallows and sat amongst cypress knees, kicking the water, whilst I sat on the bank.

You said, My mama shot somebody. Why she done that.

I told you it seemed the man startled her and she had mistook him for one of the men who robbed the stagecoach and who she'd thought might be coming back.

You said, She never done that before. My daddy shot lots of people, but not my mama.

I asked did your daddy fight in the war. You answered he did, and that he shot people whilst he was fighting and then come home and shot more. I inquired who he come home and shot, and you said you didn't know, as you did not see it happen.

You said, He don't live with us now. He lives in the woods.

I said, And where is it you live.

You answered you lived in your home at your farm but left there and went to live with your mother's friend, and now you was going to some other place.

I asked where her friend you had been with might live.

Back at her house where we left her, you said.

I figured that to be Fredericksburg, as that was where Dickie had said you boarded the stagecoach. I inquired did your daddy still live in the woods near your farm.

You owned as he did. You said, He lives with a swamp fox.

A swamp fox, said I.

A big swamp fox, you said.

I said, Is that so. And what does the swamp fox look like.

I never seen it, you owned. My mama's scared of it.

You ventured it likely had a long tail like a rat's, and said, My mama had a fight with my daddy about him being in the woods with it. She told him, Don't you never bring that swamp fox into my house!

I could not get to the bottom of what you was saying, and figured it was none of it true, as who ever heard of such a creature.

It's got a bounty, you said.

How so, I asked, and you owned you didn't know what a bounty might be, but the swamp fox had a big one.

You got out of the water, and we pitched rocks, and then your mother come searching for you. She had on a dress somebody must of bestowed her. It did not sit right, as it did not look to be made for a woman in her state.

You was excited to show her the whittled dog, and she took it and had a good study of it and said how she liked it, and thanked me for making it. She told you Mrs Reed had set food on the table and you was to put your pants on and go inquire if you might have some.

When you had gone, she brought up the matter of the coffin. She said, He'll likely get a indigent coffin. Did you mean your offer of shoring it up.

I told her, Yes ma'am, I meant it.

The way she looked, it seemed like the heft of the baby inside her was almost nothing compared to what she carried on her shoulders. She expressed she was sorry there would be no stone on the grave.

I could not see how a stone would be any use without a name on it, however I could not see how it would be any use for me to say so, neither. I offered I could give her a ride back to Comfort if she cared to go that way, given how her things had been taken.

She replied she meant to arrive to be with her cousin in New Orleans before the baby come. She worried it might come too soon. She said, If I can get on to San Antonio I'll be all right. I have my ticket money from there.

When we was back to the house I sought out Dickie in our room. He had on a different and cleaner shirt and pants and looked better. He'd got them out of his large bag, which you might recall had not been stole by the thieves like those of your mother and Mr Pate, on account of him and myself had brought it along from Comfort.

We have got to see to Nell Banes, I told him. What is your plans.

Same as before, he said. To get to San Antonio and get on a stage to Indianola.

I asked how he planned on doing that.

Horseback, he said. Mr Pate's seeking a saddle mount so he can ride ahead and telegraph Ficklin, so I told him to find me one as well. My Ficklin ticket paid me through to there, so they owe me that.

Nell Banes' ticket paid her through, same as yours, I reminded him.

Yes it did, he replied.

So how is the Ficklin going to do right by her, I asked. She's worried the baby will come before she gets where she's going.

That's not my issue, he said. I believe Mr Pate said the Ficklin will put her up here at the Reed House until they get hold of a coach.

She's not been told that, I said. How long is she going to be stuck here.

I suppose it'll be a good while, Dickie said, but unless she wants to ride horseback, at our pace, in her state, which I would think risky, I don't see how anyone's going to do any better than put her up here. You're taking on troubles that don't belong to you.

Had I not taken on yours, I answered, I would be home in Comfort right now without hers to worry about.

Then you aught not make a habit of that, he said. If you're so worried about her, you're the one's got a wagon.

I recalled him that San Antonio was thirty miles off and my mare was wore out on fifteen.

He said, Go pester Mr Pate and leave me alone about this. I got enough trouble from this bad tooth.

Outside the window, buzzards was hovering about the wagon in the yard, as they have a nose for death. We went out and waved them off, and I hitched up my mare and with some effort talked Dickie into coming along to the undertaker to discourage the buzzards whilst I drove.

We arrived there and I made deals as to a grave and a coffin. The indigent coffin on hand was not poorly made, but I give it a decorative touch and carved AT REST on the lid.

Me and the undertaker removed the body out of the wagon whilst Dickie moaned of his tooth. Then Dickie demanded I take him back to the Reed House. He informed me he was done being hindered and aimed to get going with Mr Pate as soon as mounts was found.

But I will tell you, Tot, the notion of what he'd said about me having a wagon was stuck in my mind. I reasoned that the woman in Comfort whose house I lived in could do without me for a few days.

Dickie, I said, I got a idea. We can let two mules and switch out the rigging and make good time that way. We can travel the day, stop the night, and reach San Antonio in the morning. I can then turn around, come back, return the mules, and head back home with my mare, whilst you and Nell Banes can carry on to Indianola. It would cost you and me some money and time, but save us our scruples.

Dickie declined to be interested or help me out. He was set on arriving to San Antonio as soon as he could, to catch the next available stage to Indianola. I was therefore left to consider the prospect myself.

I went back into the undertaker and asked if he knew of a couple of mules I might let.

He said a old man two doors down might have a mule or two, as he was known to do some trading in mules and horses.

I walked over there and knocked on the door, whilst Dickie stayed in the wagon. The old man come out and led me around back of his house and showed me two notch eared mules that was sisters. They was sturdy and barrel bellied and well enough shod, but was cheap on account of being poorly suited to one another.

One does her part in a pinch, the old man said. The other holds back. This here with the shoulder patch is the good sister, and this other here is the bad one. They both answer to being called Sister. Neither is broke to the saddle. If you take the one, then you take the other. Both, or neither. The good one's trained for the left, and the bad one for the right. If you get that wrong, they won't budge. I charge five dollars for a San Antonio turnaround.

I asked if he might settle for four, and he agreed to it.

Dickie had not yet paid what he owed for my hire to Boerne, so I went back to the wagon and required he give me the money. It was twelve Mexican coins worth a dollar apiece, plus fifty cents. I paid four of the coins to the man and tethered the mules to the wagon. We returned to the Reed House and found Mr Pate in the wagon yard, saddling a horse he'd let. It appeared bad tempered, holding its air to prevent a tight girth, and Mr Pate give it a knee in the belly to yank the girth a cinch.

Where's mine, Dickie asked. Did you get two.

Couldn't find two, Mr Pate said.

You don't say, said Dickie. I paid for a Ficklin ticket to San Antonio and you owe me the means to get there. If a coach is not to be had, then I need a horse.

Mr Pate stated again he could not find but one.

Then give me the funds to find one myself, Dickie demanded.

You'll not find a sound one, Mr Pate said. I been told that a cattle crowd come through town and bought all there was. This grouchy one here is what's left.

I have urgent business! Dickie proclaimed. How long am I to be left in Boerne before you come up with a way to get me to San Antonio!

Mr Pate said he supposed it would be some days.

Some days! Dickie yelled.

I then proposed a idea to Mr Pate. I said, I've let these two mules and was thinking to take Mrs Banes to San Antonio myself. I can take the mail and Dickie as well, if the Ficklin will pay me.

The offer interested Mr Pate, the mail being the Ficklin's main charge, and getting it to its destination being central to their government deal.

Pay you how much, he inquired.

It'll cost me four days all told, I said. I've paid four dollars to let these mules and I'll need to pay for their feed on the way. I'll have to board my mare here at the Reed House whilst I'm gone, and that will cost something. Also we'll have to stop for the night. I can do the whole deal for twenty dollars.

Mr Pate said, What was you planning to do with these mules otherwise.

Take Nell Banes and Tot, and not Dickie, and not the mail, I said.

The Ficklin could pay you five dollars to take them as well, he offered.

No thank you, I told him. That's not a fair bargain. I don't mind doing a woman a favor, but I don't care to be cheated. I'll need the whole twenty if I'm to carry the mail and Dickie.

Dickie told Mr Pate, That is the least the Ficklin can do for me!

Mr Pate said, Bills have to be sent up the line. The Ficklin would not approve that amount.

All right, I said, if Dickie pays board and lodging for the night, for me and Mrs Banes and the boy, and feed for the mules, I'll settle for twelve from the Ficklin. I'll be out the let for the mules and my costs on the way back, but twelve would pay for my time.

Mr Pate agreed the Ficklin could spring for twelve.

Why should I have to pay the expenses! Dickie demanded of me. You was thinking to carry Nell Banes and the boy for free. What do you care if I come along or not! I've paid my fare already.

Not to me you didn't, I told him.

Mr Pate said, If we make the deal, a receipt will have to do for it. You can tell Mr Reed to board your mare on the Ficklin account. Dickie Bell here will need to pay room and board overnight tonight for you and the woman, wherever you stay, and other expenses incurred. That's the deal. When you get to San Antonio, deliver him and Mrs Banes and her son to the Menger Hotel. The Ficklin has a account there and I'll see to those arrangements. Take the mail to the livery station across from the Menger. You can collect your payment there, and board the mules overnight. Folks awaiting the mail will find it a favor it's not further delayed.

Dickie fumed he was being cheated and further acted the skinflint, but what other choice did he have.

Mr Pate inquired of my full name and went to the desk and took paper from a Reed House ledger, on which he wrote, I, BERNAN PATE, DO STATE THAT BENJAMIN SHREVE IS OWED OF THE FICKLIN STAGE LINE TWELVE DOLLARS FOR SERVICES RENDERED IN DELIVERY OF PASSENGERS AND THE MAIL.

He give me your mother's pistol and advised I keep it until she might want it. He then mounted his horse and eyed the notch eared mules that I'd let.

That one there on the right is a loafer, he said.

How do you know, I asked him.

I rid myself of that pair on behalf of the Ficklin when I come through here last time, he told me. They're trouble. They don't care much for each other.

When Mr Pate had rode away, Dickie flew off at the handle and kicked at dirt. He cussed Mr Pate and me too. He stated he wanted a drink. I told him I knew of but one place where he might get one, that being a store called Staffel's known to serve beer and schnapps. He went off with his small drawstring bag of the unknown prized contents strapped onto his belt.

I borrowed rigging out of the livery, settled with Mr Reed to feed and care for my mare on the Ficklin account, hitched up the sisters, careful to hitch the good one to the left of the bad, as advised by their owner, loaded up your mother and you, said so long to my mare, and was ready to get on our way when Dickie returned and made plain, in his way of being, that he'd taken in too much liquor. He was not walking straight or talking right. He climbed onto the seat in a wobbly manner and avowed in a somber tone, as if stating facts of actual consequence, which they was, although only to him as yet, that treasure was a mysterious matter.

It does not lay where it's left, he said. It moves of its own will.

He awaited our response to that, and when none of us come up with a thing to say, he declared in a muddled fashion, There's always the question of whose is it, and who's got it, and who else wants it, and how they might get it.

This got your interest, Tot, and mine too. You asked him who did and who would.

He said, Who knows. He went on about treasure. Buried, it'll be dug up! Lost, it'll be tracked down. Had, it'll be taken. Hid under a heap of rocks or a pile of dirt, it'll take flight like a bird. If you hunt for it, you won't find it. If you don't hunt for it, it will find you.

We none of the three of us knew what to say to any of that. It had nothing to do with us or our journey to that point. However, I recall your consternation upon trying to figure it out. I recall how I sat in the driver's seat, and you sat between Dickie and me, and your mother sat on the mail bags in the back, as that was the most comfortable place for a woman in her state. She had on a hat plaited of straw that somebody at the Reed House give her, and held in her lap a bag of assorted items bestowed on her and you. We awaited Dickie to say a thing further of what his statements intended, but he become mum. He held close in his possession the items of greatest importance to him, those being his large leather pouch of coins tucked in his coat pocket, and the small tapestry bag of the unknown vital contents that was tied at his belt. It was straight up noon by the sun.

*　*　*

We took the stage road and passed the saddlery and meat market and mills on the Cibolo, then worked our way through a herd of cattle at the watering hole and pulled on down the road. It was a rough ride for your mother and she suffered. However, her thoughts remained inward and I wondered about them. The best I can say of the afternoon is that we was moving faster than we had with my mare, although the bad sister nipped at the good one and was generally bad.

We drew up at the store in Leon Springs and found the

postmaster awaiting us, as Mr Pate had passed through and alerted him we was hauling the mail. He's a Prussian and goes by the name Topperween. He sorted the mail and we struck out and got some distance and arrived by dark at a way stop called Moos Homestead. I had been at Moos back in the winter when hired by a German to haul a large load of pecans to San Antonio and there retrieve a piano. That was a good time as I had sole command of three fat yoke of oxen drawing the man's truck wagon with about eighty bushels of pecans loose in the bed.

Mr Moos therefore remembered me when we arrived, and hallooed me with friendly greetings. You and your mother was shown a room and took supper with the family, whilst Dickie and me was shown to a loft for sharing with drovers and teamsters. We ate outside with the teamsters for seventy-five cents apiece. They said a number of things of interest to me about Kansas laws that hampered drives from passing through parts of the state and caused roundabout miles that fatigued cattle, there being no market for stock when a buyer can count the ribs. Dickie stayed up playing at cards with them, but I was spent and turned in.

The men come in late to the loft and kept me awake, so I took a blanket and went out to my wagon where it was parked in a large shed alongside other vehicles and stored tools and contraptions. I was making my pallet in the wagon bed when the shed door pushed open a portion and your mother appeared there. She did not come in but remained at the door. It was dark in the shed, and the light from the moon was behind her, and I could not make out much of her features but I knew her by the ill fitted dress. She looked spent and untidy. It seemed like a while passed until she spoke up, but it was maybe not more than a minute. Her voice was quiet and hard to make out.

She said, I got things need to be told. Can I say them to you.

I told her, Yes ma'am, you can.

She said, I was clear who he was when I shot him. I took aim.

I said, I think I supposed you might of.

He was my husband, she said in a fixed way. His name is Micah.

I answered nothing to that, as nothing come to my mind but a muddle of thoughts as to what it might mean to shoot your own husband and the reasons a person might do it.

She said, I seen the thieves had his horse and saddle and figured that he was near. When he come running at me, I shot him right off so Tot wouldn't see him. How am I going to live with my son, now that I killed his father. What can I ever tell him.

It was plain from the way she spoke that regrets was taking her off like floodwaters, like she was borne away from all she knew of herself.

She said, I had to tell somebody.

I said, Yes ma'am, I figure you did.

She said, But for being apart from my son, I believe I can bear hell if I go there. Do you think I'm certain to go.

How might I of answered that, Tot. I strain to be a person of faith and find my way to a life that means a thing or two, and most days I lack much idea what I aught to do to that end, other than pull my weight and make a living. I can't answer questions like what she was asking of me, as who knows anything of the life after this one, if a person is honest, yet I wanted to help her find some measure of peace of mind. I will tell you, I was attached to my father before I lost him, and to my sister before she took off from my life, and to my step mother, of sorts, who tried to help raise me, despite we did not get along. I have been attached to folks I've met up with and taken meals with. Yet these cares was mostly slow grown and come to me over time, whereas what I felt for your mother, whilst she stood in that shred of light thrown from the moon behind, come at me all at once, and unforeseen. The questions in my mind of why she done what she did, and why she had hold of the gun, and what your father intended when he charged up to the door, those questions went to the back of my thoughts. The only thing I could think about was how I might stop her from being so scared.

You won't be going to hell, I told her. You have my word on it.

This come out of nowhere and not from particular knowledge of what the Lord might say on the matter, but I figured the burden of guilt she carried might not be nearly as heavy in actual fact as what she bore it to be. I can't say if she trusted my words, but the way she stood seemed to ease a little.

I said, If there's anything I might do for you, I will.

She said, I was finding my way all right, but that's turned.

Whatever I might, I will, I told her.

You're nice to me, she said, and then owned that she had better get back to the house, as you was asleep and might wake and miss her, and I agreed, and she went out and left me asking more questions than I am accustomed to asking.

Tot, I have told you straight out what your mother told me, as I before stated I would be honest. I hope it is right to of done so, as none of this could be easy for you to know. In my own life I have found the truth neither harder nor worse than what I might conjure of what it might be, and I prefer having it laid out plainly, to lurking about in the gloom.

* * *

In the morning we rolled out for San Antonio, your mother seated on mail sacks in the back that yielded somewhat to her condition. You sat between Dickie and me and at times crawled into my lap to act like you was helping me at the reins. I wished for eyes in back of my head, that I might see how your mother fared, as she did not say much the whole ride and kept her thoughts inward. I felt strongly bound to her by what she had told me. She was wearing the straw hat given to her in Boerne, and the blue dress again, not the ill fitted one, despite it was damp from her having washed it. She looked chilly before the day warmed.

We come into town at noon when church bells was ringing the hour. Mexicans stopped their business to take off their hats whilst the ringing went on, as they are devout people for the most part. The roads was crowded with commerce. We made our way to the Menger Hotel. It is a large hotel nearby the Alamo. I left you and your mother and Dickie there for the time being, intending to come back and see you and your mother was properly settled.

From the hotel I pulled to the livery alongside and had to wait my turn to get in, as the road was clogged on account of the federal quartermaster using the Alamo for a depot. The bad sister pestered the good one whilst we waited. Who knows what went on in the minds of them two.

When we got in, I left the mail at the Ficklin desk and asked the man there if I might get paid what Mr Pate had promised. He said Mr Pate had alerted him to expect me, however there was not cash on hand and I would need to come back in the morning to collect it.

I had not planned on staying the night, but now figured I'd have to, and that maybe Dickie would share his room. I left the sisters and my wagon with the hostler and told him to charge the fees to the Ficklin, as that seemed fair enough, and inquired as to which stage would be going to Indianola.

The hostler replied that the Risher and Hall had the Indianola route, and pointed me to their office. I stopped in there and told the man that I'd like to book three passengers for Indianola.

He said, The Indianola stage left this morning.

I was sorry to hear that. I told him that these passengers had missed that departure on account of the Ficklin that they was traveling on from Comfort being held up outside Boerne, and asked him how might they get tickets for the next stage.

The Indianola stage was a triweekly, he told me. The next would depart on Monday, this being a Friday, but he had already sold those tickets. The next after that would depart at eight in the morning on Wednesday. I inquired if there was another line going to Indianola and he said there was not.

I then asked could accommodations not be made on his Monday coach for a woman in a family way, traveling with her small boy, and he replied he could not throw booked passengers off his stage to make room for them that had missed their departure on account of the Ficklin's bad luck of being held up. If all stage lines was to make good on misfortunes of other stage lines, he said, every one of them would go bust, as stages was lucky ever to get where they aimed to be going, given mischief and other hitches. He said should some of the Monday passengers fail to show up, arrangements might be made at that time for the passengers in question.

It's a bad time of year to be going to Indianola regardless, he said. Last year this time the whole place come down with the yellow fever.

I found the exchange disheartening and decided I might drink a beer to think on what to do next. Down the street was a Mexican bar so I went there. It was a small place with a number of men in close quarters. Some was playing at dice games and cards.

I stationed myself at a table off in a corner to be somewhat out of the smoke. Most of the patrons was Mexicans, however I noted three men nearby who was not and who was disagreeable in the way they handled theirselves and demanded beers. They appeared sinister but not quick, which give me a wary sense, as who ever knows what might come loose from folks of that sort. They cut plugs of tobacco and gnawed them and spat on the floor. I could not see their faces clearly, on account of the smoke, but the way they acted intruded on my thoughts, which I was doing my best to mull. I overheard them argue on which of them might go to some certain place, I could not make out where, but I made out plainly that none of them wished to go there, and that their desire not to do so come from the chance they might be known later as having done so.

One of them said, My face is the most known. I can't go.

Another offered they flip a coin as to which would go.

Another said, There's three of us, idiot, how we going to flip a coin.

One of them offered, We flip a coin between two of us and

whoever loses flips with the other of us, and the loser of that flip goes.

One of the other two cursed and stated, That's unfair to the two who's got to flip twice, as their chances is doubled.

One answered, So we flip on who has to flip twice.

Another said, We flip three times to see which of us two has to go first and face double chances and flip with the third.

They squabbled on this and become angry amongst theirselves. They could not figure it out. I could not figure it out neither. Then it come to me they might do one flip each, and the one with the odd flip would go to the place in question that none of them wished to. I thought it a clever idea but forbore putting it forth, as these men was surly enough with one another that I could only suppose how surly they might be with me. However, the more I thought on the idea, the more clever I found it, and I give in and offered it.

I said, It's not my business, but you all might just each flip once, and the odd flip loses.

Tot, I will tell you, that was a large mistake I made. They turned their heads my direction, all three at one time. Evil is not a word I naturally use, but here I can think of none better. The look in their eyes about knocked me out of my chair. If you have witnessed a horned frog do its trick of spitting blood out of its eyes, you will know what I seen in that moment, times three.

I thought, I am a gone case, they are fixing to jump me.

However, they kept to their seats. Their stares went on. I bore up as long as I might and then turned my attention to my beer. I will tell you, I was shook.

It was then a man come in, sat hisself at the darkest end of the bar, and drew the attention of these men by his attire. He was dark and looked to be mostly Negro and maybe part Indian or Mexican. He was past his prime and scarred up, and one of his arms appeared useless. He wore a turban about his head and a number of accouterments such as necklaces made of metal trinkets and whatnot. Also a federal army jacket, although of a paler color than most and badly used. His trousers and shirt was regular but his shoes was moccasins and his belt was wove with beads. His hair was gray and come out from under his turban in a long braid. He carried a large poncho and a good sized cowhide travel bag with the hair still on. These he laid on a stool alongside him and ordered a bourbon whiskey in a friendly manner in Spanish from the Mexican tending the bar.

One of the three men I aforementioned said to the others, Take a look at that.

They soon commenced to call out and taunt the man about a Indian scalp nailed to the wall behind the bar.

They said, You! Old man! Might you be missing something! Might that be your hair up there on the wall!

It made no sense, as he appeared to have plenty of hair. He paid no attention to them, and they become agitated, saying, What are you. A Indian, a Mexican, a soldier or a nigger.

At some point he took note of them in a offhand way, and replied in English a good bit better than theirs, yet with a foreign aspect I had not before heard, how the scalp on the wall was not his, but might likely be one he had lifted, as he had lifted a good many, so many he had lost track, and how many had they lifted.

I could not make out if he was in earnest. The men did not

seem to know how to answer, and appeared perplexed as to how to insult him if they did not know what he might be called.

You got a federal soldier jacket, they said. You a federal soldier.

May the federal soldiers rot, he said.

Then you a Mexican or nigger or Indian, they said.

He give them a steady look and replied he would buy a drink for whichever of them might guess.

They each one laid out a option, there being three, and he shook his head to all three, and drank down his whiskey, laid down his money, took up his bag and poncho, and loud enough so they might hear, told the bar tender, in English, that he intended to find a establishment with patrons that was smarter. He said adios to the bar tender and spoke a few remarks to him in Spanish, which was plainly comments about the men and amused the bar tender greatly. He then walked out.

One of the three men remarked, That son of a bitch.

Another offered, How about we go after him.

Another continued to puzzle what he might be called. He said, I bet he's one of them nigger soldiers, on account of he was wearing a federal jacket.

They took up a debate about this, as the jacket was too pale a blue but did appear to be federal army attire.

One of them declared the man must be a Indian on account of the beads and trinkets, as who else wears those.

Why the hell would he say he's lifted scalps if he's a Indian, one of them said.

Maybe he's Apache and they was Comanche scalps, another maintained, and they commenced to debate if a Apache might speak both English and Spanish, as he had done, and to argue on if Apaches favored turbans such as he had on, and if Apaches' skin was ever that dark as his was.

One hollered out to the bar tender, You! Was he a Indian, or what.

The bar tender called the man a cabrone and went about his business.

God damn it! the man hollered. What was he.

The bar tender cursed him in Spanish.

I expected there might be further trouble from those three. However, they made note of the Mexican patrons taking stock of their measure, and how they was outnumbered. They threw down their money and left.

These events was to figure in how things played in your life, Tot, and your mother's, and mine, and not even to mention Dickie's, down the road.

* * *

I went from the bar back to the Menger to look in on you and your mother. I had not before been in a place so nice. It has nearly a hundred rooms for guests and a number of rooms for parties and whatnot, as well as a large eatery and a saloon. The ceilings is high up and the moldings as fine as what I might carve myself, if ever hired to do such work. The carpets and furniture appeared first class.

The clerk was a friendly young fellow about my age and we struck up a conversation. He showed me a book signed by guests in earlier times, one being Sam Houston who wrote his name very large. It said Sam Houston and horse! He said the hotel had indoor privies with cabinet chairs that had chamber pots placed inside them. I had not heard of such a chair and got him to show me in case I might someday find there's a market for those in Comfort. It was a sight.

I inquired how I might send a note to your mother up in her room, as I did not know what room she was in and did not think it right to go up there myself. He allowed me paper to write a note and offered he would deliver it. I wrote to your mother how the next Risher and Hall headed to Indianola was set to depart on Monday, but the seats was already sold, unless folks did not show, and the next after that would depart on Wednesday, that being five days off. I said I would be held up overnight waiting on my Ficklin payment and intended to stay with Dickie. I offered did she want me to take you for a look about town.

The clerk delivered the note and come back down the stairs, and you along with him. You was excited to go with me.

We went out and had a good time of it and seen a mix of people like you never saw before, such as French people speaking French, and others speaking whatnot, and a great number of Mexicans. We viewed the town squares and some churches and a variety of canals as well as the Alamo, although we could not venture within the Alamo, given as it was guarded. You had heard tales of what went on there and doled out more questions than I could answer, and we come on a number of people out selling sham items they claimed was Davy Crockett's. These was mostly shot pouches and hats and rifle parts. Mr Crockett could not of had that number of hats if he wore a new one each day of the week. You was interested to see so many Mexicans about. Mexican ladies was puffing smoke out of their nostrils, and you liked watching that. There was also dogs of the black hairless breed running about in the streets, and you was taken with them.

As well, we had our likeness made on a whim when we happened onto a small wooden building nearby the Masonic lodge that had a sign out front in the shape of a camera advertising a picture gallery. The sign said, Henry Doerr's photographs and stereoscopes. There was tintypes of folks tacked onto a board alongside the entry. The owner Mr Doerr seen us being interested in those, and come out and said we might have one made of ourselves for twenty-five cents apiece. I thought we might make a gift to your mother if we had one done of you. Thereupon we went in.

Mr Doerr went back into a room and come back with a small square of metal that was wet with solutions and meant to become the likeness. He stood you before the camera and had you hold your hat. He said you was to remain still and not twitch a eye for ten seconds. To help in the effort he set up behind you a stand with a grip to clamp on the backside of your head and help you keep still. You did not like the arrangement and become nervous of the situation. You would not go through with the plan.

I asked would you be all right if I stood alongside you.

You agreed how that would do, and Mr Doerr brought forward a taller stand for myself and settled the back of my head into the grip. You then commenced shaking your head and said you did not want a grip on your head and you wanted to leave. I talked things over with you, and we agreed that I might place my hand on the top of your head to help you stay steady, and there would be no grip used. I done so, and held my hat with the other hand, and you held your hat as well. We looked direct at the camera as instructed, and Mr Doerr counted the seconds. Right about when he reached ten, maybe nine, you turned your head to look up at me.

Mr Doerr said, This will be a smudged image. I'll do you another for free.

He then done so, and we was grateful about that. We stayed around, waiting for it to dry. Mr Doerr had a good time with us and showed us his camera and how it worked, and took us into the room at the back. He can do other sorts of photographs considered more perfect but they take longer and cost more. Tintypes is made of iron, not tin, as a point of fact, he told us. When ours was done we was happy to see it, as we looked nice in it.

We left there and sat on a bench at a canal and ate cornbread crackers and beef hash with peppers. Stray cats roamed about, and you said a thing I will not forget. You said, My mama and me had a cat that couldn't see nothing. I found it out in the woods. It lived in our yard but it got hanged.

I thought you must mean something other than what come out of your mouth about it being hanged. I asked you, Hanged how. What does that mean.

Like a sock, you said. At the clothesline. I seen it there.

I will tell you, that stopped me. I said, You mean it was dead.

Yes sir, you said, it was hanged and I cried about it. Mama got it and we buried it.

Who hanged it, I asked.

My mama said it was the swamp fox hanged it, you replied. She took me and my dog in the wagon, and we gone to a freeman's house and she give him my dog and said would he look after him.

She told him the cat got hanged. The freeman asked who done it, and she said, The swamp fox. She whispered it but I heard her. Why you think she whispered it. I cried to give up my dog. She said we was going to come back for him, but that was a lie she told. Why she told that.

Tot, I struggled to make sense of what you was saying. It give me the worst feeling about what your life was, and what your mother had gone through. I offered maybe you would get your dog later, but you looked doubtful about it. You said the dog I'd whittled for you had the same look about him as yours. You was carrying him in your pocket.

I took you back to the Menger when we was finished seeing sights. The dark thoughts would not leave me. Upon entering I seen a stack of newspapers and asked the desk clerk might I have one. He said I might take one free of charge, as by now he knew me. His name was Albert. He also give me a key for Dickie's room, which he said was alongside your mother's, Mr Pate having retained both rooms at the same time. He said Dickie was not yet back from when he went out.

I read the paper whilst you romped about on the stairs. There was stories of a stage line down to Monterrey, Mexico started up, and a raid on a din of gamblers. Mostly I was happy to read that a eight year old girl who Comanches had carried off from her home on the Guadalupe, ten miles from Kerrsville, had been rescued in the Frio Canyon, although her father and two other children taken at the same time was still missing and likely killed.

When I turned a page, a story called FICKLIN STAGE HELD UP ON WEDNESDAY, WEST OF BOERNE caught my eye. I read this with a great deal of interest to see if details was correct. It related the Ficklin was held up by four young thieves posed as Comanche Indians, and said the passengers was a man and a woman and child, along with the stage driver, by the name of Mr Edward Pate, by whom these events was reported, none of which four individuals was harmed in the occurrence, and all of which was brought along to Boerne by two charitable men that come along in a wagon. By this it meant Dickie and me. It maintained but one person come to be killed in the incident, he being a nameless fellow picked up on the road by the occupants of the wagon and having rushed at the Ficklin, unprovoked, unbidden, and unknown to the woman, who then fired upon him, on account of not knowing his intentions, and felled him with a quick bullet from a Hammond Bulldog she carried. The story furthermore said the deceased was transported to Boerne in the wagon and the county marshal there was alerted and now currently in search of the thieves, one of which went by the name Maynard and possessed a father known also to be a thief hisself, as apples fall close to a tree. At the end was some added details of a recent Comanche attack on a Ficklin station out west and a Kickapoo raid on the Eagle Pass route, both of which mishaps caused delays on the San Antonio mail and would mean a fine to the Ficklin, as attacks was no reason for being tardy.

You and myself went up and knocked on your mother's door and she opened it and become nearly white when I showed her the paper. She asked me right off, Does it give my name. Does it say where I'm headed.

I told her it did not.

You was pulling at me to give her the tintype of us, but I said it was not the right time. She paid you no mind but took the paper and leaned at the door and read what it said. Afterward she seized hold of herself like she might be sick, and called you to come inside the room, signaling me to come in as well. It did not seem right that I go in, however she was urgent and we entered.

She took up a hotel stationery and wrote me a note that said, HIS UNCLES WILL TRY AND TAKE HIM.

I have kept hold of the stationery and can tell you I am writing exact by the word.

I was shook, and replied underneath, WHO IS THE UNCLES AND WHY WILL THEY TRY AND TAKE HIM.

She wrote, SWAMP FOX MEN. BROTHERS TO MY HUSBAND.

It come to me then, and I wrote, IS SWAMP FOX A PERSON.

She replied, YES, EVIL.

HOW MIGHT THEY KNOW IT IS YOU AND TOT IN THE STORY, I wrote.

HAMMOND BULLDOG, she wrote. THEY WILL SUSPECT ME, THEY WILL PUNISH ME. LAW CHASED THEM FROM THE SWAMP. THEY HAVE A HIDEOUT AT A FARM NEARBY TOWN HERE.

WHY IS THE LAW AFTER THEM, I inquired.

She replied, WHERE IS MY HAMMOND. MR. PATE GIVE IT TO YOU.

I drew it forth from my satchel and give it to her whilst you was jumping about at the window and not seeing what we was doing. There was then a knock at the door. I called out who was it and Albert from the desk replied it was him. He said a reporter from the paper was downstairs asking if he might talk to your mother.

Your mother become alarmed at that notion and opened the door and said, Tell him I won't talk to him.

Albert and me went down to the lobby and told the reporter

the woman he had come to see wished not to talk nor be named in the paper. He was a pushy fellow, but we remained firm until he give up and quit the hotel.

I returned to your mother's room and told her the reporter was gone. I then retired to Dickie's room to await Dickie so we might think what to do for her in the situation. After a short while, here come Dickie with a mouth full of cotton, his tooth pulled. He hailed me with greetings I could not fully make out, on account of the cotton, except that the greetings was not entirely friendly, as he did not expect I would be in his room.

Unplug your mouth, I said. We got a issue. The Monday stage to Indianola is taken. The next is Wednesday. Nell Banes needs out of town sooner than that.

He fished the wad out of his mouth and replied, Are you telling me we can't be on our way until Wednesday. That's five days. I have important business and now I am cost more days! Is that what you are saying.

I agreed he was cost. I said, However, the issue is her. Put your thoughts to it. We got to help her.

He pitied hisself and claimed he was dogged by bad luck. He had thought he was soon fixing to head to Indianola to catch a steamship to New Orleans and pursue his important business, and fixing to be famous in the newspaper as well, and he was not happy there was hitches.

I asked what did he mean about being famous in the newspaper.

He said a reporter from the San Antonio Express come to halt him outside the hotel and ask if he was the fellow held up on a Ficklin, to which he'd replied affirmative and made statements.

I said, I just spoke to that man and sent him away. You did not give him Nell Banes' name or say where she's headed, did you.

Why would I not, he replied.

Tot, I did not have liberty to explain to Dickie the full where-withal of your mother's troubles, so I could not very well say. I told him, We have to advise her what's happened.

Dickie did not want to face her if she was to be unhappy. I didn't much neither. However, we gathered our wits and knocked at her door.

She opened the door and Dickie said, I told the reporter your name. I didn't know not to. He waylaid me on the street.

She become very still upon hearing this news. There was no blood in her face of a sudden. She asked Dickie what exactly did he tell the reporter.

Dickie owned as he had told him the particulars of where the Ficklin had started from, where it was headed, how it was held up, who the passengers was, and that him and the woman and boy, who was you and your mother, was all headed to Indianola. Also that your mother was in a maternal condition. Another way to put it is that he had told him everything. The reporter had said he would write the details for tomorrow's newspaper.

Your mother's eyes was fixed on Dickie whilst he owned up to this. But she did not appear like she saw much of him. It was like her sight had turned inward. She moved aside that we might enter the room, and then closed the door and turned the key when we done so. We all become silent. It was late day and the window at which you was standing allowed in a streak of sun that laid sharp across you and onto the carpet and onto your mother.

You took in the quiet amongst us and become uneasy, and said, Mama, talk, I don't like when you say nothing.

What she said at that time was to me and Dickie and was spoke in a still manner, like a vast calm come over her. She said, Tot and me need to start to Indianola. Please. Will you take us.

It was that direct a request, made in that sharp stretch of light, yet it settled in such a soft way I hardly figured the command it would seize of how things played.

I will tell you that Benjamin Franklin noted thirteen moral virtues in his autobiography, one of them being resolution. He maintained how resolution requires being resolved to do what you aught, and then doing what you resolve. Resolve is what your mother done in that moment. No matter this nor that, she intended to see you was safe.

My answer to her was foregone, as I cared for her by then in ways I did not yet own to myself. I believe I was glad for having the request put to me so frankly.

What took me aback was Dickie. I had thought him a passer by in my life, and in your mother's, and maybe a passer by in his own, given as how in my dealings with him thus far he had needed a push to do right. I had therefore missed the fact his heart was decent. I have known mules to behave like him, refusing to budge forward, or turn this way or that, but when given their heads and a loose rein, they'll start in the very direction they had declined to go. Likewise, Dickie found hisself with a loose rein in that time. He did not so much as blink at the question your mother put to us. He must of forgot his vital bag of secret contents that was tied at his belt, and his important business, and his hurry, and his lost days.

He must of forgot how travel by wagon was slow and could cost him more days to his destination than a wait for the Risher and Hall. Or maybe some guilt, or conscience, was seeping into him for talking to the reporter and stirring up this problem for you and your mother. Whatever the reason, he give one nod and it become plain to me of a sudden that him and me was soon to be heading to Indianola with your mother and you in my wagon.

*　*　*

Tot, I avowed to stick to the point and not go on about other things, but I will tell you one spare fact. For a long time it had been my hope to complete two things in my life, which was to visit the sea on some occasion and to drive cattle north on another. The first of those was the earliest dream of mine. In my younger years I got hold of a book about a whale who went by the name Moby Dick, and I read it many times over, as it was mostly all I had at that time in the way of items to read. From it I learned of such things as ship rigging, and what skrimshanders and such things is, and the meaning of words such as abaft and halyard and scuttlebutt, and also which side of the ship is leeward, and the manner in which a ship hoves out, and hoves to. Whilst living in Comfort I had seen pictures of the sea and spoke with Germans who told me tales of sailing across it. Nevertheless I could not call up a sense of the place, by which I mean the smell of salt they talked of and how waves come and went on the sand. It was my hope to do so, and I would be dishonest to claim I wanted to go to Indianola only on account of your mother needed a way to get there. I was glad for a cause to go on my own account, as well.

But by then it was too late in the day to set out, so we was stalled for the night. We was not worried about that, on account of we did not figure on trouble, as how would your father's evil brothers know we was in town. Even if they had happened on the newspaper that day, and figured it was your mother fired the Hammond Bulldog, as they knew she had one, and even if they could of figured it was your father she killed when she done so, how would they know that her and you was brought by me from Boerne to San Antonio in my wagon, as the paper had only said that the passengers was taken as far as Boerne. Tomorrow's paper would say otherwise, as it would contain the information Dickie had told, and let on that we was in town. But we would be gone then.

I made haste to the office of Risher and Hall in the livery and told the man there to expect that you and your mother and Dickie would be on the Wednesday stage to Indianola. This was a ruse, and not true. It was a ploy. I told him to tell any men who come by and inquired of you and your mother that you would be on that Wednesday stage, the Monday stage being full. The ploy was to give us a start ahead on the road, should the brothers think to pursue us. By Wednesday we would of covered some miles.

I bought food in the plaza with money Dickie had paid me and took it up to your mother and you in her room. When I went back to Dickie's room he was not there but returned soon with a dress he had got for your mother to make up for what he had done. It was scant up top and I told him it was not suited for her. He went to her room regardless and give her the dress and come back bringing you with him, as you was bored being alone with your mother.

We three had a good time in the room. The window was over a side street with a good deal of commerce to watch. Dickie laid about on the bed and recounted stories of lost treasures found and buried by drunks who could not later find them again, and treasures buried in dunes of sand that shifted and lost the markers.

Winds change, Dickie said, and whatever a dune might shelter, it will hand over in time.

You bounced about on the bed and into my arms and enjoyed the tales a great deal, although most of them likely was lies. I borrowed Dickie's razor and you liked watching me shave, so I showed you how it was done.

Then a knock come at the door. I called out who was it, and Albert from down at the desk said it was him and to let him in in a hurry. When I done so he stood in a state of alarm, breathing hard, and said three drunk men had appeared at the desk asking for the Ficklin's passengers that was held up.

They're looking for Mrs Banes, he said.

I asked how they knew she was here, as the Risher and Hall ticket man was to say otherwise in the case of his being asked.

It was the clerk at the Ficklin desk informed them, Albert said. He told them the Ficklin passengers was likely in town, having come along in a wagon with the mail, as he figured the fellow who brought the mail probably brought passengers. It's known that Ficklin travelers is put up at the Menger, so they come here looking. I denied I had a record of Mrs Banes, but they didn't believe me. They're yelling how they think their brother was murdered. Right now there's two of them banging on doors downstairs and a third said he's headed up here.

Albert then took off, saying he'd send to the federals at the Alamo to help us, as they was the nearest law.

Dickie and me could now hear the loud turmoil downstairs. We argued our options and thought up a hasty plan. I was to take you back to your mother's room and stay with the two of you there, whilst Dickie would stay in his. You and your mother would hide by the bed. If the men should knock on our doors we would claim we had not seen any woman nor child anywhere on our floor.

You was privy to the goings on, which agitated you. What men is looking for my mama, you asked, and would not give up asking whilst I carried you to your mother's room.

When she opened the door I related the situation and advised her to hide, whilst I would come in and guard the door.

She took you out of my arms and set you down and seized hold of your shoulders and said you was to stop asking what you was asking, and be fearless, and not make a sound, not one whimper out of you.

She tossed her dresses under the bed to hide how a woman was in the room, then got hold of her Hammond Bulldog and pulled you behind the bed and laid down on the floor with you.

Nearly at once come a uproar in the hall from the direction of the stairs. It was some distance off, as between us and the stairs there was about eight or nine rooms each side of the second floor. I readied my rifle and placed it beside the door. I checked and checked again that our key was turned and the toggle set. I put my ear to the door and distinctly heard the tromp of a pair of boots down the hall and the pounding and shouting of such things as, Open up or I'll shoot the lock! Folks within the rooms mostly refused and swore. I heard one lock get shot at. The disturbance moved in our direction, room to room down the hall, and imparted to me a powerful dread that grew worse as the noise become closer.

I will tell you, if there is a thing harder than facing danger it's knowing it's headed your way. I commenced to sweat and fidget. You piped up a time or two and your mother whispered at you to keep quiet. A few times she raised her head from where you was hid, and I seen by her look she was scared. I guess we all three hated hearing the racket and waiting for it to get to us. Dickie's room was alongside ours and would be arrived to first.

When the pounding arrived to Dickie's door the blows was so hard things shook. You whined and your mother shushed you.

I heard Dickie open his door and demand, What the hell do you want by knocking like that.

The man replied in a slurred nature he was hunting a woman and boy.

I seen no woman nor boy, Dickie avowed, and shut the door. This seemed to finish the matter, therefore I thought to try the same tack. Yet when the fierce beating occurred on my door and I gathered my wits and pulled the door open, I will tell you, Tot, all bets was promptly off. I laid eyes on the man and was stopped by my own surprise. You might of figured already, on account of how I have laid things out, but I did not at that time expect that the man before me would be one of the three with the evil stares who I seen in the bar, arguing over the coins.

Nothing useful come out of my mouth at that moment. I believe my jaw might of just dangled. The man did not appear to observe this however, as he was notably drunk. His eyes did not settle on me right off, but rolled about. Then of a sudden they alighted on me like they settled to roost. He had a six-shooter with the hammer already thumbed back. I can tell you, I was scared. My rifle was there in my reach, primed and ready to fire, and my hand itched to get hold of it. But I had a feeling that grabbing it might be the wrong move and start things on a path that would not go well for you or me or your mother.

He said, I know you.

I replied I did not think he did, and that I was not sure how he might.

You was the son of a bitch in the bar, he said.

I maintained that whoever he saw in a bar was not me.

His eyes was squinted but there was evil in what portion of eyeball might be seen. He grinned in a weird manner and said, I'll shoot you if you're lying to me. He then backed up and looked at me from a foot or so further off. He said, You made smartass remarks of flipping coins.

Whoever done that was not me, I restated. I know nothing of flipping coins. What might I do for you otherwise.

He kept up the evil look at me.

I nearly give in at that time, and snatched up my rifle, but figured he'd shoot me before my finger even got close to the trigger. I might of done better to answer the door with my rifle already aimed at the man.

I'm hunting a woman and boy, he said. Have you seen them. Lie and I'll shoot you.

How old is the boy, I inquired.

This high, said he, and indicated, more or less, how tall you was.

I seen nobody that size today, I told him.

He continued to squint at me in a way that become so cold hearted I felt sure he would shoot me. I feared you might make a noise from under the bed, either before or after he pulled the trigger, and he would then search you out. It was plain that any attempt to appeal to the man would turn out useless, on account of his eyes bore a shortage of reason, and mercy as well. So it was a question what aspect of his I might even petition. I did what I might to stand the man's stare without quaking and hoped for your silence under the bed. At last he took a step back and commenced to turn from me. I had my hand on the knob to push the door shut and was feeling a sense of relief, but then of a sudden here come Dickie from behind the man and struck him hard on the head with the butt of his Whitney. The man dropped down to his knees and looked up at me, whereupon Dickie thumped him again a time or two until he toppled onto his side, stone cold out, and laid prone in the doorway.

I said, Why did you do that! We was rid of him!

Not so! Dickie said. He offered to shoot you!

He was off that notion! I argued. He was leaving! We was done with him!

Dickie however did not regret his rash behavior and was glad to of knocked the man out. We felt of the man's breathing and found him vital although not lively. We dragged him within your mother's room, disarmed him of his weapons, which was the six-shooter, two derringers, and five pocketknives, and shut the door to devise how to further handle the state of affairs.

Tot, you was begging from behind the bed to know what had occurred, saying, What happen! What happen! You got free of your mother and slid your way under the bed close enough to be nearly face to face with the man, and commenced to shriek, It's Uncle Dale! Mama! It's Uncle Dale! He's dead!

You was very exited about that notion. Your mother, however, got hold of you and tugged you back and shushed you and said you was not to remark further upon your uncle Dale, nor any other uncle, as they was cruel people and you was to hush on the matter.

Dickie and me then took stock of the problems to handle, which was one of your uncles flat on the floor, knocked out, two others in search of you and your mother for reasons Dickie and me remained chiefly in the dark of, and your mother having a hard time making you hush.

We expected your uncle Dale might come to, so we pulled his belt off and secured his arms with it. Dickie headed downstairs to see if Albert had got the federals from the Alamo to come help. I locked the door and checked your uncle remained vital. Your mother kept behind the bed, as she did not want to chance your uncle seeing you, nor her neither, if he should arouse out of the stupor.

She signaled she had something to say, so I went over and got down at her level and she whispered how it was crucial for her to get you out of there yet she feared the other two brothers might be out in the hallways.

I advised, The federals is likely on their way to help us, so it's better to wait.

She had hold of your arm so tight you was whining of how it hurt. She had a firm grip on the Hammond with the other hand and it was aimed at Dale. The aim appeared true from what I could see. I did not doubt she had good enough reason to shoot him. However, killing a disarmed person did not seem the right idea and I hoped she would not do it. She had already done it once. How might we even explain the matter this time. I could not picture that she would blow a hole in your uncle whilst you was there, and yet she did appear ready, and she knew more of the man than I did and more of his deeds and what peril he posed to you and her too.

I whispered at her, If you shoot him there's two brothers left to come after you. I'll keep a eye on him. You just keep Tot quiet.

She said, Tot's hard to keep quiet.

She spoke this into my ear in barely even a whisper whilst you was complaining her hold on you was hurting your arm. However, you heard what she said and become silent as a rock of a sudden. It was strange how that happened. It seemed when she'd hushed you, you was deaf to her, and noisy, yet when she whispered at me, you was all ears, and heard her, and turned solemn.

You said, Mama, I'll be quiet.

She considered you and asked if you might be quiet like a possum. You showed her you could, and laid still and closed your eyes as if you was one playing a dead one.

I got up and stood over your uncle and watched for a twitch. This give me a chance to study him. He was worse looking than his brother that was your father, who I had deemed to be not bad looking, and he was distinctly poorly kept up. He also appeared older. His hair was a muddy color and greasy. It laid over his collar. His trousers was patched and his boots decrepit. His mode of breathing was somewhat like growling and moaning. I figured as long as that noise remained steady then he was sound out.

You kept quiet and fairly soon Dickie and Albert returned with two federals from the Alamo. One was a private and one was a sergeant. The sergeant was notably short and had a brisk way and spoke in a Yankee manner.

He looked at your uncle laid out on the floor and remarked on how he was hit pretty hard. Which one of you hit him, he asked.

I hit him, said Dickie.

More than once, it appears, stated the sergeant.

Whatever number of times it took, replied Dickie.

With what did you hit him, inquired the sergeant.

My pistol, Dickie said.

There's a city ordinance against concealed weapons, the sergeant advised him.

My pistol was not concealed when I hit him, Dickie owned.

Your mother at that time stood up from behind the bed, and the sergeant seen she had hold of a pistol.

He said, Ma'am, if the pistol is loaded, put it down on the bed please.

He then required I place my rifle on the bed as well, and Dickie his rifle and pistol too, given as how the army does not favor folks going about armed, concealed or not, despite folks will do it regardless. He inquired of your mother if she might like to sit, as I guess he seen she appeared feeble and her hands unsteady, and not even to mention her family condition.

She did not sit, but rather asked in a hurry, Did you get hold of the other two men.

The sergeant replied that the two had fled upon seeing him enter the hotel. He ordered the private to remove your prone uncle from the room, upon which the private dragged your uncle out to the hall and remained out there to watch him. The sergeant then asked Albert to recount what occurred, whereby Albert told how three men had arrived drunk and armed to the hotel and commenced pounding down doors in search of your mother.

You was still under the bed acting like you was a possum playing a dead one. Your mother looked under at you and remarked how you had done a good job being quiet but was now to go with Dickie Bell to his room so she might talk with the sergeant.

You crawled out disgruntled about leaving, and said, Why do I have to go. I want to talk to the federal too. Why can't I talk to the federal.

Your mother was anxious, however, and warned you not to argue with her.

You went off in a sullen mood with Dickie, who was no more glad to leave than you was.

Your mother and the sergeant and Albert and me was then the ones remained in the room. The sergeant took out a record book and a pen and asked your mother what she might know of the three men, and why they might be after her.

She said, They are brothers, and Swamp Fox men. Do you know who I mean by the Swamp Fox.

The sergeant had his eyes on his book and his pen set to write, but it was like somebody jerked his head up with a string when she said that.

Cullen Baker, the sergeant said. Cullen Montgomery Baker. The Swamp Fox of the Sulphur, up in the three state corner. Is that who you mean.

Your mother owned as it was.

The sergeant then become single-minded and dogged in his questions and asked if she knew where the two fled brothers might of run off to.

I will tell you, up to that point in my knowledge of your mother she was one to keep her thoughts private, but now they come out. She replied that the Swamp Fox gang had a place they sometimes hid out at a farmhouse nearby a mission called Espada on the boundary of San Antonio, but she did not know whose farm it might be, nor where that mission precisely was, as she had never before been in San Antonio nor even in the county. She said the two that run off bore marked resemblance to the one laid out in the hall, being about the same height and hair color and likely wearing attire once decent but now down at the heels from hanging about in the swamps. The one in the hall was Dale, she said, and the others was Silas and Murry. The sir names was all Banes.

They been with Cul Baker a long time, she added. They have killed a number of freedmen, and federals as well. If you're a Negro or a soldier, they'll kill you for no other reason. They was with Cul Baker the Swamp Fox when he laid into the soldier squad out of Jefferson that was taking supplies to Mr Kirkman of the Freedmen's Bureau.

The sergeant yanked open the door and ordered the private to go in haste to the Alamo and alert the captain that one of the Swamp Fox clan, by the name of Dale Banes, was held at the Menger, knocked out, and two others, of medium height, dark unkempt hair and shabby dress, both by the sir name of Banes as well, was fled and loose about town, perhaps heading south toward Mission Espada. He said to request for men to be sent to the Menger to take charge of the captive and for them to bring a stretcher along.

The private took in the orders and left in a hurry, whereupon the sergeant instructed Albert to go out to the hall and keep watch on your uncle Dale for the time being. Albert went out to do so.

The sergeant then asked your mother why the brothers had sought her, and she replied that she had reported some of their deeds to Mr Kirkman of the Freedmen's Bureau and she feared they was out to take her son from her.

He asked why they might want you, Tot, and she said, He's their kin, and I'm taking him to New Orleans to get him away from them.

Kin in what manner, he asked.

Nephew, she told him. They're brothers to my husband.

Where is your husband, he inquired.

Deceased, she said.

Deceased by what means, he asked.

Killed, she said.

Killed by who, he inquired.

She did not own it was by her. She said, There's enough folks, aside from the law, would of wanted him dead.

The sergeant pressed if she knew anything further that might prove useful in finding the others of the Swamp Fox clan, as the army had failed to track them, on account of Cullen Baker had local folks in the corner regions harboring him and his men and supplying their needs.

Your mother replied, They was one place when I left that region two months ago and they'll be some other place now. They move about in the bottoms with likeminded men. They was with Bob Lee's gang in the Black Cat Thicket south of Webb Hill for a time, and with Bickerstaff's clan a year back.

He asked would Mr Kirkman of the Freedmen's Bureau attest to what she'd said of these brothers and who they was, and she owned that he would, as they was well known by him to be part of Cul Baker's band. She said, Mr Kirkman knows their names and faces as well. They was with the gang when it fired on him before, and they've threatened judges and preachers who is trying to keep the peace. They make no secret who they are and what they do.

The sergeant said, Are you aware there's a large reward offered for the killing or capture of Swamp Fox men.

Yes, she replied. It's well known of. A thousand dollars for Cul Baker and lesser for his men.

That being the case, said the sergeant, if the man out in the hall is who you say, then Mr Bell in the next room is owed some money. Proof of your statements will be needed.

Mr Kirkman has plenty proof, she said. He's got affidavits from freedmen, and whites as well, including myself, about Cul Baker and Dale Banes and the rest of them lawless rabble and their deeds.

Tot, I will tell you it occurred to me that the risk your mother had undertook in reporting to Mr Kirkman about the Swamp Fox Cul Baker and his gang, and in having signed affidavits against them, should of earned a reward for her and not played out so Dickie would get it. Dickie did not even know who Dale Banes was when he whacked him over the head. I wondered if he might share his prize with your mother, and maybe even myself, as we was part of the situation, in a way, and in need of traveling money. However, I did not seriously count on he would, on account of why would he.

The sergeant finished making his notes, returned his pen and record book back to his pocket, charged me to help Albert watch over Dale in the hall, banged on Dickie's door and told him to go to the Alamo and report to the captain there about a reward he might get, and took off in search of your two fled uncles.

Albert and me was relieved when three soldiers appeared shortly and bore Dale off on a stretcher.

* * *

Your mother took you back to her room, and then Dickie returned from the Alamo in a cross mood and found me in his.

He said, I'm owed four hundred dollars in legal tender for my prize and they won't pay me. They say it's the state owes it, not the federals, on account of Governor Pease was the one offered it. For me to get hold of it, they have to send a telegraph to some kind of subassistant commissioner of the Freedmen's Bureau, up in some subdistrict of the corner counties, Kirkman by name, and he's got to come up with vouchers about the man's crimes sworn to from folks around there. Then the whole of it goes to the pen pushers over in Austin, who will sit on the papers until I'm dead.

He went on about not getting a fair shake, and how he had complained of that fact to the captain, and how the paper collar people was going to cheat him out of his rightly earned funds, and how the captain had become tetchy and told him his other option was to haul Dale Banes to Bowie county hisself and turn him over to the sheriff, either alive or otherwise, to attain his remittance, and did Dickie care to do it that way.

He said, It's more trouble to get my money than it was to knock the man out.

Whilst he grumbled, the light become sparse outside and the streets went quiet and I lit the lamp burners. Then your mother come to the room with you and asked could the two of you stay the night with us, as she feared your uncles might return and take up where they had left off.

We thought it a good idea for her safety and yours, no matter that it would be strange. We offered you and her might sleep in the bed whilst Dickie and me would mind our own business on the floor. She laid on the bed with you and worked on getting you quiet. You was confused by events and for a long time kept asking about things.

After you was finally asleep a soldier knocked and entered and shown me a voucher to sign, maintaining how I had seen Dickie knock Dale Banes on the head with his pistol. I signed it and Dickie looked hopeful, despite his earlier complaints, to see his reward might be underway.

The soldier then told us Dale Banes had passed on from the blows, and his body was to be carted up to the sheriff in Bowie county as proof of his demise, and did your mother have any instructions about who might be notified up that way, as she was kin.

On hearing Dale was dead, Dickie become dumbstruck and wordless, as I guess it had not occurred to him, nor fully to me neither, that the man would perish.

Your mother, however, appeared to play things through in her mind in no time at all. She replied to the soldier that Dale Banes was not her blood kin, only kin by her marriage, and she wanted her name kept out of matters when his family was told of what happened, as she wanted nothing to do with them.

The soldier answered he would relay those wishes to the colonel, and he went off.

Dickie then sat in a chair and said nothing, and your mother got on the bed with you whilst you slept, and I sat on the floor, and we none of us said anything for some time. Dickie was notably somewhat astonished that he had killed the man.

After a while he said, I swear I had no idea he would die.

Neither me nor your mother remarked to that.

Did I strike him that hard, he said.

Which strike do you mean, I replied. You hit him three or four times.

I didn't expect to kill him, he avowed. I must of got carried off. I never killed anybody before.

He plainly felt strange to of done it. A dark feeling come over us all, along with the actual darkness already settled upon the room. I turned up the lamp burners, yet the room was large and the ceiling high, and two lamps was scant light for the range. The windows was open but their bottom portions was shielded in wove wire cloth to fence out mosquitoes, so the flames was mirrored only in the upper portions and failed to offer much further light. Not much of a breeze passed through the wove wire, and the room was considerably warm.

Your mother commenced to pet your hair whilst you slept, and then commenced to tell things to Dickie that I recall as if by the word. She spoke in a slow manner and nearly a whisper and seemed to set her attention on petting your hair instead of on what she was saying, as if her thoughts and her words had nothing to do with one another. Yet I had the feeling that what she was saying had dug its way into her thinking so deep it was there for good, at practically all times, and had been so for some while.

She said, Dale kept a list of the names of Negroes he killed. I would guess it was more than a dozen. He claimed he wanted to thin them out a little, as there was too many for his taste.

She got quiet after saying that, and then she went on in her quiet way. She said, It was women as well as men, and one child I know of he killed. The child was a boy about ten, maybe twelve, and Dale seen him on the road and took him to the woods and tied him to a tree and lit into him with a black snake whip for having failed to tip his hat to him. The boy's brother found him tied to the tree when the family went looking. He had give up too much blood to live. His family learned of who done it, and told the sheriff, and the sheriff asked Dale about it, and Dale replied how it was a shame the boy had not lived long enough to learn to tip his hat. The sheriff did not take Dale in, for fear of being severely punished by Swamp Fox men if he tried, but he did alert the federals, and they come and arrested Dale and had him locked up. However, the jailer then let him go free and he returned to hiding out in the swamps with Cul Baker and the rest of them.

She become silent again for a time, and at other times as well, but the words all come back to me now as a piece, despite they was parceled, on account of her voice stayed at the same level and she kept on petting your head even at times she was silent. The words was harsh, no matter how soft she spoke them. It did not seem the halting manner in which she spoke was to conjure the words, as they appeared already fixed in her mind, but rather it seemed she figured to let them out in a measured stream, or they might come out in a flood.

She said, As well, there was a freedman Dale killed for no other reason than he was working a farm on his own account and making a good living at it. Dale and Cul Baker and some of them others showed up to his house one night and beat up his wife for not fetching a light for them prompt enough. Dale shot the man and made the woman light up a broom so he could see he was dead. He shot him a time or two more, for the fun, whilst she held the broom on fire for light. Folks learned of it afterward, and the freedmen and a couple of white folks reported what had took place, and they all paid for telling it. It's a known fact, if you tell things like that on Cul Baker's gang they'll pay you a visit. They'll shoot your goats and shoot your hogs. They'll go on a dog killing spree. They hanged a blind cat that lived in our yard, so I would take note of their meanness. You teach freedmen to read, you're paying for that with a whipping of one kind or another, no matter you're black or white. Any white person pays a Negro fair wages is set for a hard time. And if you was to manage to bring Cul Baker before the law, and collect that thousand dollars offered by Governor Pease, then you better pack up your things. Cul and his men hate anybody stood for the union, and hate the government, and would just as soon kill federals as freedmen. Some of the locals think Cul Baker's a hero. They give his gang cover so soldiers can't catch them nor take them in. The judges can't hold proper court, neither, on account of the juries is scared.

Your mother finished saying all that and kept on petting your hair. Dickie sat in his chair and made no remark for some time. I guess he took in the point she might of been making, that Dale should of been caught and tried and killed by the law some time ago, and what Dickie done was a favor. She declined to say it outright, but her statements stacked up.

She then laid down close beside you. Dickie got up and snuffed the lamp burners and laid on the floor with his head on his traveling bag and his money pouch, with his vital bag alongside him. I sat with my back to the door.

I thought maybe your mother and Dickie was both drifting off, but then Dickie whispered at her, Who was it you killed on the road back there, if I can ask you that.

It was a stretch of silence that followed. I wondered if she would tell him the truth like she had told me. He plainly was on to the notion. The quiet went on for so long I figured she wouldn't. I figured she might of gone to sleep. I think maybe five minutes went by before she said, It was my husband, Micah Banes.

I recall hearing Dickie suck at his gums where the tooth had got pulled, whilst he thought on what she had said. After a time he commenced to snore and I heard no more from your mother.

* * *

Tot, it was a odd night we passed there in the Menger. I kept mostly awake with my back to the door to stay certain nobody entered. At times I went to the window and looked down at the street. There was street lights around the corner on the main roads in the plaza, but they threw only a dim light to the window. The room was mainly dark, and yet I did not feel I aught to look at the bed, or at your mother asleep, as that would be a trespass, so it was hard to know what to look at. I had not before stayed in a hotel room, nor stayed the whole night through in a room with a grown woman other than Juda who raised me. I felt strange about it yet wanted to be there.

Dickie appeared to be having a solid rest and giving no thought to any of that. Mostly I sat with my back to the door and kept my rifle near me and laid my head on my knees and stared at the floor. I thought on the fact that Dale Banes was dead and wondered if I was right to be happy about that, as I was, knowing what your mother had told of him. I contemplated the evil he'd done to others, and how the boy he took to the woods might of tried to appeal to his mercy and seen how the man was shut to him. He'd been shut to me in the same way whilst he stood in the doorway with his pistol aimed at my belly, and who can say why he made up his mind to turn away when he did, and start down the hall, before Dickie struck him. It was nothing I said to plead my case that so inclined him, but maybe some chance thing, or likely that I am grown, and white, and not black, and we was not out in the woods.

My thoughts of that boy would not take their leave but returned all night long. As well, I thought of my younger years, as they come to me on account of the sense of danger skulking the other side of the door. I had many times likewise sat at the door of my home near Camp Verde, before I left there for Comfort. Me and my sister was there on our own after the time when our father passed, and there was a number of perils. Having my back to the door at the Menger was different from doing it back in our home, on account of the room I was in at the Menger was larger than our house, and contained proper lamps and no stinging and biting creatures and no pig shat on the floor. However, the feeling I had whilst listening for trouble took me back to my home and my sister, who as I afore-mentioned is gone from my life for now. The gloom come over me, and I missed that little girl.

From time to time, other thoughts come to my mind, such as what I might find in Dickie's bag of secret contents if I was to peek within it, which I did not do. Also whether or not the room we was in might of been stayed in by Sam Houston or other folks of impor-tance, and why I had felt the strong way I did about Dickie giving that scanty dress to your mother. I was bothered that he had done that, despite that she had not wore it as yet. What was he thinking, to buy such a thing.

I thought of the woman in Comfort whose house I room in, and wondered if she was all right feeding her chickens and such, and if she might be worried about where I'd gone off to for more nights than I'd told her. As well, I questioned how I had got myself onto this journey, and what for.

Mostly, though, I missed my sister, wherever she might be, and thought of you and your mother there on the bed, and thought of Dale Banes and his gruesome deeds. Many thoughts rattled along that track, with nothing to yank them off it, not even hardly a passer by making noise out in the hall.

Now and then you made snuffling noises or spoke things in your sleep I couldn't make out, and your mother whispered at you, and you become still. She got up to go to her room once, I suppose to make use of the chamber pot or take care of some private need, so I seen that she got there and returned without any disturbance. We did not exchange words on the matter.

I must of slept at some time before daylight, as it was near dawn when I awoke to the screeching wheels of Mexican carts out in the streets and your mother standing over me.

She whispered at me, You're still sitting up. Did you get no sleep at all.

I got up and told her I must of got some, and asked if you was still sound asleep, as you appeared to be.

She whispered you was, and said how I must be tired. It touched me that she should note that. I don't recall any person ever took note of that but my father. I let on to her how I was all right.

She asked if I'd keep a eye on you so she might go to the washroom down the hall. I watched that nobody laid in wait for her whilst she went, and watched that you slept.

When she returned, her and me roused Dickie and you, and we four collected up our things and went down to the hotel desk. There was newspapers there, and your mother and Dickie and me looked at what the reporter of yesterday had wrote about us. He told further details of the holdup, and where we come from, and who we was by name, and where your mother and you was headed. These was all details told to him by Dickie. He quoted Dickie a good deal. The brothers now would know exactly where you and your mother was going, and it was Dickie's doing. I seen he felt ashamed for being a loudmouth, so it was no use to remind him of it now.

We did not see more of Albert. I left a note for him, to thank him for his help to us, then we took our leave of the Menger.

*　*　*

When we was outside, your mother put on the hat afforded to her at Moos Homestead and set the brim low, so not to be known if your uncles was out and looking for her. Your own hat sat low on your head regardless, being too large for it, so that was a help. Your mother asked me if you might walk with me to appear like you was my son and not hers. You and me therefore walked together. You acted frisky and jumped about.

I took you along with me to the Ficklin office within the livery and asked for the payment they owed me. Your mother and Dickie stayed outside whilst we was inside. It was a different man at the desk from who I'd talked to the day before, and he said he knew nothing of such a payment. I showed my receipt from Mr Pate but he still knew nothing about it. He said no cash had yet been delivered that morning, but if I returned at five in the afternoon the fellow on duty at that time might know something.

I said, Is he the person who was here yesterday.

He said, No, that person comes in only on Friday.

Is there another Ficklin office in town I might look in on, I asked.

No, he replied. Just this one.

Is there one in Indianola, I asked.

No, he told me. Risher and Hall has that line.

The idea of having no funds, either going or coming back, worried me, as you might imagine. I took you back outside and told your mother and Dickie the money was not there and I did not know when it would be. I told them it might come at five in the afternoon, but if we was to wait for it, we would have to stay in town for another night, and I didn't think it a good idea.

They agreed we would need a decent head start on your uncles if they was to come after us, as they would likely be horseback and traveling faster. So it was a quandary. Your mother had in her purse what she'd meant to pay for the coach fare, but it would not go very far in the way of supplies for our travel. Beyond that, she had only boat passage to pay at Indianola. I myself had nothing but what was left of what Dickie had paid me to bring him from Boerne.

It was decided therefore that Dickie would have to pay our expenses if we was to get out of town. He was not happy about it, but he agreed to it, and bought us tamales and Mexican ginger-bread pastries shaped like pigs from cart vendors. I appreciated the food, but felt his way of handling the situation made me look like a scrounger. I would of preferred he advanced me the money so I could buy my own tamale. Benjamin Franklin hisself owned how pride is a hard thing to tamp down, and how on occasion when he did do it, he then become prideful for having done it.

We stopped at a bank, it being the first national one of San Antonio, and Dickie went in and changed out a bunch of his Mexican coins for U.S. specie. His coins in general remained a mystery to me as there seemed no limit to their numbers. When they was scant from the money pouch they appeared from the large travel bag like the fishes and loaves. That bag should not of been on the coach waybill starting out, given how many coins was in it and how coins and treasury notes and all forms of money is not allowed in the coach boot, but Dickie had disregarded the rule, being the sort who would.

I took you with me into the postal office and sent a card to the woman I board with, saying how I was delayed a number of days and hoped she would not have too much trouble without me around to help out. I sent a card to Mr Reed in Boerne as well, and asked if he might look after my mare for a few days longer, as she is a good mare, and I am fond of her, and if he would please tell the man who let me the mules that I was delayed. I promised I would somehow pay the amounts due, although I owned I was currently unsure how.

Your mother spent some of her dollars on toiletries and a hair comb, and also a serape to hide her condition and further hide who she was. She bought a canvas duffel as well to put her things in, as she now had the two extra dresses. Dickie bought us a tarpaulin for the wagon, bar soap, some wool Mexican blankets, a cushion for your mother, and food stuffs, largely cornmeal and canned goods and peaches, along with a few cooking utensils. Also ropes to encircle us when we slept, as that is supposed to keep out snakes, although I do not see how.

For myself I bought a cheap razor with the money left over from Dickie's payment to me for his ride to Boerne. I had not brought my razor from home, as I had not thought to travel so long. It has a black cowhorn grip handle. It was my father's possession, which he left for me on his passing.

You went along with me then to retrieve the mules. The livery master showed us a map of the route we was to take. It was the main one to Indianola and sufficiently traveled, Indianola being a large port and heavy with commerce, second only to Galveston which lies up the coast. I made out we could not reach the first town by dark but would come on a halfway station called Stellerman's.

Church clocks was ringing eleven in the morning by the time I got the sisters hitched and we was loaded and on our way.

*   *   *

I had not before traveled east of San Antonio, nor been so far from home, and neither Dickie nor your mother had been on our route at any time before either. We was all nervous the Banes brothers might somehow learn that you and your mother had left town early by other means than the Risher and Hall and come after you sooner than later. That was a solid concern. Nevertheless I was happy, on account of where we was headed and you and your mother being along. Dickie was not bad company neither, although he talked a great deal. A little of him could last a long way.

Your mother sat up front on the cushion Dickie had bought her, and you sat between her and me. Dickie reclined in the back and snoozed.

When we left the town and entered the wider spaces, I whispered to you if it might be time to give your mother the tintype of us.

You was excited about that notion, and I took it out of my satchel and handed it to you, and you give it to her and said, Mama, me and Benjamin got it for you! Benjamin's holding my head! It's for you!

She viewed it for a long time and told you it was the best belonging she ever owned.

You explained about the camera, and how it worked, and claimed the man had tried to put what you called a pitchfork on your head to make you hold still.

I recall how your mother appeared whilst she regarded the tin-type, on account of she smiled and I had not seen her do much of that. Her hair was a plain color and had no curls, and it was tied at the back, yet there was pieces come loose from under her hat that looked nice in how they fell. She had on her serape. She placed the photograph in her handbag in a careful manner.

We traveled through the afternoon and come on the halfway station before dark. There was a uproar going on when we pulled in, Mr Stellerman having gone off to poison a pack of wolves that had bit up one of his fillies, as we later learned, and the dogs having used his absence to tear apart two pigs that was in the potato field. The woman of the house was out hollering and whipping at the dogs to call them off the pigs, however with no success at it, as she was past her prime and they was large and blood thirsty. It was a loud upheaval as the pigs was not going to die easy and was squealing and trying to run off.

We pulled up and seen the trouble, and Dickie and me got out to help curtail the beastly party the dogs was having. Your mother wanted to keep you in the wagon, but you escaped her and run about screaming at the dogs with your hands over your ears whilst we tried to get them off the pigs.

You told them, Stop it! Stop it! Stop it! You was wild the whole time they was killing the pigs and screamed nearly as loud as the pigs theirselves, as it was a terrible sight to behold.

After a tussle, me and Dickie and the woman, who was Mrs

Stellerman, got hold of the dogs and tied them up in the barn. One of them had a nest of puppies in there that she should of been looking after, instead of being out ripping up pigs. Mrs Stellerman was glad of the aid and offered we could help ourselves at the well and feed the mules and camp in the yard without charge. We was a little beat up from the ordeal, with Dickie's arm bit and both of us scratched up. I was lucky my spectacles wasn't broke. You was wore out and crying, and your mother looked done in. Mr Stellerman arrived home shortly and was pleased we'd been there to help, although the pigs was perished.

The yard being fenced and well protected, we turned the sisters loose to take their leisure. They got along well enough when they was not hitched together. A wagon bearing a load of wool pulled in for the night a while later. The drivers was surly and had nothing to do with us, not so much as a tip of their hats.

We made our fire and had supper and then Mrs Stellerman come out. She told your mother she did not feel right leaving her to camp outdoors in her state, and offered did she want to come in and bring you with her to sleep in the spare room. Your mother welcomed the relief, but you did not want to go in with her and asked could you stay with me and Dickie. We swore to take good care of you, and your mother agreed to this after discussion.

When she was gone inside you laid out a blanket alongside mine in the bed of the wagon, and Dickie laid his on the ground alongside what remained of our fire and encircled it with his rope to keep snakes from crawling in with him, as he believed it could. We sat up awhile and he recounted stories of treasures guarded by banshees, and of witching for silver with divining rods, and of how a pack load of gold will sink deeper in the ground six inches every ten years.

That makes no sense, I said. There's hard ground and soft ground. There can be no standard sinkage rate.

We argued about that and a few other matters, as I felt he was showing off for you with pure lies. You was impressed with the stories, which was all right by me, except I didn't want you misled when it come to things that made no sense at all.

I told you, He's only telling tales. They're not all true.

Dickie said, Everything I told you tonight is the gospel truth.

Is the banshees he told of nearby us, you asked me.

I assured you they was nowhere near and told Dickie to hush about those, as he was scaring you.

Dickie thereby went to sleep. You and me laid awake in the wagon bed and stared at the stars. We talked of the manner in which bright stars was laid out in forms, called constellations. You had a lot of interesting things to say and a number of questions, and I did my best to answer with facts and not the kind of nonsense Dickie had put into your head. However, when I offered we should close our eyes and sleep, you was back on the matter of banshees. Nothing I said made you feel any better about those, and you commenced to fidget and sit up and look about. It become plain to me you would not sleep. After a while you asked could you sleep with your mother.

The house at that time was dark and I did not know which room your mother might be in. I did not think it right to knock at that hour, nor to peer in the windows. However, I did not figure it too impolite for you to have a look in, so we went to each window and I got down on my knees, and you climbed on my back and had a look in every window. You could not see your mother and was upset about that. We returned to the wagon and you commenced to get worked up and cry. Nothing I said was a help. I was glad when three puppies come tumbling out of the barn upon hearing the disturbance, as they got your attention. They was sweet puppies and I put them into the wagon with us so they might make you feel better. It was a tight fit, with them and me and you and my toolbox and the supplies, but well worth the discomfort, as they burrowed down alongside you, and you become quiet, although still awake.

I believe you might of remained awake all night had your mother not come to the wagon. I guess she knew you might miss her.

You seen her and sat up and said, Mama!

She said, Tot, I been missing you. Do you want to come sleep with me.

You was already climbing out of the wagon before she finished asking. She give me a nod and the two of you went off to the house. The puppies was well settled, so I allowed that they slept where they was, and laid there looking at stars, and thinking of you and your mother, and feeling put out with Dickie for scaring you about banshees.

When I heard Dickie wake and turn about on his blanket I figured to tell him I had a few bones to pick with him, as they was starting to mount up.

However, he beat me to speaking. He could not of seen me from where he laid on the ground, and I could not see him, so how he even knew I might be awake, I can't figure. Maybe he didn't care if

I was. He might of been half asleep hisself and sleep talking. However, what he said was clear, sensible language and appeared flat out thought out.

He said, You know, there's knuckleheads that'll take off riding along a ledge halfway down the side of a bluff. It'll get thinner and tighter until they're snugged against the wall, with a steep drop down below and a high wall alongside. But they'll keep on going. Then of a sudden they go around a bend, and whoa, the ledge has petered out. There's no room for the horse to turn around, and it can't walk backwards on such a narrow stretch as that. They're stuck. That could be you, my friend. You're on a ledge just like that. I seen how you look at Nell Banes. For your own peace of mind, I advise you don't go around the bend.

He said that and then nothing more. It did not call for a answer and I give it none. However, I give it thought. I give your mother and you a good deal of thought as well, as not much else seemed to stick in my mind. I laid there staring at stars whilst the puppies rustled about me, and after a time I owned to myself how Dickie had made a worthy point, though the ledge was likely too far narrowed already for that to matter.

* * *

In the morning Mrs Stellerman give us a good breakfast of batter cakes and molasses and we collected up our things and pulled out for Sutherland Springs, twenty miles off.

Dickie sat in the back and talked. He said, Tot, I'll tell you a riddle based on a true case. A stagecoach hauling the mail out west come under attack near Fort Concho and the mail was stole.

When the mail didn't arrive on time, a party was sent to look for the coach and found it out in the brush, a ways off the road, the driver bound by one leg to the back, and dead. He had been scalped and dragged a good distance. It appeared the Indians done it. The mules and harness was gone and the coach fully cleaned out. How do you think authorities knew it weren't Indians who done this, but rather was outright white thieves.

Tell me how, Dickie! Tell me how! you replied.

Two ways, Dickie said. Number one being the fact the mail was entirely missing and not scattered. Warriors have no use for our mail nor any currency might be in it. Number two being the manner in which the tracks of the coach run through the brush. There was no brush laid low in the path, but rather the brush had been skirted. Therefore it become evident the coach was skillfully managed. So who might do that. Not Comanches. Not Apaches. Not any of their stripe. They are skilled horsemen, not drivers of mule teams. So it was brainless white thieves or bandits got hold of that coach. They dragged the driver and scalped him, in which order was not made clear and was beside the point regardless, and then taken off with the mules and the mail, thinking they'd fooled their way out of being caught by diverting folks to a goose chase after Indians. They was later tracked down and met their fates. So let that be a lesson in how you can't trick people smarter than you.

Or better, let it be a lesson not to murder and steal, said your mother.

It's that lesson as well, agreed Dickie.

He went on about a number of other things, such as a time he had in Carson City out in Nevada when a wind called a Washoe

Zeffer come up and tore him off his horse and hurled him up in a dust cloud so thick he lost track of his whereabouts and never again found the horse, which he said was a good creature and about which he still wondered where it might of ended up. He said whilst he was in the Washoe Zeffer he saw children take to the air like they was birds. Two of them was later found with broken bones against a barn alongside the saddle his horse had wore.

He talked as well of wildcat mines, and a coffin peddler he once traveled along with, and a old plug horse he once had, and worms and lye in a lake named Mono Lake, and gulls' eggs turned to stone there. He said you could dip your clothes in Mono Lake, just one dip, and they'd come out looking like they was brand new, except for having so many worms hanging on them like strings that had to be cleared off. You was very excited about the worms, and he told you there was so many in that lake you could dunk a bucket and come up with more worms than water. There was flies a foot thick about the whole border, he said, and you could stir them and turn the sky black, such hordes of them took flight.

I will tell you I envied his journeys and the tales they afforded him, as I didn't have much likewise to offer you nor your mother.

We arrived at Sutherland Springs toward evening. I was tired of driving and tired of listening. I believe your mother was the latter as well, although you was neither, as you encouraged Dickie along. We pulled up at the store and postal office and found the owner out front closing up. I called out to ask what he knew of the town and where we might stay for the night, and he thereby come to the wagon and give us a earful.

He said there was a hotel we might stay in, although it had

gone downhill in the war and currently was infested with bugs due to folks he called low lifes traveling through, there being a good deal of cattle traffic passing on the Chewawa Road and the Goliad Trace, and foreign immigrants taking the trek inland from the port at Indianola. He made clear he did not like immigrants, although I could not see how he'd have much business without them.

He said we was better off sleeping outdoors alongside the mineral springs up the road, as they provided rejuvenation and was well kept up by folks in the town for bathing and healing. The black spring was reserved for men, as it was the most potent and stank the strongest, and the white one was reserved for use by women. There was a third one too, called Sour Spring, which contrary to its name had refreshing waters for drinking.

Methodists was camped at the Sour Spring until yesterday, but they've most of them gone by now, he said.

He pointed the way and we drove that direction and onto a narrow trace through a large forest of giant oaks that trailed gray moss as thick as curtains. The sun was low and the light yellow. It come through the branches in a weird way, as the moss swayed in the breeze and give the sense of things being topsy turvy. We all become quiet whilst passing through this forest, even Dickie, as the place seemed to call for a certain respect.

The trace led us along to a spring we guessed to be Sour Spring, as it was neither white nor black and the banks looked downtrod by the Methodists. A family of five lingered on the far side, and we hailed them, and hollered was this Sour Spring and was it good for drinking. They replied how that was correct. They come around and greeted us and asked did we want to take supper with them.

The woman offered how she would show your mother the way to the white spring to refresh herself from traveling.

You was shy of the kids, Tot, as they was all bigger than you, but after a time you warmed up and left to the other side of the spring and romped about with them. Your mother went off with the woman, and took with her the scanty dress Dickie bought, as I suppose she wanted a change from the other two.

Dickie ate and kept watch on our wagon whilst I went to the black spring and stripped off and laid in it. I was surprised how it bore me up. My hands being hard used, a bunch of skin come off in the black water. I believe if I'd stayed there longer the water might of ate to my bones. I'd planned on shaving my face but thought better of that, as I figured it might cause sores.

I dunked in a cove of the sour spring to wash away some of the smell, and got back to the wagon at dark. Crickets and frogs was cranked up and there was a breeze. Dickie asked would I keep my eye on his important bag of the secret contents whilst he went for a soak in the black spring. He said he would be a while. I agreed, and he went off with his beard scissors and a bottle of whiskey he'd bought in San Antonio.

I made my supper and sat on a log beside our fire and watched across the way. You was over there, moving about the family's campfire, roasting things on sticks and running about with the kids, and you come to the edge of the water and hollered to me. You was a small shape out there in the dark, yelling Benjamin! and waving your arms about. That was a nice event, hearing you holler my name over the water and seeing you being so happy.

Your mother then returned from the spring with the woman

and joined you at their campfire. Her hair was tied up and she had on the dress Dickie give her. It was a nice scene over there, with the light the fire shed into the darkness and onto all of you, and the fireflies flashing about in the forest behind you. I was fully sunk in the way I felt for your mother and you by then. I knew in my own mind that you would be passers by in my life, as we'd have to part in Indianola. And yet watching you and her over there in the light of the fire, against the dark of the night, I allowed myself to wish otherwise.

When the two of you come back to our side of the spring, you said you was still hungry. Your mother agreed you might get peaches out of the wagon. Dickie remained off soaking. Your mother and me sat at the edge of the water whilst you rustled about in the wagon looking for peaches.

Do you like this dress Dickie give me, she asked.

What could I say. It was scanty up top and it showed a great deal.

Do you like it yourself, I asked her.

My belly's too big to look nice in this, she allowed.

She looked better than nice in it to me. She'd slackened the laces to make more room for the baby.

The baby's moving in there, she said. He's rambunctious.

She took hold of my hand and settled it onto her belly and asked could I feel him move. I could hardly believe she did that, but I felt great having my hand on her that way. The baby moved a time or two and I felt it. I had not felt such a thing before excepting with nanny goats that was having issues getting their kids out and needed my help at it, and a time or two with sows about to farrow.

This was altogether a different occurrence for me, and I would of liked to keep my hand there all night long.

She said, I'm fairly sure he's a boy. What do you think I should name him.

What names are you choosing from, I asked her.

She said, I'm thinking maybe I'll name him Benjamin to remember you by, as I'm grateful to you.

Tot, I will tell you, I would of been glad to hear that idea except for how it meant she was thinking never to see me again after Indianola and would need some means, even aside from the tintype, to recall me. Even so, I told her I would appreciate that a great deal.

She asked if she smelt of the sulphur, having washed her hair in it.

I told her I did smell sulphur but thought it was coming from me.

She said, I hear the soaking is good for the baby. I'm scared having the baby without my mother to help me. She helped me when I had Tot, although she was sorry I'd chose the husband I did. My father was finished with me for having done that. I wish I was home with them now.

This must of made her reflect on home, as she talked of the crops they grew, which was a feast of corn and sweet potatoes, beans and pumpkins and tomatoes and onions and other things, like yellow squash. She said they had pigs and goats and two good dairy cows and it was a nice piece of land they was on. She figured her parents would live there forever, but she wasn't sure she would see them again. She had two brothers as well who was younger, and she said she missed them.

We sat awhile there in the dark after she spoke of these things, listening to frogs having a time on the banks and loud crickets and katydids in the forest. The Methodist family across the way laid their blankets and let their fire burn low.

Whilst we sat, your mother said she shouldn't of married your father, although at the time she had liked him. She said she'd seen him around town when she was a child and he was mostly grown up. And one day when she was thirteen or thereabout he'd stepped up at the general store and paid for a bag of flour she'd come up short to buy. His family was pitch farmers that owned a good patch of pines and was well off, and he was nice looking back then. She could not say if he was a good person at that time, but he was a better one than he later become. When he returned from the war she was fifteen, and he took notice of her, and things transpired, and then you was on the way, and they got married. She said she liked him all right until she learned of the cruelties he was up to. The pitch farm went bust on account of the slaves become freed, and at that time him and the whole Banes family commenced to torment people.

Did he torment you, I asked her.

It seemed like she replied not to me but to the water we sat looking at, as she did not turn her head my direction. She said, He give me cause to torment myself. I was scared to cross him for a time. There's things weigh on my conscience.

A notable stillness come over her then, to the point it seemed like she disappeared and left only her voice talking. She become doubly invisible as she did not look at me, and I therefore felt I aught not to look at her neither.

She said, There's things would not of happened if I'd had the right courage. My husband was going off a lot, coming home mostly to have privilege with me and to see Tot. His brothers was sometimes with him, and sometimes Swamp Fox men was. Sometimes Cul Baker hisself. None of them told me what they was off doing, but I should of known. I even believe I might of. I can't say when I crossed from not knowing, over to being sure. I heard rumors of what they was up to, but I was too scared to find out. I was scared to ask Micah of his part in it. He got rough with me sometimes. He was not so rough with Tot, but aimed on raising him up to be one of them, and that scared me even worse. Then one day I was told that him and the others had acted the animals, taking their turns at having their privilege of a Negro girl no more than twelve years old. It was so heinous a crime I doubted it might be true. When Micah come back to our house after I heard that, I asked him straight out if he'd took part in it. He wouldn't answer, and said to stop asking, and I didn't stop, and he went crazy at me. He hollered yes, yes, yes, that he done that, and done all them things. They all done all them things, he said. I felt sick in my stomach hearing that, and when he was gone I thought to report the crime to Mr Kirkman at the bureau, but I was too scared. There was people in town that would see me there and tell Micah I done so.

She stopped talking after she told me all that. I didn't think I should say anything, as it seemed like she'd almost forgot I was there.

But then she said, Later I did tell Mr Kirkman, but Micah and them had done other things then that might not of happened if I'd gone sooner. I acted cowardly, plain and straight. Do you have any thoughts on the matter.

Tot, I had plenty of thoughts on the matter, but they was about these men, and not her. I said, None that's directed at you, Nell.

She still did not look at me. Instead, she looked back to see you was not up to mischief and noted that you was fine, just plucking up grass at the edge of the light of our fire and urging one of the mules to eat it, despite the mule did not want it, on account of she could get it herself.

Your mother then continued to face the water, and after a time, she said, But yes, there come a time I did at last go talk to Mr Kirkman.

I inquired what prompted her finally to do that.

She sat with her knees pulled up to her chest and her arms wrapped around them. She said, It was a time when the whole Swamp Fox gang was all camped at our house. Micah and his brother Silas intended on going to town for supplies and asked my help at it. I took Tot along. And there was a thing took place in the store too cruel for me to tell you about, as I did nothing to stop it. There's shame on me for that. You wouldn't care for me anymore if I told you. I can't even hardly care for myself.

She said this in earnest, and I replied how I didn't think it could happen that I would change my opinion of her, and how if she'd like to tell me, then I would listen.

Well then, she said, let's see what you think of me after.

And she went on to tell me. She done so in the way she had, of stopping and starting and seeming like her words was aimed to the water or the air or some other person who was not there to listen.

There was times whilst she spoke that her voice was so quiet it was drowned by the crickets and katydids and the croaking frogs, and I couldn't plainly hear what she said. But I understood enough of her words to make out this horrible tale.

There was a little girl, maybe three years old, in that store they went to, she said. This little girl was with her daddy, who was a freedman your mother had seen about town. She wanted a penny whistler and her daddy didn't buy it for her, and your uncle Silas seen her begging for it and offered he'd buy it for her hisself.

Your mother said she got a bad feeling upon hearing that offer, as she figured it for a trick, and the daddy did too, as he looked doubtful.

Silas told the girl to take the item and run on, and she picked it up, and then Silas hollered at her, Girl, don't you steal that whistler! He snatched it away from her and threatened to give her a thrashing, and her daddy stepped in, and Silas hollered at him about raising a thieving daughter. Silas said, She needs a beating! He told his brother Micah to get hold of her, and Micah did, and her daddy put up a fight for her, and Silas drew his pistol and struck the man on the head. He said, She gets beat, or you get beat for raising a thieving girl.

Tot, the girl was not quite your own age that you are now while I'm writing, but nearly. You was seeing all this that happened and was confused and upset, as it was your daddy holding the girl and keeping her from her daddy. She cried and struggled to get to her daddy, and your mother started begging your daddy to turn her loose, and he wouldn't. It was a awful scene that happened. Nobody within the store stepped in. They was all scared like your mother.

Even the man at the store counter just watched and did nothing. And here's the thing your mother felt so ashamed of. She just grabbed you up and got out of there.

It's a hideous thing to know of myself, she said. That I turned my back on that child. I should of fought for her. I can't ever forgive myself that I didn't. I did nothing but go outside and stand there with Tot and try to breathe. I heard Silas in there beating the man and I did nothing. Tot was upset and asking me what his daddy and uncle was doing and if we could make them stop it, and it was like my mind quit working and my self just froze. It was like my ears stopped hearing that child screaming for her daddy whilst he got beat. And yet afterwards the sound come back to me all the time.

Tot, it's a hard tale, and likely a hard one for you to be learning about all these years later when you read this account, if you do read it. I am sorry to have to know it myself, but it did nothing to turn my feelings against your mother. It was plain how angry she felt at herself, and the awful regret she had. What good would it do for me to think less of her, too.

I asked her what happened after, and she said your daddy and uncle Silas walked out of the store toting supplies like nothing at all had occurred within. It was not spoke of all the way home. Nothing was spoke of. But your mother couldn't forgive herself for how she'd acted, and could not forget standing outside that store, just froze by fear whilst the freedman took a beating and his little girl wailed and screamed for him.

Then arrived a day, she said, when the men was gone back to the swamps, and her feelings of guilt was so harsh she could not reckon with them. She left you in the care of a neighbor and went to town and told Mr Kirkman what had took place. And just as she'd figured would happen, somebody seen her do that, and your daddy found out about it when he returned from the swamps. He took her out back of the house and put a knife at her throat and said if she was to go to Kirkman again and snitch on the Swamp Fox he would kill her hisself. He then give her a thrashing to prove it, and left back to the swamps.

Your mother took off afoot that night with you and went to town, and woke up Mr Kirkman at his house, and told him where she knew the men was hid out, so he might call on the federals to go after them. She named all the men that was accustomed to be with Cul Baker. She told of everything she knew that they'd done. Mr Kirkman give your mother and you a ride out of town before daylight, and you two got rides from strangers all the way west to Fredericksburg. She had a friend lived there and had heard the German folks in those parts did not harbor gangs like Cul Baker's.

It was a long, long way to go, she said, quite a journey, and but for the kindness of strangers, she and you wouldn't of made it. She would of preferred going home to her family but knew your daddy would look for her there. Or if he didn't, his mother would, her being the cruelest of the whole family and the most vengeful.

I don't know how Micah found us all the way out to Fredericksburg, she said. I guess Swamp Fox men have friends anywhere I might go in Texas.

She supposed the information she shared to Mr Kirkman is what rousted the gang and forced them down to their hideout near San Antonio. She said, Now Micah and Dale is dead on account of me, and the other two brothers will never give up trying to chase me down. If they was to go home without taking revenge, their mother would send them back after me. She'd take my son, for taking hers. She'd put forth every effort to raise him up to be Micah.

We sat a minute after she told me all that, whilst I tried taking it in.

Then your mother said, Am I ruined in your eyes.

Tot, I can't even tell you how far off she was from ruined in my eyes, and how sad I felt for the freedman she'd told of, and his little girl, and how angry I felt at your father, despite he was dead, and my thoughts of his brother Silas. I couldn't think how to explain what I felt, so I just told her she couldn't be ruined in my eyes no matter what, and how I thought she'd got up more courage than most people do.

She didn't make any response to that. I think she didn't fully believe me. I recall how she snugged her knees tighter against her and stared at the dark water.

You was meanwhile having a time on your own, nosing about things at the wagon. But right about then you come running to us, dangling a lengthy object by one end like it was a snake and yelling at us to look at what you'd found. It was nearly a foot long and I made out that it was a necklace strung with a number of jewels. You jumped about with it, being excited.

We stood up for a closer look, and your mother took the necklace and give it a good long study and said in a measured way, Tot, where did you find this.

In Dickie's bag! you replied. In Dickie's little bag!

I was nearly knocked over to hear that, having puzzled over the contents of that bag for the past several days. Furthermore, I recalled that Dickie had asked me to watch the bag whilst he was soaking. You can imagine how ashamed I felt at my failure.

Your mother said, Tot, you should not go searching in people's bags! That was Dickie's private belongings!

Straightaway when she said that, you become forlorn, and ceased your jumping and appeared at once down at the mouth.

It's my doing, I said. My fault, not his, Nell. Dickie charged me to watch the bag and I went off and left it.

Your mother asked you where the bag was, and you said it was in the wagon. You said, Mama, don't tell Dickie what I done. He might get mad.

He won't get mad at you, Tot, it's my issue, I told him. It's my doing. He should get mad at me.

Your mother sent you back to the wagon whilst her and me went to the fire and sat close to it to have a good look at the necklace in the light of it. The necklace was the most unforeseen item I ever held in my hands, and I guessed it to be worth thousands or millions of dollars. How Dickie might of got hold of it, neither of us could fathom. It seemed to contain diamonds as well as a range of colored stones and jewels. Also pieces cut of a tortoise shell. A large stone in the center took in the firelight and appeared to shoot the flames right back out.

Might this necklace be stolen, I wondered. If Dickie come by it fairly, why would he not of told us of it. And how had he come by so much money as he carried in his bags. That was a puzzle as well. I recalled how troubled he was in Comfort when the stage took off with the bag, and how he had later mentioned to me that his life underwent a surprising turn near the Horsehead Crossing out west. I'd asked then if the turn was upward or downward and he had replied it was upward, and that it entailed the bag and its contents and his need to travel to Indianola and what his fortune might be from there. Furthermore, I recalled his relief and delight to rescue the bag from the thieves that held up the coach, and how he had kept it close to him ever since, right up to the moment he'd asked me to mind it and taken off for a soak.

I wondered how angry he would be at me, and what he might do about that. I had come to think him a straight up person, yet might there be points about him still to surface. Might it be safer not to let on we'd seen the item.

I puzzled over these thoughts whilst your mother stirred up the flames to shine more light on the necklace. She was pretty whilst she did that, Tot. You watched from the wagon to see what we might be saying amongst ourselves. I stated my thoughts to your mother and she agreed it was better we not let Dickie know that we'd seen the necklace. She went to you and asked you to keep quiet about it on account of Dickie might be upset.

I meanwhile returned the necklace into the bag and took the bag and went looking for Dickie, as he'd been gone a long time. He was belly up in the black spring, bore up by the water, bobbing about in the moonlight. I called to him and he did not answer. I plunked a stone his direction, and he startled and come upright.

You looked like you might be dead, I said.

He replied, I was sleeping.

He swam to the shore and put his clothes on. I give him the bag. He'd emptied a good third of the bottle of whiskey he'd took, and appeared sluggish, but he'd trimmed up his beard and was better looking than I would of thought. As well, with the bad tooth gone his breath was improved.

When he and myself got back to the wagon you was already asleep. Dickie commenced to admire your mother's dress that he'd gave her. He was not coarse in his comments but I wished he would not make them. I admit I was jealous of him having money, and tales, and a nicer look with his trimmed up beard, whilst I was less husky, with not much to regale, and currently without funds of my own.

I could not make out if your mother welcomed Dickie liking her dress or didn't. I asked did she want me to string the tarp over herself and you in the wagon, so she might have privacy in the night.

She declared it was not worth the trouble, as she liked the fresh air.

Dickie and me laid out our blankets nearby the fire, circled the ropes around them to keep out snakes, in the case that might actually have a effect, and went to sleep.

Some hours later you come over the side of the wagon and laid down by me. The fire was burned down, and the night was chilly.

You whispered at me, My mama's sleeping.

I said, Yes, I know.

You said, I don't like her sleeping.

I asked why that might be.

Who's going to look after me when she's sleeping, you asked.

I'll look after you, Tot, I replied.

I'll sleep here with you, you told me.

All right, I said.

We can't tell Dickie we seen the necklace, you said.

That's right, we shouldn't, I answered.

Why, you asked.

He might be upset to know it, I said.

You agreed with that, and snugged down and went off to sleep.

Having you there alongside me recalled me of younger days when my sister would burrow under our quilt to keep herself warm. I sometimes nagged her about her feet being so cold on me. She was strong minded, and hard to put up with, but what would I give to have that little girl back in my life. A lot, that's for sure. I would give a great deal just to know where she is and if she's all right. I wonder if she thinks about me. I think of her nearly all the time, which is more than I would of expected.

So there I laid, alongside you, listening to a pair of owls who-whoing to one another, and missing my sister, and liking having you there with me, and considering what I might do after parting with you and your mother at Indianola. I would be making my journey back home on my own, that's what. I would reunite with my mare in Boerne and settle back in my board with the widow in Comfort, and go about carving cabinets and chairs and other items. Maybe someday I would get some news from my sister, of how she was doing just fine somewhere and didn't need me to be waiting on her or worried about her. If that should happen, I could sign on to drive cattle up north. I would just up and take off from Comfort.

However, with you there asleep alongside me, and your mother close by, even a real adventure like that seemed rather pointless of a sudden. My life looked like it might stretch along somewhat of a empty road.

* * *

Fog stole in overnight and sank a dark feel on the whole place, so we found ourselves in a mood to head out as soon as we roused from our beds.

Dickie built up the fire and your mother made coffee and hasty hotcakes. You hollered across the lake to your friends, but the fog was too thick to see over there and you got no answer. They must of packed up and gone on. I went to the woods and hunted branches to use for tarpaulin stakes in the case of encountering rain in the day, as it appeared that we might. From what I recalled of the map, we had quite a distance to cover before our next stop of Ecleto.

Regarding the necklace, you was good at keeping the secret whilst eating your breakfast, but not so good at appearing as if you had no secret to keep. You looked every which way but at Dickie, even when he was speaking to you. You hummed to yourself in a fashion that hinted you might be trying to keep some thoughts out of your thinking. It was plain to your mother and me the secret was eating at you. Me and her shared a glance about that. Dickie, however, was not attentive, as he was queasy from drinking the night before.

Our drive back through the forest was unnaturally strange. The long moss hanging from branches was hard to make out in the fog, being the same gray color. The strands was like damp hair practically slapping our faces before we knew we was on them. I had the feeling the day was not starting out right. You rode up front with your mother and me whilst Dickie sat alongside my toolbox in the rear of the wagon amongst our bedding and rations.

We was about a hour along the Goliad Trace when Dickie come back to life and told of a time when he chopped off the head of a rattler and the head jumped up and bit him. He said the fangs sank in and would not let go and he had a time pulling the head off him.

I doubt that happened, I told him.

You'd be surprised to know it happens quite often, he said.

It's a guaranteed fact I would, I owned. Are you saying the brain, the eyes and the fangs was all behaving like nothing untoward had took place between them and the length of the body, as if they was still one piece.

I am, replied Dickie.

How would a head jump with no muscles to carry it off the ground, I asked him.

I was wore out on his stories, on account of he had so many. Benjamin Franklin said to avoid trifling conversation and only speak what benefits people, but Dickie had never read that and I doubt could of held to it. At any rate, you liked the tales, Tot, and I think your mother mostly did too, as they took her part way out of her own reflections, which appeared to be mostly burdens to her. I felt jealous of Dickie in that regard, as well as in other regards aforementioned.

He went on about wildcat mines, and Mormons driving their wagons out of the Great Salt Lake City to Soda Lake and hauling off loads of free saleratus to sell at twenty-five cents a pound. He told of a swindler he knew who salted the shaft of a silver mine with melted and blackened half dollars to pass off as findings and raise the worth of the stock, who then encountered some trouble with the investors when one of the shards turned up engraved with the head of the liberty lady.

We kept a steady pace. There was gray clouds before us and black ones behind us that seemed to be following close on our heels and approaching ever closer. The sisters was frisky, sensing a storm. We rested them briefly a time or two but mostly pressed on. We met a few freighters and wagons of people who asked how far behind us the storm might be, as they was going straight for it. A wagon of immigrants who was not Germans hailed us, but we could not make out what they was saying, other than that they was headed to San Antonio. I think they was Checks.

By midday it was dead dark behind us and looked like we was fleeing the night. You turned and sat backward and watched the dark come. Lightning shone like embers within the clouds and stayed trapped there for a long time before breaking out in branched shafts that struck the ground. Thunder cranked up so loud it seemed like we had a cattle stampede after us. We was traveling a stretch of road at that time with nothing but grass and cactus and scattered patches of brush alongside, no sign of a farmhouse anywhere near, and evening was coming on.

When a spattering rain started, your mother and Dickie and me agreed we could not out pace the storm. We spotted a good sized oak tree off the road, but chose to remain in the open on account of the lightning chasing us. I pulled off the road and Dickie and me unhitched and hobbled out the mules. We strung the tarpaulin over the wagon bed at a good slant that would drain. Thunder was shaking the ground by then and rain drizzling down.

Prickly pear was the devil, the skies being so dark we could not see much of where we was stepping whilst we secured the tarpaulin. My spectacles was so drenched it was like I had gone for a swim with them on. The wind picked up further and become loud but not howling, there being nothing for it to howl against other than us and our small wagon and our two mules. The mules stood side by side, no matter if they disliked each other, and put their rumps to the winds.

When things was situated Dickie and me got in the back of the wagon under the tarpaulin with you and your mother. Your mother had on her serape. You and her was both damp, and Dickie and me was wet. We tossed aside our pocketknives, and everything else metal, and stayed clear of all hardware on account of the lightning. It was a tight squeeze amongst our gear and we was nearly on top of one another and feeling the mood of excitement commonly brought by electric storms. You was in my lap, and your mother had her shoulder up against mine. I remember her shoulder being there, as this is not a thing I would ever forget. It was dark there under the tarpaulin, but we seen each other in traces of lightning shed through it.

Our supper was bread and corn relish. We enjoyed it a good bit. Your mother and myself was crowded so close I could feel her breathe. I will tell you, I was every inch around the bend for her at that time. However, it did not seem right to let on about that. I brought up how Benjamin Franklin come into his knowledge of electric storms.

Dickie talked of large wasps known by the name tarantula hawks giving a poison sting and dragging helpless tarantulas off in a state of stiffness, as if they was froze, and burying them alive. Why he'd got onto that topic during a storm, in the midst of no place, I don't know. He went on about tarantulas froze so stiff they could not twitch a leg. Then of a sudden he disrupted hisself and asked why you and myself and your mother was all on one side of the wagon, there being better room over on his side. He said, Tot, Do you want to come over here where there's more room.

Hearing that invitation, you become nearly as still as the poisoned tarantulas, on account of the thought of sitting near him recalled you about the necklace and the wrong you'd done in taking it out of his private bag. You snugged against me and put your head down and would not answer him nor entertain any notion of moving to sit by him.

He become puzzled and asked what was the matter.

I said, We're settled in over here, so we're all right.

He looked us over in chance glimmers that come through the tarpaulin from lightning. Is there something I've not been told, he asked.

You could not hold out to the question, Tot, and shouted, I looked in your bag! I'm sorry! Now I'm in trouble! We was not supposed to say. I think you're going to be mad! Are you mad!

You put your hands over your ears in the case that he was.

Dickie appeared considerably stunned by the news. He asked which of his bags you'd looked in, although he must of had some idea.

It was the little one! you told him. The little one with the necklace in it! I'm sorry!

I could not at once tell what he felt about this, if he was angry or maybe disheartened, as his face become blank upon hearing it.

Dickie, it's my fault, I said. You asked me to watch the bag last night and I forgot about it. Tot didn't know any better than to have a peek in it.

Did you not see any reason to tell me, he demanded.

I guess I didn't, as no harm was done, I allowed.

Your mother then took over explaining and said how we'd kept the occurrence to ourselves, not wanting to make him mad or upset. She owned it had been a bad idea to do so.

Cold crept in whilst we waited to see how he might take that. We sat in the thick dark, listening to rain smack at the tarpaulin over our heads and awaiting for Dickie to answer, as he was not hasty to do so.

After a time, I said, Dickie, it's not my business how you come by the necklace or what you intend on doing with it, but it would be good for us to know if somebody might be after you for it.

I wish you would of been honest with me, he said.

We should of, I agreed.

It's a matter of trust, he declared.

I apologize, I told him.

To answer your question, nobody's after me, he said. Nobody knows I got the necklace.

Where did you get it from, I asked.

Hole in the ground, he said.

You claim you got the Mexican coins out of a hole as well, I recalled him. How many holes of riches might there be.

Same very large hole, he proclaimed. Out west, alongside Horse-head Crossing near Castle Gap.

Who might of buried a bunch of coins and a necklace like that, I asked him.

I will tell you something, he said. When a man's been seeking out treasure his whole life, and not yet found any, and he's afoot in treacherous country he might not get out of and happens upon a patch of dirt that looks to be dug not too long ago, and finds it to be a hole of riches, then he is not much inclined to ask questions like that. His sole question is likely to be how quick he can get what he's found out of Texas, where somebody might be missing it.

And do what with it then, I asked him.

Sell it, said he. I figure New Orleans has prosperous buyers. That's why I'm going.

About that time, it crossed my mind how the spatter of rain on the tarpaulin now sounded like pebble hail bouncing off it.

I said, Hold up. Is that hail.

We all become quiet and listened.

It dang sure is, Dickie noted.

Your mother asked would the tarpaulin hold firm against hail stones. She was notably nervous about it.

I told her I thought that it would. These are small ones, I said.

At times small ones give way to big ones, she said. Her voice had a grave and solemn tone when she spoke this. She must of fore-saw what would happen.

It happened faster than I would of thought. Thunder crashed over our wagon. A harsh wind wobbled the tarpaulin, tugging it to and fro. Then it was like a herd of buffalo dropped on us.

You jolted within my lap and let out a holler. Your mother reached over and grabbed you. The sisters shrieked in alarm. The stakes holding the tarpaulin give way and it fell down on us, trapping us underneath it. Hail nearly as big as horse hooves pounded upon it, knocking us over our heads and our whole bodies. I strove to push the canvas upwards to ease the stones from striking so hard, but it was soaked through and taking a beating and we was pummeled beneath it.

There is no knowing how long that would of gone on had a powerful wind not, of a sudden, took hold and carried the tarp away as if it weighed no more than a sheet. It went flying off after the mules. They was headed out for the oak tree we'd noted off in the distance when we stopped, their pace hindered to a hopping fashion on account of the hobbles. The tarpaulin flew out past them and tangled and rolled through brush, and the next I saw, it was stuck in a stand of cactus way out beyond the lone tree.

Your mother crawled over on top of you and tried to cover you up from the hail that now fell directly upon us. I did what I could to cover you both. However, those causes was lost. We was none of us any match for such hail. It battered us fiercely. I grabbed up one of our blankets and threw it over you and your mother and myself. We strove to get out of the wagon and climb underneath it. Dickie was headed the same direction. Despite him and myself did what we could for you and your mother, there was no saving any of us by any of us others. If we got knocked in the head by too many stones we would be senseless. It was a scramble.

We all four did get under the wagon yet found it a sorry hideout. A large patch of cactus pierced us with thorns. However, thorns in the flesh was a good deal better than stones to the head. You did holler about the thorns nevertheless. Your mother and Dickie and me had long ago learned how hollering makes no difference, but you was still of a age where it seemed like it might.

Our problems was only just started at that time. We was soaked wet and cold. The north wind had found us. We was beat up as well. Our belongings was all getting wet and walloped up in the bed of the wagon. I worried about the mules. No matter the bad one being ill tempered, she did not warrant the thrashing her and her sister was taking. As well, I felt the need to see to your mother. I asked her if she was all right, and she maintained how she was, but I feared it was not the case. She was a skinny woman, as I afore-noted, and close to her time. She was trying to keep you out of the prickly pear and the nettles. Her serape had dropped off and her scanty dress was soaked through. The skirt portion was soggy and heavy and tangled with thorns.

Dickie and me begun to bellow at one another over the racket of hail, regarding how we might get blankets out of the wagon. We took hold of the blanket I had brought down, and pulled it firm between us, and stretched it over our heads as a pretty good shield. We climbed up into the wagon bed and grabbed what blankets and things we could carry, our knuckles getting pretty well pummeled by hail. As well, I retrieved the bag of items given your mother at Boerne and Moos Homestead. The blanket we held over our heads barred most of the hail from smacking us but was hard to keep a tight grip on, as wind was trying to tear it out of our grasp.

It was a wild and messy time. Dickie and me could not easily hear what we was yelling to one another, given the thunder and hail and wind. We hauled what we could under the wagon. Your mother laid the blankets over the ground between the stands of cactus. They was wringing wet, but sturdy wool, and kept us off most of the bristles and out of some of the mud. I was sorry I'd steered the wagon clear off the road when halting. We would of been better off in the center where we would of been spared the barbs, although the mud would of been deeper there.

We then settled onto the blankets and Dickie commenced to yelp about how his vital bag had gone missing, as it was no longer tied at his belt.

Well, Dickie, nobody took it! I hollered.

I got to find it! he said.

I assured him no thieves was lurking about in the hail to snatch it, yet he worried over the matter as if worse trials was not going on.

By then you was shivering hard enough that your teeth was clanging together and you could no longer fret about thorns. Your mother got your wet clothes off you. She helped you into the pair of trousers given to you in Boerne that was in her bag. Her blue dress was in there as well, and mostly dry. She turned her back to Dickie and me and changed the dress out for the sopping scanty one she had on. She was entirely business about it, being chilled and worried about you and the baby, and not a finicky woman. Myself and Dickie was both respectful and turned our backs, as she was close by and she must of been nearly naked. We did not have a great deal of room to move, the floor of the wagon being close over our heads. We meantime took off our sopping shirts and wrapped ourselves in blankets. They was damp but better than nothing.

That was our situation. We was all four shivering cold, bunched together under the wagon, hemmed in by switchgrass and prickly pear. Hail hammered the wagon above us and the ground alongside us, tearing things up. It piled itself up in the grass and mud. You was interested in the sight but miserable. It was a terrible night for you, and a awful one for your mother and Dickie as well.

However, it was a splendid night for me. I could not get over how close your mother sat to me. Our sides was pressed against each other's. You was snugged mostly into her lap and partly into mine. I wanted to get you both in my arms and keep you two warm, but lacked the say so to do so.

There we sat. Dickie and me shouted to one another over the storm about his lost bag, and about the poor mules, and when the storm might move on, and other such things. Time and again you declared you was hungry. Your mother then leaned her head on my shoulder. I hardly breathed for having it there. I had certainly never felt so alive and cozy whilst nearly frozen to death. I put my arm over her shoulder and she did not seem to mind having it there.

It was a long, long, wet night, and the storm was brutal. The hail slackened to pebbles the size of buckshot, and then passed on, but the rain kept at it. The ground was thoroughly flooded. Thunder become more distant, but lighting kindled the clouds and flared up into chain lightning. It showed us sights we was sorry to see, the sorriest being one of the mules standing without the other, under the lone, far off tree. We could not make out which of the two she was, nor where her lost sister might be.

I stared a great deal at the darkness, searching for that gone mule. I awaited bursts of light to show her to me. The sight of her sister under the tree, with the branches whipping about in the wind and lit up by lightning, settled profoundly into my brain along with the smell of the wet ground, and the shine of ice that laid on it, and the sight of the tarpaulin out there lodged in a stand of cactus, and the dark of the gone mule.

Another vision revealed in the shards of light was that of a rangy creature running about in the rain after the hail had ceased. We thought him to be a coyote and then wondered if he was a dog. We felt sorry he was so addled. You asked might we feed him and make him our dog. He pestered the mule a time or two and she kicked him away. At times he become no more than a shadow streaking about in the dark. After a while he seemed like he vanished and I was glad about that, as he was unnatural and acted rabid.

Your mother drifted partly asleep and leaned more easily into me as the night went on. Despite my arm was cold and stiff for being around her shoulders, I would not of budged and bothered her sleeping for any offer of any prize of any kind I might name.

*   *   *

So passed the night. It withdrew to a gloomy dawn and the rain give way to mist. The ice commenced to melt but the air stayed frigid. The ground was a slurry. Dickie roused and ventured out and found his bag with the necklace in the muddy road. He was joyful to have it back. There's nothing beats when you can break even by finding what you once had but lost.

We then had to hunt for the mule. Your mother snugged close to you and dozed the best she could in the cold as I took my leave.

Both Dickie and me was half naked, our shirts being wet and too frosty to put on. We did not care to get our blankets wet by taking them with us into the drizzle, and therefore struck out shirtless with a rope for catching the mule.

We found her in less than a jiffy. She was reclined on her side nearly under her sister's nose, felled by a sizeable branch that laid heavily on her neck and pinned her. Her sides heaved in a harsh manner as she sucked in breath. She was the good mule of the two. I owned to myself how I had misjudged the bad one, who appeared to of guarded her through the night, as it seemed she was loyal in bad times even if bad in the good ones.

The down mule was seriously hurt and plainly bewildered. Her hobbles was tangled in brush and she was badly bruised by the hail, with large welts on her. Both her and her sister had taken a hard beating.

Dickie and me commenced to lift the branch off her and disentangle the hobbles and remove them. The mule moaned and grunted a great deal. We dragged the branch away, and she rose to her feet in a labored manner and acted spooky, like she'd been knocked in the head. When she let us get close we examined her legs and discovered one of them injured, although no bones appeared to be broke.

She won't be drawing our wagon today, Dickie said downheartedly.

Nor any time soon thereafter, I held further.

We become silent and stood looking at her and wondering what to do. We did not have any workable ideas, and was posing a few thoughts that was not worth much in the way of solving our issues, when of a sudden we heard your mother holler your name in a desperate manner.

We turned, startled, and caught sight of you, Tot, in the damp gray of the morning, headed out for the shadow creature we'd spied in the night. You was holding out some morsel of food you clearly intended to offer. But right off the animal sprang at you in a dead on run. You stopped in your tracks, spun around fast, and fled back for the wagon as quick as your legs could take you. Dickie and me took off for you, but we was unarmed and far away and could not head the animal off before it caught up to you and got hold of your leg.

Tot, I will tell you what, it's a fact how a mother will attempt to rescue her children with greater vigor than she can muster even to rescue herself. She will do it with greater passion. I have seen this happen before. What your mother done at that moment was a feat. She grabbed her pistol out of her bag and loaded a cartridge in it and run to reach you in time to take aim. How she done it so fast confounds me, given how she was close to her time and large with the baby. She fired into the creature. It yelped and dropped, but continued thrashing about, its teeth gripped onto your leg. Your mother run close, and loaded another cartridge, and fired again, and then the animal moved no more.

You laid on the ground, screaming, It come and bit me! You was pitiful in your amazement at how it had turned on you when you meant it no harm.

But worse to see when we reached you, and worse by far than many disheartening things I have seen in my life as well, and I have seen a good many, was the look of the animal that laid dead. It was a wretched coyote, hairless with mange, scrawny and covered with sores. The mouth appeared to drip in a manner your mother and Dickie and me beheld at once, and knew the possible meaning of. Your pant leg was rent where the teeth had laid in, and we yanked the pants down whilst you wailed in the icy mud about how the creature had bit you. The place it had bit was the back of your leg just over the bend of your knee. Already a bruise was rising.

Your mother knelt in the grass and held you still and studied the marks of the teeth. Her face went stark white. She looked to Dickie and me, and whilst no actual sound come out of her mouth, her eyes was plainly asking, Is it rabid.

Neither of us could think what to answer right off, as we both feared it likely was so. She knew this from seeing our faces. She turned and crawled a few paces away and vomited on the ground. Dickie and me got hold of you and scrubbed at the wound with ice that was melting around us.

Your mother crawled back over. Her hair dragged into her face. Her voice come out strange, like she was half strangled to death. She asked could we help her make out for sure if the flesh of your leg was broke through.

We settled you down on your belly and held you still. You bawled whilst your mother and Dickie and me got as close of a look as we could in the muggy light. The wound did not bleed a great deal, but the puncture marks was plain and appeared sufficiently deep for poison to of sank in.

Your mother got to her feet with trouble. Your cries went down to a whimper. She stood with her back to us for a long minute. When she turned back around to us, a stillness was come over her. She said in a calm and steadfast manner, Where can we find a madstone.

* * *

After she asked that question, Tot, I had but one purpose in my life. I forgot the hurt mule, and the miles we yet had to travel, and the parting in Indianola I dreaded, and the empty life I feared I would live when our time together was over. I forgot the cold drizzle around me, and your uncles who was after us, and I could not even of told you what day it was. The question would not of come to my mind, as time of a sudden had no standing other than how many hours it might take me to find a madstone, and whether or not I even could.

My thoughts at that moment was thus. Ecleto is maybe eight miles off, maybe even ten. The only way I might get there is to ride the bad mule. I was told by the man I let her from that she's not broke to the saddle. I don't have a saddle regardless, mine being back in Boerne. I know nothing about Ecleto. It's said to of been a muster station during the war, but the war is currently over. It might now be only a way stop. It's unlikely I'll find a madstone there, as those is hard to get hold of. Folks that have them is often stingy at lending them out. I seen but one in my lifetime, owned by a man in Bandera, passed down in his family and brought from Poland and kept locked up in the Catholic church. Bandera is far away, back in the hills near Comfort. How might I even hope of finding a madstone anywhere near here, other than seeing a uncommon white deer, who happens to carry one in the gut, walk right up and offer itself for the killing.

The words I heard myself speak was, I'll find you one, Nell.

It seemed a reasonable thing to say, as how could I of said otherwise, despite otherwise being the only reasonable answer.

I wonder at many things concerning your mother, Tot, but what caught my mind at that moment was how stanch she appeared for your sake, whilst in private she was coming to pieces. On account of how calm she acted, you thought you had nothing to worry about at that time. You got to your feet, and ceased to whimper, and leaned down to look at the dead coyote. I believe you was feeling the beast had betrayed your kindness. I also believe you took note of how it had suffered, being so thin and pitiful and having a bullet into its chest and its head. You bent down low, with a hunch to your small shoulders. Your pants was still halfway off. You eyed the coyote close up for a long, long minute, during which time a silence come over your mother and Dickie and me, the sounds of the morning hushed by the mist drifting down. The notion never entered your mind how the misery of the wretched coyote might very well be your own, in time.

*   *   *

I put on my shirt in haste whilst your mother and Dickie sorted amongst our provisions and found something to feed you. I then went to the tree and roped the bad mule, puffing a few breaths into her nose to get her to know me better.

Sister, look here, I told her. I was advised you're not broke for riding, but myself and you have got urgent business to tend to.

I brought her up alongside the wagon and tied the wagon reins shorter. It was just as well that we had no saddle, as we had no time to accustom her to it. I got in the wagon and leaned on her to acquaint her to my weight. She was so jumpy when I got on her I had to remove my spectacles to keep them safe. I laid face down on her, backwards, my head to her rump and my legs locked under her neck, and from there I seized hold of her flanks down under so she could adapt to having my full self on her. Dickie led her about for a minute with me laying on her like that. She swung her head back and laid into my ribs, but otherwise she did fine, and eventually I sat up and turned to the front and took the reins without her getting too aggravated about it.

Your mother called me aside to talk at that time, so I tied the mule and we walked a ways from the wagon. She tried to hold back how afraid she felt for you, but her hands kept making fluttering motions like birds' wings.

When we was far enough off so you couldn't hear, she stopped of a sudden and turned to me, and stated, I want you to take Tot with you.

I felt stunned by the notion of such a charge and did not have a ready reply.

She said, I know for a fact it's hard to get hold of a madstone, no matter you said you could do it. If there's none to be had in Ecleto then it's better for Tot to be with you. You can take him on down the road and keep searching.

I warned her the roads was mired and the mule chancy and likely to pitch us.

There's worse dangers than that, she said. If Tot's here with me and his uncles catch up, they'll take him.

I recalled her how the brothers had probably not started after us yet, as they would be thinking to catch her boarding the Risher and Hall on Wednesday, this being but Tuesday.

Once they start out, they'll come fast, she replied. If Tot gets pitched from the mule and gets hurt, he'll get better. If he gets taken by them, he won't. They'll turn him into his daddy.

I asked her what they would do to her if they found her and Dickie stuck here.

She flew off at the handle and yelled at me, saying, How can I even think about that when Tot's in danger of getting the rabies!

She appeared about to break down but held up. She was scared, she owned to me.

It's my fault it happened, she said. I was asleep when he went out to feed the coyote. I feel so afraid it's like I'm on fire and can't get it off me. I need to pace about but I can't appear scared to him. He won't go if he sees me scared. We've not been apart a day in his life.

I can't even tell you, Tot, how sorry I felt for how things stood. Her hands fluttered about. They would not be still. She got her small handbag out of her pocket and pulled out what was left of her money, including that which she had for the boat passage.

Pay what you have to, she said. Whatever you have to. All of it.

I took it from her and vowed how I would take care of you and bring you back safe very soon. But these was false promises altogether, as there was no guarantees, and she and myself both knew this. Even if I should find a madstone, it might help or might not. It's a known fact that they work on a whim. I think she believed this was the last she might ever see of you.

* * *

My ride with you started poorly. You was wary of the mule and did not regard a madstone worth leaving your mother for. You did not know of the risk of rabies, nor what a madstone was, and you was not taken with Dickie's tale of madstones being magic with powers to heal up wounds. I believe you had long since figured how Dickie's tales largely was nonsense and you did not think your wound awful enough to need healing, despite the coyote had frightened you a great deal. You bore leaving but kept on asking why you should have to go. I believe you understood there was things hidden from you and qualms we was not speaking.

So me and you started southeast toward Ecleto on the bad sister with you in a tense and balky temper. The sun broke through the mist and dried up the air and shone harsh in our eyes, yet the world appeared dark to me. Patches of road was like hog wallows. You sat before me and kept a good grip on the mule's scanty mane. She halted a number of times. It was tricky to get her going without making her jump and act crazy. You was fierce to stay on. A ways down the road she become compliant and settled into a rapid walk, which I did not then allow her to slacken, our time being essential. We come on a immigrant wagon, as well as a freighter, and I hailed them and asked did they have a madstone. But I could not make myself understood to the immigrants, and the freighter did not have one. The morning grew warm and you nodded off, being tired out by the night before.

I cannot exactly explain to you how astray my thoughts went on that ride, rambling in dread stories of folks dying from rabies. I knew of the awful treatments and the potions forced down the throat or hosed up the back end, and of folks roped to trees, kids tied down to their beds or smothered between mattresses when the raving took over. None of the cures was said to of worked except madstones, and then only at times.

I once knew a farmer in Kerrsville who died of the rabies. Before his passing he called on me to bring him a load of cypress shingles to fix up his roof. Him and me got to talking whilst I was unloading the shingles. He told me a twitchy raccoon had leapt on him from the rafters out in his barn five days back and bit him. Rabies was going around at that time to such a extent that people was killing their cats and dogs without provocation, to be on the safe side of things. He feared he was living on borrowed time and wanted to leave his family a good roof on the house. His wife give me meals with the family and I stayed for a couple of days to help out with the roof. I witnessed how fast he went down. His wife cut flesh from the bite and applied caustic that left a raw hole in his arm but didn't cure him. He become woozy and sick. His muscles cramped up and he walked bent over and suffered a palsy. A doctor come and offered some potions, but the man was then churning out such a amount of spittle he could not swallow even a teaspoon of water, and he declined the offer of things going in from the other direction. He knew he was past hope. I finished the roof and said my farewell, and a few days later heard how he'd told his family so long, and gone out with his gun and took hisself out of his suffering.

These was my thoughts on the ride to Ecleto, Tot. You was asleep and sagged forward, so I pulled your hat off to keep it from dropping and kept my arms about you the best that I could whilst trying to manage the mule. Holding you like that give me the sense that you was my kid. I could not see how your mother was standing her worry, my own being nearly intolerable.

* * *

It was thus we arrived to Ecleto right about noon and found it not much of a town. The main street through was nearly all there was to it. The yards was slurries. Folks was out patching up damage undergone from the storm, and dogs run about barking at us and worried the mule. Coops was busted and chickens was loose in the street as well. The swing station, when we come on it, proved a mere meager affair of a office, a privy, a goat pen, a shed, and a poorly kept barn for the stage mules.

I woke you and tied the mule at the post, and you and me went inside. There was a great deal of goat shat on the floor, as the goats must of been brought in out of the hail the night before. The station keeper was at his desk but rose to greet us, and I explained to him at once, whilst trying to convey my concern in a way that would not worry you, that you had been bit by a sickly coyote and we was in need of a madstone.

The man eyed you, and then took a look at me and appeared to understand my fear for you and my need not to frighten you of the situation. He spoke in a careful manner, saying, Well, son, if there was a madstone anywhere here in Ecleto I believe I would know about it. Which way are you headed.

He was old and bald and there was not much flesh to him. His right eye did not turn in the socket, as it appeared to be glass. It was blue and did not match the other.

To Indianola, I told him.

Then maybe on down the road in Yorktown you might find one, he said. It's a bigger town than here. But to be honest, I'm doubtful. Victoria you might find somebody's got one.

How far is Yorktown and Victoria, I asked him.

It's twenty miles on to Yorktown, and a good stretch further on to Victoria, he said.

My hopes had hung on, but now they give up. Our time was too short to travel that far. I could not think of a workable plan, and felt light in my head and sick at my stomach.

The station keeper told us to wash from the bucket out on the porch and help ourselves to cabreeto for fifty cents each if we should want it, whilst he planned to go knock on doors and ask if by chance there might be a madstone he might not of known of.

Meantime you was making friends with the man's dog. It was a small white wiry haired creature infested with fleas and ticks but wagged its tail like it had no troubles.

So there we was, me having no hopes and you playing with the dog, unaware how much risk you was in, and the station keeper fixing to go knock on doors, when out of a back room appeared a person I had not expected to see. He wore the peculiar attire of a patched up federal army jacket somewhat paler in color than most, along with a great number of necklaces strung with trinkets, a belt woven of beads, moccasins on his feet, and a blue scarf wrapped like a turban atop his head. He was dark skinned, quite tall, past his prime, and appeared to of known rough times. His hair was gray colored and hung out from under the turban in a braid down to his belt. I knew him right off as the strangely outfitted man I'd seen in the Mexican bar in San

Antonio, as there could be none other like him. I was nearly as dumbfounded to see him there as I was by what he then stated.

He said, I have a madstone in my bag.

I stood but half believing I'd heard the words right whilst he fetched his traveling bag from the room he'd stepped out of. It was the cowhide affair with the hair still on it that I'd seen him bring into the bar. He laid it down on the table, opened it up, and dug about in it, using only one arm to do so, as the other hung limp in a lifeless manner. After a moment of searching, he brought out a stone nearly perfectly round, two inches across, of a spotty gray color, and held it for us to look at.

His attire and general appearance had got your attention, Tot, despite you was on the floor with the dog. He offered the stone to you, and you was notably wary of him but got up from the floor, and took it, and felt of it.

I could not think of sufficient words to state my feeling of joy and gratitude at having my hopes restored, but I give it a try and stumbled my way through a few I come up with, and told him my name.

He replied that his name was George in English and Hor-hay Elveraz in Spanish. He preferred that I call him Horhay. He instructed me to soak the stone in milk and put it to use. His speech had a odd measure in how the words was put and where they was paused, but there was no fault to the actual English as far as I could make out. In the Mexican bar he'd spoke Spanish and English and seemed easier with the Spanish, but he did not look like a Mexican.

The station keeper told me to take a bucket and rope from the wall of the porch and go out to the pen and catch the large one-eyed nanny who'd lost a eye to infection, as she typically offered good milk.

She's hard to catch, but easy to milk, he told me. Get her into the barn and she'll go to the stand. There's feed in the bins. She's got a soft udder and good long teats and you'll get her milked out in no time. I'll feed this boy while you're at it.

I went out and spotted a bunch of does standing about in the pen. They yelled at me when they seen me coming. The one I was after seemed like she knew I was coming for her. I had a tussle to catch her. Her friends was all yelling about it. After I got her into the barn she become sweet as pie and jumped into the stand to await her feed and the milking.

I milked her in haste, fearing how time might cost us, and pretty soon Horhay come into the barn. It was mostly dark in there on account of the shutters was closed, but bands of light shined through gaps in a wall and laid stripes on us, top to bottom. Horhay stood mostly straight up but appeared like he listed off to the side, on account of his slack arm sagged and the stripes of light angled on him. He was quiet, and the place was quiet too but for a couple of stage mules milling about in their stalls and the milk squirting into the bucket and the nanny crunching her feed.

Dust hung about in the air and seemed to blink off and on whilst drifting between the bands of light, and this somewhat mesmerized me, as I was entirely worn down. Had I not been so worried about if the madstone would cure you or not, I might of fallen dead asleep on the milking stool whilst staring at bits of dust.

I said, Do you think the madstone will draw out the poison.

Horhay replied he had never put it to use and couldn't say if it would, or how it might do it. He said he carried plenty of sundry charms, and objects from his people, and a rosary that a Mexican soldier had presented to him, and yet was not certain if any of these could work miracles. However, he had lived longer than he deserved, he said, and through more than he expected, and who could say why.

I asked who his people might be, as he had made reference, and he said they was Seminoll. I had not heard of them. I asked where he got the stone, and he said from the gut of a deer he killed some years ago.

I've been told a white deer is best, I offered.

It was not white, he said.

I asked how we might know for sure if the stone was drawing out poison when we applied it, and he said it would stick to the wound and then take on a green color when placed back in the milk.

He inquired of our situation and I told him how we had become stranded, and how your mother awaited us back at the wagon with Dickie, and who Dickie was, and how we was hoping to get to Indianola.

He said he was headed the same direction.

I owned I had seen him in San Antonio in the Mexican bar when three men was pestering him, and he said he remembered the men.

They're after the boy and his mother, I told him. They come into the Menger looking for them, and Dickie struck one and killed him, but it's likely the other two is still coming for us.

When I had enough milk in the bucket, I put the nanny back

in the pen whilst Horhay took the milk into the station. I come in and found you eating cabreeto and beans and telling the station keeper and Horhay about the coyote. You called it a rabbit coyote and wove a long tale about the attack. The station keeper boiled up the goat milk and soaked the stone in it. He moved about with a cane and threw bites of cabreeto to the dog. We stood you up on the table and took your pants down and had a good look at the bite marks at the back of your leg. Horhay took the stone from the milk and held it against the marks. I broke a hard sweat waiting to see what would happen. You was not worried yourself, being blind to your risk of the rabies and busy chewing on ribs and tossing bites to the dog.

When Horhay give the stone a tug, it did not stick to the flesh as it should of, and my hopes sank low and my fears rose so high I could hear my heart thump. He applied it another stretch of minutes, then pulled it away and dropped it into the milk, and stirred it about, scooped it out with the spoon, and I was knocked nearly out of my boots to see that it come out a pasty green like the back of a dollar bill. I kept on staring to see if that could be true. I looked to Horhay and seen by his grin that it was. The station keeper hisself stood alongside the stove with his mouth dropped open. There was a part of me grasped how thin my hope must of actually been, to find myself so surprised that the stone had appeared to of done as intended.

I then walked out of the building and into the yard and sat on a large rock and give over to my feelings, there being too many to rope in. I outright cried, and felt stunned to think you was saved, and stunned to know how scared I'd been that you wouldn't be.

I cared about you too much for my peace of mind, and owned to myself how I had not cared about any two people, save my father and sister, like I now cared about you and your mother. I had made peace some time ago with the fact of my father's passing, and just about come to terms with missing my sister so much, but you and your mother taking your leave was yet to be gone through, and the work to get over the loss was yet to be started.

I thought to go through it right then and there, telling myself that you would live, and not die of rabies, but you would be doing that living elsewhere, off in places I'd never laid eyes on and might never would, and I would need to accept how we would be strangers after a time. The relief I felt at having you saved made plain to me how I would feel about losing you, and I told myself, Suffer it now, not later. Go through it now. Get it behind you.

I did what I could in that regard with my thinking, which was not much, then went back inside where the station keeper and Horhay was applying the stone once again as a matter of being thorough. The station keeper was named Cooper Sandler, as I should of stated before now. You was impatient with standing, and laid on your belly upon the table. Horhay applied the stone and waited, and dropped it into the milk again, and stirred it up, and spooned it out, and it come up no greener this time, and he pronounced you entirely cleaned of the rabies.

Mr Sandler brought out peach brandy and offered a toast to you. He called you a brave boy, and you grinned a great deal to hear that. You then commenced yanking ticks off the dog.

I will tell you, Tot, I would of liked to of laid down and slept at that time, but my thoughts was fixed on the current trouble of having your mother back at the wagon, worried out of her wits, and only one mule to pull the wagon when we should get there.

I posed these worries, and Horhay granted he would ride to the wagon with us. He said his mare had a cold jaw when it come to the bit, but she would be willing to hitch with a mule, and she was luckily gray, that being the color that mules prefer in horses they're made to hitch with. His mare and the mule could draw the wagon back here to Ecleto, and we would figure things on from then.

I offered some of your mother's money to pay for his trouble, but he declined to take it. He retrieved his mare from the barn and we three set out.

*   *   *

I will say this about Horhay's mare. Her jaw was certainly cold to the bit but she was a headlong plug horse and kept ahead of the mule, being part mustang.

I asked where he had got such a mare.

From the army, he said.

I asked was he in the army.

He said he had dealt with the army, but he was not ever in it.

Our mule tried to keep pace with his mare, so we made better time than you and myself had made coming. We encountered drovers headed to Indianola with a large cattle herd from up the Goliad Trace, and Mexican carts with sundry wares going that way as well. The cattle took up a stretch of road and we had to slosh through wet prairie to skirt them. By and by we spied my wagon ahead, with your mother pacing about it in the harsh sun of late afternoon, and Dickie watching for us.

Your mother become unnaturally still when she seen us approaching. It was like her feet was suddenly welded tight to the ground and she couldn't move. She hugged her arms about herself, like she was holding herself up, and we hurried the mounts forward. When we was up to her I halted and let you jump down, and she let go of herself and grabbed hold of you and locked her arms about you but fixed her eyes on me whilst waiting for me to say if you was all right. She was gripping the tintype picture we give her of you and me.

I said, He's fixed up, Nell. It's thanks to Horhay Elveraz here. He had a madstone, by a miracle. We put it to use, and Tot's going to be just fine.

She did not hardly believe me, and kept on looking at me and Horhay on our mounts whilst clinging to you and gripping the tintype. It was like for a minute she wouldn't allow herself to believe me, as if fear had taken such a tight hold of her that she couldn't escape the grasp of it right off. But when it seemed to dawn on her that we was telling the truth, she put you down and pressed her hands together as if thanking the Lord, although she was looking at Horhay. He alighted and give her a nod. I suppose he would of taken his hat off, if it was not a turban of scarves instead. For a minute, then, she broke down, and cried even whilst she was thanking us over and over.

Dickie meantime, whilst we'd been gone, had tried to set the coyote carcass alight, as he figured creatures might scavenge from it and spread the affliction. However, there being no dry wood at hand, the carcass was merely charred. You wanted to have a look at it and started to pester your mother about that, but her nerves was frayed, and she told you she'd had enough of the creature and you was not to go near it. She kept hold of your hand.

Horhay and Dickie and myself meantime harnessed the mare and the bad sister mule to the wagon and tethered the injured sister to the back, so we might lead her along to Ecleto. We then all of us loaded and started out, skirting the hub deep mud holes.

* * *

It was about dark when we pulled up at the Ecleto station and was greeted by Mr Sandler. He showed you and your mother across the road to a family he had arranged would give you supper and a clean bed.

Horhay seen to the animals whilst Dickie and me tied the tarpaulin over the wagon in case of more rain. We washed in the creek and returned to the station and helped ourselves to supper. Mr Sandler give us boiled cabbage and side beans and dined with us, as he lived at the station. He agreed he would board and feed our lame mule until I returned this way in a few days, and Horhay kindly offered he'd travel with us to Indianola, that being where he was headed as well, and his mare having done all right being hitched.

It was a interesting meal. Mr Sandler got in the cups and talked in a heated manner of the president getting hisself impeached in recent months over affairs which I knew nothing about and which he claimed was crimes and misdemeanors, and how Congress was all handing out favors and bribing each other for votes on that matter and other matters as well. He cursed how Texans should not of pulled out of the Union, as we might never be let back in it, when even Louisiana was already let back in. He said Sam Houston had foretold rightly the Union army would take hold of the Mississippi and cut Dixie in halves and blockade the ports to starve people out, and that Texans was too stupid to of listened to him, and now was all down at the heels. The folks who'd gone bust on Confederate bonds was even stupider, he said. His glass eye got stuck on me a time or two like I was to blame, despite I'd had nothing to do with any of that.

After a time, Mr Sandler retired into his room with his dog, and Dickie laid claim to a cot in a back room where Horhay had slept the night before. There was half a dozen cots in there but Horhay said they had bugs. He got hold of a broom and swept goat shat out of the main room, and laid out his poncho alongside the table. He took off a gun belt. The holster was a California slim jim with toe plugs, very nice. The pistol appeared a strange one.

Horhay noted my interest and showed me the trigger design, whereby the bottom trigger could cock the hammer and turn the cylinder and the upper trigger could fire the piece. It was a six cylinder with a rifled barrel. He joked of how a man with but one useful arm was in need of at least two triggers. He then untied his scarf from his head, removed his jacket and necklaces and his attire but for his shirt and drawers, and laid down on his poncho.

I meantime fetched my rifle and a blanket out of the wagon. The blanket was damp and had a unsavory odor, being wool, and it was stuck full of prickly pear thorns from the night before. I spread it over the table alongside the lantern and commenced plucking the thorns out. I'd been at this a minute or two when I noted Horhay had sat up and looked at me.

Where will you go from Indianola, he said.

Back to my carpentry business in Comfort, I replied.

You care about the boy and his mother, he said.

I granted how that was true although I had not planned on it being so.

It's hard to gauge from the riverbank the strength of a current, he said. It can appear smooth on the surface, but if you put one foot in it, it carries you off.

I conceded how that was what had happened.

Yet you are staying in Texas and they are leaving, he noted.

I told him how your mother and you had to leave for reasons of safety, whilst I had to go back home, on account of my sister.

Your sister is in Comfort, then, he reasoned.

No, I told him. She run off a year ago and I'm waiting for her to come back. I have to look after her. I promised my father I would.

He proposed how maybe if she had been gone for a year she was looking after herself, and inquired as to where she'd gone off to.

I replied how I didn't know, as she had not told me before she left.

He surveyed me and laid back down and closed his eyes. I thought he might be asleep, so I kept at pulling the thorns. Some of them was too small to see and required I feel them out. Despite I was tired, it was a comfort to stare at the red and brown stripes of the blanket in the lantern light and move my fingers along them. It was a steady, dependable task, as opposed to every other thing in my life at that moment, which was not currently steady.

By and by, a moth found its way in and agitated itself thumping against the lantern glass, so I caught him and put him outside. The room then become very quiet. I dwelt on thoughts of you and your mother, and of my sister as well, and a loneliness got hold of me. I went line by line on the blanket, pulling the thorns, and tried not to think about how one person I loved was passed, him being my father, and how one was gone off, her being my sister, and how two that was left, who was you and your mother, would soon be taking your leave.

Then Horhay spoke up again. He laid with his eyes closed and said, I have a sister, as well. I have not seen her in forty-seven years.

His voice was deep and heavy and held a somber aspect that seemed to be caused by more than the strange way he parceled the words. It might of come from him being old and making his peace with the same sort of loneliness I myself felt, and then lasting through it for so long. I stopped from picking out thorns and the idea come into to mind that I was not alone in my aloneness. I wondered if I'd only thought that he spoke when in fact he hadn't, as his eyes was still closed.

I ventured, Where is your sister now.

He opened his eyes partway and looked at me, then closed them again and said, A long way from here.

Where is a long way, I asked him.

The islands of Las Bahamas, he said.

I asked did he aim to see her again, the question being of special interest to me on account of I longed to see my own sister and held on to hope that I would, despite there being no sign she aimed to come back to me, and no means by which I might find her, as I had no idea what direction she'd gone. Down toward Mexico, was my guess.

Horhay arose from his poncho with trouble, his knees seeming badly used up, and he sat at the table across from me. The manner by which the lantern lighted his face caused his solemn look to take root in my mind in the deepest way, the room being dark around him.

He said, Yes, I hope to see her again. It is the one thing more that I ask of my life.

I inquired if he had heard from her in those forty-seven years and he said he had not.

Did you come from Las Bahamas yourself and leave her behind, I asked, and he said he had never been to Las Bahamas and that he originally come from Florida. He explained his grandfather was a Seminoll Indian in Florida that married a Negro who run off from a rice plantation in Georgia, it being a common practice for Seminolls to take in runaway slaves and claim them and sometimes marry them and raise up children that was mixed Seminoll and Negro. Horhay's father was such a mix, and likewise married a runaway, and raised up three children, Horhay being the oldest.

I remained confused as to how his sister had ended up in Las Bahamas, and he said this was a long story.

I replied I had nothing to do but pick thorns, and there was a number of them, if he cared to tell it to me.

He asked if I knew of Negro Fort.

I never heard of it, I told him.

Tot, I hope you will tolerate my going off the track here, to relate what he told of events that occurred at that place, as well as a few other places, as I think you will someday like to know more of the man, on account of his saving your life with the madstone.

He told me Negro Fort was in Florida and when he was young him and his family was there with assorted other Seminolls and black Seminolls, when the United States army come in and blew the fort up. Horhay was seven years old at that time. His father was killed and his mother was hurt and carried off and likely was sold for a slave somewhere in the states, although Horhay was not certain what become of her. His sister was badly burned. Hundreds of people was blown to the sky, with pieces of them lodged up in the trees. Horhay escaped and went south afoot, carrying his burned sister along with him. She was but one year old and cried the whole way from the pain of the burns she suffered. They found a town and settled with other Seminolls and Negro Seminolls for a few years, but Andrew Jackson sent his Creek Indian friends to capture the Negro Seminolls that was there and scrub out the town. Whilst the town burned, Horhay run off with his sister again, down to a place called the Cape, where Cubans and British captains was putting Negroes into canoes and wrecker sloops and on rafts and taking them off to Las Bahamas where they might have some manner of freedom. Horhay did not have funds to pay for the passage, but begged that his sister be taken, whereby a Cuban man had pity on her and agreed, her being small for her age, and took her in his canoe.

She did not want to go, said Horhay.

But you convinced her, I offered.

No, he said, and looked direct at me across the table in the light of that lantern. I forced her, he said. I put her into the boat. I told the other passengers to keep her there. She screamed for me a long way out to the sea. Her cries still come to my ears. She was six years old at that time and still scarred by the fire at Negro Fort.

He said he believed now that he had been wrong and was liable for not going after his sister throughout his lifetime, but things had took place after she left, and he become older and partook in raids on white people's farms and sugar plantations, and killed white soldiers and set fires and burned crops and done the things he seen done to his people. He said the jacket of pale blue color he wore was stole from a dead soldier. He learned different Indian languages and Spanish and English and pieces of French, taught to him by a Negro Seminoll named John Horse. Him and John Horse was sometimes called on by the U.S. army to interpret and bargain on treaty terms. There was agreements, and broken agreements. After a time him and John Horse and others granted they'd go to a reservation of land out west where Negro Seminolls was promised to be free people and protected from slave hunters.

Horhay had a wife at this time, but she perished whilst she give birth to a daughter before the departure west. He took the baby along, but she perished out in the west, as conditions was not as promised and very poor. As well, white slave hunters come in and was stealing Negroes from out of the reservation. So after about ten years of this intolerable situation, the Seminolls and Negro Seminolls decided they'd had enough, and struck out together for Mexico.

It was a large number of them that went, and nine hundred miles of hard terrain they had to travel. Most of them was afoot. They took nearly a year to get down there, on account of slavers come after them, and deserts parched them, and northers froze them, and Comanches attacked them. Kickapoos joined up with them and traveled along. Texas Rangers got wind they was coming, and caught up to them when they was halfway over the Rio Grande, but it was too late. Horhay said they was all relieved to arrive on the other side of the river and get away from Americans.

When they was there, they made deals with the Mexican government to live for free on the border in trade for fighting Comanches and Apaches and American desperadoes and anyone coming over it. Horhay said he got bounties of two hundred and fifty Mexican dollars for every live Indian warrior he captured, and two hundred for those he killed and took the hair of, so it was a pretty good living. He liked the Mexicans. He become known by the name Horhay Elveraz, meaning George the Honest, as he was said to be truthful in all matters.

For quite a few years he was in Mexico, during which time things was changing in the United States. The slaves here was freed, and by and by the U.S. army gone down to Mexico and tried to get Negro Seminoll warriors down there to come back up and join up with the army and be scouts and fight off Indians in Texas and out west. They offered to pay with land in Texas.

But Horhay was not a young fighter anymore at this time. He was used up. He had a mindless arm that carried two bullets and moved only by swinging about when the wind blew at it. He had lived out most of his time allotted. As well, the deal offered did not sound like a firm one to him. Where was the land to be, he wanted to know. What was the guarantees. There seemed to be none.

So Horhay said so long to the Seminolls and the Negro Seminolls and the Mexicans and took off, planning to travel over the border into Texas and east in Texas to Indianola where he would board a boat to New Orleans, and sail across to Florida and walk about in the places where he had started. He would walk about as a free man in those places, he said. Then he would sail from the Florida Cape where he'd last laid eyes on his sister, over to Las Bahamas, where he hoped he might find her again.

*　　*　　*

When Horhay finished telling these things I could not figure how to remark on such a life as he had. Yet he appeared to await a response. When he spoke again, I understood it was comments on my own life he awaited, and it come to me that this was the reason he had told me of his.

What is your sister's name, he asked me.

Tot, I think of my sister all the time but it's rare that I talk about her, on account of not many people ask about her. The only folks who knew her is a preacher and his family, who I see on occasions and who was fond of her before she run off. The only other folks who ask about her is the Hildebrands, who run the Comfort store and the postal office within it, and who know how eager I am for her to come back. So it's seldom I get the chance to say her name to somebody.

Her actual name is Samantha, I told Horhay, but she prefers that I call her Sam.

He regarded me from across the table, waiting for me to say more.

She is my half sister, part Negro, like you, I told him.

He give no reaction to this, and appeared still to wait.

My story and hers is bound together, one and the same, I said.

And what is that story, he asked me.

It's hard to tell it, I said. I've not told it before.

But then, Tot, it come pouring out of me how Samantha's mother was not my mother, but one that come after, named Juda, who took to my father, and him to her, and how Sam had been but a small girl in a white shift, running across our dark farmyard when she caught the eye of a panther that up until that very time had been stalking the goats. She was never to be the same again, nor look the same, nor even think like she had, as she was a changed person after the panther lit into her and killed Juda who went to save her. All she thought about after that, was killing the panther and taking his hide and tromping around on it. She thought doing that would give her some peace on the matter. And when she got older, the panther come back around. Samantha and me and the preacher and a man named Mr Pacheco tracked it, but it survived us. And then it come back again, and Sam left off after its tracks, and never returned back home. The panther was known to travel a range that reached to Mexico, so that's likely where she was headed when she took off.

Horhay give consideration to this. He said, If she was to get her wish and kill the creature and have the hide, do you believe she would come home to you then.

I only know, if she does come home, she'll need me, I said. If she's still living, she'll need me, no matter what. The hide would be nothing but loss for her, as she would have nothing to wish for then, and nothing to do with her life. Her face was messed up by the panther the night it attacked her. She's a hard person to look at, and shies from people. If they look at her, she gets mad. Who would put up with a girl like that, except me. I'm all the family she's got. I guess I feel for her same as you feel for your sister, and feel regrets the same as yours, thinking I should of seen to her better.

Horhay reflected on this, and then rose and took from his bag the madstone, and laid it down on the blanket amongst the thorns I was picking. It appeared a thing of no value laying there on a stripe the color of rust, and yet it had such power to draw out poisons and heal up wounds and save lives.

I believe it is yours, Horhay said.

I understood that he meant me to take it, yet I thought it too vital a gift for him to give me. You will need it in Las Bahamas, I told him.

Or you will need it in Comfort, or on your travels someday. Your travels, from here, will be longer than mine, he answered.

I took hold of the madstone then, and felt how light it was despite the powers it carried, and Horhay's face told me he would not budge on the matter of if I should have it. Therefore I thanked him for such a treasure, and tucked it away in my satchel to keep it safe.

We was both worn down at that time, so I snuffed the lamp burner and Horhay laid down on his blanket, and I spread mine on the floor as well, and laid there awhile with a measure of peace of mind that I had not felt in a long time.

* * *

I was deep asleep when I was awakened, Tot, and seen you was crawling up next to me. I whispered to ask what you was doing and if your mother knew where you was.

You said she was sleeping.

I said, Does she know that you left her.

You replied you had snuck from the house where you'd been. You was excited about it. You said, Where's the dog, I want to sleep with you and the dog.

I told you the dog was with Mr Sandler and it was not a good idea for you to stay with me, as your mother might wake up and be worried to find you gone. You was forlorn that I meant to take you back to the house.

Somebody had lent you a shirt that belonged to a bigger boy and reached down to your ankles. I had to roll back the sleeves nearly a foot to get hold of your hand as we went out. The clouds overhead was thin and swift and at times opened up to the moon, which had become full in the days since we'd started.

The house was across the street. It was painted and kept up well. You had left the front door fully open when you come out. I returned you to it and we spoke in whispers. You pleaded at me to go in with you, and I said I couldn't but offered that you could wave at me from the window of the room where you was staying. You agreed to that idea and led me around the side of the house and showed me which window it was. You then went in the front door and I closed it behind you and walked back around to the window to wave.

I watched from outside as you entered the room and got up onto the bed alongside your mother. You settled under the blanket with her, but sat up looking at me. Your mother moved but did not fully stir. I lingered a moment to see what I might of her face, as it was turned my direction. Then the moon of a sudden appeared from behind the clouds and lit up the room.

Tot, I will tell you this about that moment. That quick

brightness give me a glimpse of the perfect life I wished to have. Each piece of what I seen, which was the bed, and you two in it, and you looking at me, and a chair off in the corner, and a nicely carved chest of drawers, with a washbowl atop it, and a small rug alongside the bed, and every factor of your face and your mother's, dug itself into my mind in that swift light. Your mother had on a white shift that somebody in the house give her. It had no sleeves to it. One of her arms laid atop the blanket. Even to now, to this moment whilst I write, and even after I stored up recollections of you and her that is closer to my heart, the look of you and her in that room remains the one deepest dredged. I felt like you was my kid and she was my wife and I was within the room instead of outside it. I viewed a whole lifetime in that light before a cloud overtook it.

You then waved at me to show you was settled, and I returned back to the station. I made a attempt to sleep but could not stop thinking of how it would be if I could marry your mother, and all the manners by which she might love me. My notions become dreams and kept me restless through the night.

* * *

By daybreak we was up and moving, knowing that if your uncles had fell for our ruse in San Antonio, and believed your mother and you was to be on the Wednesday stage for Indianola, and then had arrived to the Risher and Hall to nab you two and found you was not there boarding the stage, then they would be after us now in earnest and would know which way we had gone, the newspaper having declared that you and your mother was heading to Indianola. They would probably figure you was planning to catch a boat out, and whilst they wouldn't know how you was traveling to get there, they would be on our tail.

I inquired of Mr Sandler what time the Wednesday stage out of San Antonio customarily passed through, and he said it generally arrived to his place late Wednesday afternoon and went on to Yorktown, where it stopped for the night. From there it carried on and arrived to Indianola on Thursday, it being a two day journey by stage, considering the Risher and Hall had worthy mules and horses that was changed for fresh at the stops.

I figured your uncles would not be far behind the stage if they was riding good mounts. But if we could get through Yorktown before nightfall we could likely keep our lead on them, as it was doubtful they would make it any further than that without a rest for the horses.

You asked Mr Sandler if you might take the dog, but he said he'd promised a woman he would care for the dog until she might return for him. She had come from Indianola with the dog hid under her coat, dogs not being allowed on coaches, and the driver had got wind of her having it when they stopped in Ecleto, and he evicted it from the ride. It was nearly a year since that occurred, but meantime Mr Sandler had become fond of his little buddy and would not give him up to anyone but the woman, should she return.

Therefore we left the dog, greased the wagon's wheels and said so long to Mr Sandler. He said to take care of ourselves in Indianola, as he'd heard of a outbreak of yellow fever.

The clouds was gone by then, the sky was a solid blue, and we traveled toward the morning sun with our blankets and your mother's serape hung to dry over the sides of the wagon. The day got fairly warm. The road was flat, there being no hills in this region. Grassy prairies laid either side. The steady churn of the wheels and the trod of the mule and mare just about put me to sleep. My eyes would not stay fully open. Therefore Dickie took my place at the reins and I sat in the back nearby your mother and dozed here and there for a time.

You sat up front between Horhay and Dickie, and Horhay told you tales of the ocean, which he had not seen since he left Florida so many years back. He told how a person could build small forts from the sand and watch the waves topple them over. He said you could put up small stones to act like guards for the forts but the waves would carry them off. He maintained the waves was like white people taking over the fort, as they would keep coming and there was no shortage. I went from wake to sleep and sleep to wake, hearing him talk with you.

Thus the day passed. We stopped to rest the mule and the mare only when necessary, and to purchase provisions in Yorktown, that being a good sized town with a well stocked swing station alongside the hotel for stage travelers. There was no sign yet of the coach, so we was still further along on the road and ahead of where your uncles could ride to before nightfall, but we pushed on through to make time. The sun sank, dark set in, the mule and Horhay's mustang tired, and we pulled off into a vast pasture of prairieland and halted behind a screen of thorny mesquite and weesach that was still holding on to their yellow flowers. We collected wood and built a fire and prepared our camp for the night.

You had meantime taken such a liking to Horhay you felt the need to show off. You showed him how high you could jump and the number of sticks you could search out and bring for the fire. Your mother told you to settle down but you remained lively. We was ignorant what you was up to when of a sudden you thought of a item you figured would draw Horhay's attention. Dickie's small bag was laid alongside him, and you pulled the necklace forth from it whilst Dickie was stirring a pot of beans on the fire.

You carried the necklace over to Horhay and held it before his face and declared, Look what Dickie brought with him! He dug it up out of a hole!

Your mother and me went stone still. Dickie become like the poisoned tarantulas he had aforementioned, stung stiff, his hand froze in the air holding the spoon dripping beans into the fire. Horhay's eyes fixed hard on the necklace. A stretch of time seemed to go by.

Then Horhay looked at Dickie and said in a solemn manner, Where was this hole.

Dickie appeared to weigh if he should answer or not. He laid the spoon back in the pot in a measured way, as if to buy time to think this over. He then said, Nearby the Horsehead Crossing on the Pecos river.

You mean the ford of the Pecos near the pass through the Castle Mountains, said Horhay.

Yes, replied Dickie.

The necklace belongs to the Empress Carlota of Mexico, Horhay stated.

You was now onto the notion that Horhay's attention might now be better avoided, as he was notably somber. You was still holding the necklace but seemed to be wondering how you might rid yourself of it.

Horhay spared you of figuring that out. He took it from you and held it up to the fire and give it a close study. He said, This necklace carries a curse.

A curse! Dickie said.

A bad luck curse, they say, replied Horhay. The opal will bring bad luck.

You and me and your mother and Dickie was all confounded to hear such a thing spoke in such a heavy fashion. Had we been in town amongst people, then we might of been merely interested at the news of having a cursed item in our possession. But out in the midst of no place, shielded by only a scanty wall of scraggly mesquite and weesach from view of the road, where troubles might come from, in the dark of night with the sky stretched out and showing how small we was, and the number of stars making it plain how little we might matter to the broad scheme of the world, I admit to feeling alarm. I'd heard of the Empress Carlota but I knew nothing about a curse.

Your mother knew nothing of that curse, nor any other, nor of Carlota, and said she did not believe in curses, as life on the face of it was bewildering enough without such things. She asked Horhay, Who is the Empress Carlota and how do you know of the necklace.

Horhay stated a long answer in a short manner. Here is the facts he told us.

Carlota was married to Maximilian who was the emperor of Mexico for a time on account of Napoleanne sent him there to take it over. Mexicans primarily wanted shed of him however, as they preferred Beneeto Warez to be their president. They did not care much for Carlota neither. Warez got up a army, aiming to throw

Maximilian out of Mexico, so Carlota boarded a ship and sailed back to Europe and demanded Napoleanne defend her husband, and begged the pope to make Napoleanne do so, neither of which done so.

Therefore the Mexicans under Warez captured Maximilian and sentenced him to be executed. A portion of Carlota's riches was still in Mexico at that time, so Maximilian conspired to get them back to her in Ostria, as that was where both of them come from. He could not figure a way to get them shipped from Mexican ports, on account of Warez had taken those over, so he arranged they would be hauled north over the border and through Texas to the port of Galveston, and from there sent home to Carlota. Hence at the time Maximilian faced the fusillade and was shot to death, the treasure was in a wagon headed for Texas under the care of two of his trusted Ostrian people and four Mexicans who was loyal to him.

And who might you think was called on to guide this journey. There was mountains and risky wilderness to cross over. The party did not know their way. They feared Comanche attack. They none of them spoke any English. Who might they trust to guide them in such circumstances. Might it be a known scout and good fighter, a man who had been around for a time and knew the border regions and spoke English and Spanish and pieces of sundry Indian languages, and who was above all known to be honest. Who better than Horhay Elveraz, Horhay the Honest.

The six men in charge of the wagon of riches went to the town of Naseemeinto where Negro Seminolls was stationed and requested for Horhay to guide them.

Horhay declined, saying his people had kept on good terms in the country by not taking sides in political fights.

You are not asked to take sides, they replied. There is no fight, as Beneeto Warez already is victor. It is a matter of doing a favor for a woman, so she might have her jewels returned.

They said that the treasure consisted of silver platters, gold vessels, bags of coins that was Ostrian and Spanish and American, and a number of jeweled pieces. They told Horhay he might have his pick of these treasures for payment if they should reach Galveston safely. The only item he could not choose was a opal necklace rumored to carry with it a curse.

It is a favorite of the empress, a prized jewel in her collection, the Mexicans told Horhay. It must be returned to her.

So Horhay agreed to the journey. After crossing the border into Texas, whilst on a trail around the mountains, the party come on a gang of four seedy looking Americans. Horhay knew this breed well. They was known in Mexico to commit crimes and loot towns and string people up, and he had dealt with such.

These four men struck up a conversation with the party. There was nobody but Horhay who understood what they was saying, on account of it was in English. However, all amongst them knew the word Comanches. Even the two Ostrians knew it. They noted how the ruffians was excited and pointing the very direction the party was currently going. All but Horhay become alarmed and believed they was headed straight to a tribe of Comanches.

Horhay asked the strangers to give a account of the Comanches they was claiming to of seen, and how many there was, and what they was wearing and armed with.

The men said they theirselves had been riding peacefully from Missouri to Mexico and come on a raiding party that give them chase a mile or two off to the east from where they now stood. They give details of attire and weapons. They pointed out a remote route to evade these Indians, saying, We will lead you.

Horhay knew their statements did not make sense. Their horses did not appear jaded. What they reported did not hold to how Comanches, nor any other Indians, was usually attired and armed. Horhay therefore reasoned there was no Indians. He figured these men for liars hoping to lure the party off to a place of advantage and rob them and do them all in.

In Spanish he stated this very thing to his companions and advised they keep to the route they was on. But the Ostrians become balky. They did not speak English nor much Spanish and could not make out what anyone said. They got badly worked up and commenced to shout curses at Horhay in their language. It was plain they believed he would lead them into a band of Comanches.

The ruffians meantime stood by, watching to see how things played.

Horhay become impatient with the Ostrians. He laid out how they could follow the way he stated, or could take their wagon and put theirselves in the hands of these four outlaws, and he would head back to Naseemeinto.

They chose to go with the outlaws. Two of the Mexicans chose the same, on account of they was overly loyal to Maximilian and did not want it said that they had turned back. The other two of the Mexicans trusted in Horhay, and turned back with him, leaving their fooled companions on a poorly chosen and ill fated path.

Tot, that was the last Horhay seen or known of those Ostrians and their wagon, or those two Mexicans who went with them, or of their treasures, until the moment you dragged the necklace out of Dickie's small bag and held it before his eyes.

I will tell you, the story was a lot to take in.

* * *

So there we sat, taking stock. As I seen it, we had a dark night about us, a dying fire before us, and a cursed necklace amongst us. We had your two uncles after us. We had one horse, one mule, and a wagon. We had Horhay with his limp arm and his long past, and Dickie with his hopes for the necklace now dashed and turned to dread of its curse, and me with my ache for your mother who was destined to take her leave of me, and you with a life before you and a look of puzzlement on your face. We had your mother and her sweet baby to be. All together, it was a untidy mix of items. We none of us made any comment for quite some time.

Dickie then said, That does not any of it sound true.

Horhay replied, I agree. It does not.

When Horhay made no further statement, Dickie said, But you claim that it is.

I do, Horhay said. It happened not long ago.

Then what am I to do with this necklace now, Dickie asked.

Nobody stated a answer. I recall katydids making a racket, is all.

Is the curse real, Dickie asked Horhay.

Horhay answered by asking him if he had seen anything near the hole where the necklace and coins was buried.

A broken down wagon not too far off, Dickie told him.

Horhay said nothing to that.

And bodies, Dickie then added.

Bodies! I said. You told us nothing of bodies!

How many bodies, Horhay inquired.

Two bodies, Dickie replied.

Horhay asked was they Mexican bodies, and if they wasn't, then how might they of been clothed.

They was not Mexican and was clothed regular, Dickie said.

Then they did not belong to the Ostrians, Horhay stated.

They was missing some clothes and some parts, Dickie owned.

Mutilated, Horhay asked.

Yes, Dickie said.

Describe them, Horhay told him.

They had not much left of their faces, Dickie replied. I think there had once been a scar on one of them's neck, but the flesh was dried up, so I can't be sure. The other of them had a crop of red hair, from what I could see of how much was left.

I know of these features, Horhay said. Two of the band of four Americans we encountered had such features. What distance from the hole did you find them.

Five or ten minutes afoot down the trail, Dickie said.

And how far was the hole from the wagon, Horhay asked him.

Five or ten minutes afoot again, Dickie said.

Ah, said Horhay. The story falls into a line.

How so, inquired Dickie.

Horhay related how the location of these discoveries, many miles to the north of the Mexican border, would indicate the

Americans had been headed back to their homes in Missouri, bringing the wagon and loot they had stole after slaying the Ostrians and the two Mexicans. Along the way, two of them must of fell out with their two companions, and killed them as well, then continued on with the treasure. The wagon must of then broke down nearby Horsehead Crossing of the Pecos, leaving no method to carry the treasure. Hence, they thought to bury it and return for it at a later time. They carried it off from the wagon to a place where it might be hid, dug the hole in the ground and buried the necklace and coins. Perhaps they buried the other items of treasure in other places close by. And then they continued on. A short time later they was attacked and murdered. The treasure and their two bodies laid undiscovered until Dickie happened upon them whilst making his way alone, afoot and disheartened, out of El Paso where rumors of silver had turned out a bust.

But do you believe the necklace carries bad luck, Dickie asked. I have got to have the answer to that. The necklace is my whole fortune.

Horhay give him a look from across the fire. He said, Maximilian is executed. Carlota is now a widow. It is rumored she has become insane. The Ostrians and the Mexicans who transported the necklace cannot be found. Two of the thieves rot in the wilds, victims of their companions. Two have been murdered and butchered. But who am I to say if the necklace is cursed.

We allowed these words to settle on us. The flames of our little fire licked at the darkness. Horhay arose and offered the necklace over to Dickie.

Dickie took hold of it with a sorrowful look, and stood, and paced about the fire. He become very upset and then become sulky and sour. He said, I've come on one good thing in my life, and now I am told I am cursed by it. I should of seen this forthcoming. It was likely the curse that give me the trots and got me arrested in Comfort. Probably the curse is what rotted my tooth that had to get pulled. It was likely the curse that put me onto a stagecoach with a woman who is pursued by thugs, and you see where that now has brought me. Also, a hailstorm struck us. That was cursed luck. The storm crippled the mule, by double cursed luck. And now the curse has forced me into a pasture of cactus and needled shrubs with the only alive person who knows of the curse and whose horse happens to be the one drawing our wagon. I am faced with a terrible choice of what to do with the necklace, and choices like this is curses theirselves.

Your mother said, But look here, Dickie. You having your issue in Comfort and getting delayed there saved Tot and me. Had you not got a ride with Benjamin, and the two of you come along when our stage was held up, we would of been stranded. And now we're not. That was no curse.

A curse for me but not for you, Dickie replied. I'm the person dug up the necklace. It and the specie. And now it appears the necklace has brought me bad luck, and the specie is mostly spent on trying to get you and your boy to Indianola. I could of got hold of a horse in San Antonio and been on a ship to New Orleans by now for less money. I been skinned out of my last dollars by doing a favor.

His blaming of Nell made me angry. Don't you fault her, I advised him. It's not her doing what's happened. And maybe if you was on a ship to New Orleans the bad luck would sink it. How would that suit you.

Yet he continued to pity hisself and swear at his luck for coming upon a cursed necklace. It was a bitter pill and a difficult situation, but there's times a man has to get hold of hisself and pipe down. I seen by the manner your mother went at the task of tidying after our meal that she was impatient with Dickie.

She said, You have got your tooth fixed, Dickie. You've been paid a bounty on account of being with me. The hailstorm is passed. The hurt mule will heal. We'll be in Indianola soon. You can sell the necklace or do whatever you want with it there. You can take it on to New Orleans. I'm grateful to you for all you've done for me. But there's no point to you complaining. We've all lost worst things than fortunes.

Still Dickie did not spare us of his frustration. He stalked about and declared he intended to bury the necklace. He rummaged about for the spade in my toolbox and strode off into the pasture with it. You and myself and your mother watched him go. You made no comment upon the matter and appeared perplexed to see Dickie upset.

Horhay said nothing in all this time. He laid out a bed by the fire and prepared to sleep. He unwound his turban and let his hair loose and allowed you to see how long it was and to feel of it. You was extremely taken with it. Your mother laid out a bed for you and her in the wagon.

Meantime I grew worried about Dickie and his poor spirits and went off and found him. He'd dug the necklace a shallow hole. I noted he'd placed it a pile of stones for a marker. As I afore stated, it's hard for a person to part with his hopes.

So long to my fortune, he said in a doleful manner. Him and myself stood in the dark and cast a last look to the heap of dirt over the necklace. We then walked back to the fire and nursed it up and laid our pallets alongside it.

* * *

Thus commenced a night I will not forget, on account of what happened next.

Whilst watching the embers burn down I dropped into a deep sleep on my blanket, then awoke to someone touching my shoulder. I said, Go back to your mother, Tot.

Your mother then whispered, It's Nell.

I come wide awake, thinking there might be trouble. She did not appear worried, however. She had on the white shift somebody give her to sleep in, and she was a beautiful sight.

She whispered at me, Come back to the wagon with me.

I of course done as she said. She got in the wagon and indicated I was to get in it as well. I lifted the toolbox out to make room and done so. She wrapped her arms around me and I laid alongside her. I can't even explain my feelings. You was asleep on the far side and did not hardly stir. Your mother and me spoke in whispers.

She said, I wish I was married to you, Benjamin.

I said, Nell, I been feeling that way the whole time.

If Tot and the baby was ours, I wouldn't be leaving, she said.

If you stay, we can get married, I told her.

I would if I could, she said. But the Banes family would come after us. They never give up what they think they got rights to. They kept hold of their slaves for I don't know how long after they was declared to be freed. A long time. The mama is the worst of the family. Worse even than her husband. Tot cried every time we had to go visit them. Micah's mama would put the whole Swamp Fox gang after Tot and me if she knew where we was. She'd not give up looking. And how could I live with making you unsafe as well. Do you think you might come to New Orleans with us instead.

Tot, I would of surrendered every item I have a claim to if I could of been free to say yes to that. I would of give up my hopes for going along on a cattle drive and owning my own cattle some-day and living my life in Texas. I would of thrown my dreams out to the winds and left my mare back in Texas despite how she's gone through so much of my life alongside me and been my most loyal companion. I would of left behind my customers, and all my work tools, and said so long to the Hildebrands who run the Comfort store and the postal office. I would of walked off from my whole life for you and your mother. But my duties was laid out for me a long time ago. They was set for me by my father.

I said, Someday I might can go to New Orleans, Nell, but I can't do that anytime soon. My sister might come back and need me. There's nobody who could do for her but myself. If she was to come back and look for me and learn I was moved off to New Orle-ans, there's no chance she'd follow and search me out. She wouldn't have means to. She would go off again. I would lose my one chance to help her.

I then told your mother about my sister Sam and her troubles, and how she's my half sister, her mother not being my mother, but one that come after. I told her how I had promised my father that I would look after her, and why she might need such looking after, being part Negro when folks is not always friendly to that, and scarred up as well, and too smart and stubborn, and younger than me, and a girl. My steadfastness for her, despite how she chose of her own accord to take off and leave me behind, is not easy to understand, and yet your mother did understand it when I told her all this, being the sort of person who could. We talked a good while about Sam.

Your mother then asked who else I missed in my life and said she would like to know things of me that I had not told her before, on account of I had not told her much. So I said how I missed my father a great deal, and how my mother had passed when I was born, before I could build up memories of her, making it hard to say if I missed her.

There was other things that was said and occurred between us, and by and by she asked had I been with a woman in my lifetime, and I owned to her as I had. She wanted to know who was it, and I told her it was the widow in Comfort whose house I room in.

Is she a old widow, she asked me.

No, I said, she's a young one.

Do you love her, she wanted to know.

Not in the manner that you might mean, I told her. Not with my heart. She's come to my room on occasions, is all.

I think maybe she loves you then, your mother said.

I explained how that was not the case, as her and myself did not even speak the same language nor own up to each other on what was the situation between us, there being nothing to say on the matter, as we both knew how things stood. She was a good woman, and missed her dead husband, and cried for him, and did not love me, although I was sometimes a comfort I think. There was nothing more to it than that.

We laid there watching the moon slide over the sky, and swatting mosquitoes, and now and then hearing creatures out in the brush. Your mother put my hand on her belly that I might feel of the baby kicking. A great deal of honesty come about between us then, and there was things took place I will not forget until the reaper should fetch me. I have not before in my life, nor since, felt so near to a person.

*　　*　　*

I awoke at daybreak and wanted to lay there alongside the two of you whilst you slept, and watch the moon fade out and the sky grow light and think things over. But there was no time, as we had to get underway. I roused myself out of the wagon and seen Horhay fixing breakfast and Dickie out in the pasture digging up his cursed necklace.

I guess I knew Dickie would do that, as I don't recall being surprised. I went over and spoke with him. He was using my spade, which he must of slept with on account of he must of figured he'd have second thoughts and dig up the necklace. I said good morning to him and he told me likewise.

He then said, It looks like you've gone around the bend for that girl and leapt clean off the ledge.

I said, It looks like you've elected to carry around a cursed necklace.

He got the necklace out of the dirt and scrubbed it on his pant leg, then said, I been thinking it over. My luck has not been so bad with this. My tooth was partly rotted back in El Paso before I come on the necklace. I recall it bothered me then. And the hailstorm was natural forces. The rest of what I figured bad luck is just things occasioned from circumstances.

I did not have much opinion about these matters, though given a choice I would of preferred traveling without a thing said to be cursed. I went off to help Horhay cook breakfast.

You and your mother then come from the wagon and we was all packed up and fed and off in a very short time.

The sun got to be blazing hot whilst we traveled. Dickie's trots returned and struck him hard. Horhay said this was caused by nerves from having a cursed necklace. Dickie bemoaned having no paregoric nor tannins nor laudanum and called on us to halt the wagon time and again so he might visit the brush.

Meantime your mother become uncomfortable with the ride. She moved about in the back of the wagon to search out other places to sit. She piled up blankets and sat on those, and tried out different places. Horhay rode up front with you and myself. Dickie remained in the back with your mother when he was not out in the shrubs.

I asked your mother a time or two if she was all right, and she maintained that she was. But myself and Horhay noted she wasn't. She took hold of her belly like she had cramps, and whenever Dickie was off in the brush, she paced in the road. At times she went to the brush herself. Her thoughts was kept private.

We traveled another spell, then a pin in the hind axletree snapped and cost us a hour to fashion out a replacement. Dickie did not help, being primarily indisposed. Horhay and me worked at fixing the issue whilst you scampered about in the road.

I asked your mother in private if she thought her time could be near, but she denied that it was. She would not budge on that notion.

I was at work under the wagon when I heard the approach of horses and Horhay hollered, Stagecoach is coming!

I scrambled out from under the wagon to flag it down, hoping that it might carry your mother in haste on to Victoria, where we could meet up with her later. Dickie run out with his pants but half up, waving his arms at the driver and trying to get him to stop, but he paid no attention to any of us and sped on.

We mended the wheel and hastened along, as our concerns was heightened now, with the stage having passed. If the Banes brothers was coming, they was likely not too far behind, although we still figured to beat them on to Victoria.

Your mother's troubles got worse on down the road. She was anxious and asked a number of times how far we might be from Victoria, but none of us knew the answer.

By and by we hailed a freighter coming from that direction and asked how far was Victoria. He replied we was fifteen miles out at the least. It was getting toward afternoon.

Meantime you seen how your mother was not acting herself and lacked her usual patience. Mama, you're grumpy, you told her.

Yes, she replied.

How come you're grumpy, you asked her.

People just sometimes is, she said.

Am I grumpy, you asked her.

Sometimes, she said.

Why am I grumpy, you pressed her.

She was hurting a great deal. Hush about it, honey, she told you.

When Dickie required another stop, she become cross with him. Can't you hold it, she said.

I'm sorry, I can't, he told her. He did appear very sorry.

You run about again whilst we waited on Dickie. Horhay and me and your mother sat in the wagon. Your mother did not look well. We was all sweating and hot. There was no shade to be had from the sun.

Your mother kept shifting about. Of a sudden she stated, I won't have my baby out in a prairie with no women about. This is false pains that I'm having.

She got out of the wagon to pace and to go to the brush herself.

I recalled how Horhay said his wife had perished when she give birth to his daughter. My own mother had not lived past the ordeal when I come into the world. Myself and Horhay sat on the seat of the wagon and watched as your mother returned from the brush and paced in the road before us. Forward and back she went, holding on to her belly. Horhay and me was both worried about her. She wore the straw hat from Boerne and her blue dress. She appeared to have trouble catching her breath.

Dickie returned, about done in by the trots, and again we started off. It was lucky the roads in this part of Texas was level and not too ragged.

Your mother rubbed at her back and her belly. By and by, she declared of a sudden, I need us to stop.

I steered a ways into the prairie and she got out and paced in the grass. She bent over and held her belly.

You asked me, What's wrong with my mama.

She's not feeling herself, I answered.

Is that baby going to come out, you asked.

Not yet, I don't think, I replied.

You wanted to know when it might.

Maybe today or maybe not, I told you. It can't be forecast.

Why, you wanted to know.

That's hard to say, I replied, having no better answer. Babies come out when they want to, is all.

You was reflective about the matter and went off and caught up to your mother. She got hold of your hand and you paced alongside her out in the prairie until you grew tired and lagged and complained you was thirsty. I fetched you back to the wagon and give you some water.

You and me sat on a blanket under the wagon for shade whilst your mother continued her pacing. Horhay sought shade from a lone post oak and Dickie kept going off into the brush.

Meantime your mother's pains become worse. I took her a canteen of water. She commenced to squat and then to get on her hands and knees but made plain she did not want me with her. There was times we lost sight of her in the grass, on account of it was spring high and dense with butterfly weeds and Indian paintbrushes and sundry other tall flowers. As well, there was rocky patches and blackbrush and dogweed. Our canteens was low and we rationed the water to save it for her and you. Even Dickie rationed the water, despite he was parched from having the trots. He asked if I thought the cursed necklace was causing the trots, and I said I thought that it might be.

You and me passed the time under the wagon. We played with

the dog I had whittled you, and I whittled a cat and a hog to go with it. You pushed them about in the dirt and had them jump over weeds and stones. We thought of what Horhay had said of the ocean, and planned out forts we would build from the sand when we should arrive to the shore in Indianola. I told you the story of Moby Dick and all I had learned of ships and rigging and whales and life at sea from the book about him. You asked that I go along on the boat to New Orleans, and I explained how I couldn't do that. We laid on our backs whilst I carved our names, Benjamin and Henry, that being your actual name, there on the underside of the wagon.

Then of a sudden your mother called out to me. In haste I got up and spied her a ways out in the prairie. She was crouched low to the ground. Horhay come over and led you off for a spell whilst I started out to your mother. I found her red in the face, in a terrible sweat when I reached her.

She told me, I can't do this without my mama. I need a woman. My water's broke. I'm scared.

Horhay and me can help you, I told her.

Can you alone help me, she asked.

Horhay knows more than I do about it, I answered. But I'll try to help you at first.

Keep Tot from seeing, she told me. Bring me a blanket.

I went for the one blanket I'd picked clean of thorns. Horhay walked you further into the prairie where you wouldn't see what your mother might suffer. I headed back out to her and she commenced pacing again but come to a sudden halt whilst looking off to the road.

I turned to see what she might be fixed on, and it was two

riders, moving in fast, both with a rifle strapped to their saddle and their pistols drawn. I did not yet make out the likeness they bore to your deceased father and dead uncle Dale, but figured I knew who they was.

Your mother sank to her knees. The riders come on apace. It went through my mind how my rifle was back in the wagon and your mother's Hammond was back there as well. Horhay's pistol was on him, but he had walked some distance with you toward the edge of the prairie by now. Dickie was armed with his Whitney pistol, but he was far off in a stand of sagebrush in the other direction from Horhay.

I dropped the blanket and run for the wagon and my gun. There was no cover between here and there and your uncles opened up fire on me like I was a jackass rabbit. I went down in a crouch and they quit their fire, but one of them rode up twelve feet distant and pulled rein, and put me clean in his sights.

Get your hands in the air! he hollered.

I done so but stayed down low, as why give him a larger target.

Your mother had got to her feet by then and was running for you and Horhay. She was hindered by weeds and thorny flowers and dogweed brush that dragged at her dress. Nevertheless, she run so fast that her hat flew off, despite there being no wind. Her dress was markedly wet with her broken water and patches of sweat. She stumbled a time or two but arose and kept going. The rider that was not watching me followed behind her, pulling up close and keeping his horse in a measured lope, its nose nearly over her shoulder. He could of readily overtook her but seemed to enjoy she was running.

Horhay meantime considered events and shoved you down to the ground and laid down flat alongside you. He drew his pistol, and yet his position was too far off to get a good shot at either one of the riders, and he did not fire.

The one that was trailing your mother spied him and hollered, Stand up and toss that gun or I'll shoot the woman! He pointedly aimed his pistol at the back of your mother's head.

Horhay stood and tossed his pistol, the risk to your mother being too great for him not to.

Your mother did not stop running. The rider stayed close behind her and kept his pistol aimed at her head. She didn't slacken her pace until she had reached you, and then went down on her knees and grabbed you into her arms and laid herself over you. Horhay stepped forward to stand between her and the rider.

The rider pulled rein and dismounted. He took stock of Horhay and yelled to his brother, who was keeping the watch over me. Murry, he yelled, I think it's the nigger we seen in the Mexican bar!

Murry likewise dismounted. He took aim at me, and shouted, The one I got here is the smartass remarked on our coins!

Their horses was blowing hard. The brother hounding your mother ordered she should turn loose of you. I figured him for the one named Silas that committed the cruelty to the child in the store and her daddy, over the penny whistler, there being four brothers, and two of them dead, and the one watching me called Murry. Silas resembled his brothers but for his hair being light, not dark, and his face being clean shaved as well. He was thin like his brothers, but looked to be somewhat taller.

Your mother did not obey him, and he become heated.

You ratted where we was hid out, he said. Cul Baker is looking for you. You set the law after us, and then you skipped town with our nephew. We got rights to the boy same as you do.

Murry's pistol was still aimed at me. He stood a few feet away, holding the reins of his horse, and kept the aim true. He hollered out to your mother, We can't find Micah and we suspect mischief from you, Nell! That boy is likely all we got left of our brother! Our mother wants us to bring him home! And where's Dale! We seen him get hauled from the Menger, laid out on a stretcher. Did this fellow here kill him. If he did, then he's done. I'll blow his head off.

I noted the pistol aimed at myself by Murry was a short bar-reled revolver. The one aimed at Horhay by Silas was a revolver as well, although with a longer barrel and it appeared like a bet-ter gun.

Answer me, Nell, shouted Murry. If you don't then I'll do it! I'll shoot him! Silas, should I do it! Might that get your attention, Nell!

I will tell you, Tot, it got mine. I did not want to get shot and did not want to be crouched like a coward if that should happen, neither. But the brothers had made it plain to me in their first round of fire that I should not run for the wagon. And where else could I run to. Around me was open prairie, is all, with hardly a stick of timber for ducking behind, just weeds and flowers and patches of brush and the one trifling post oak. There was a outcrop of rocks, but not high. The most I might do was head for the tree line off in the distance and hope Murry's aim would be poor. But how would it look to your mother for me to run off.

I arose with my hands in the air and told Murry, My name is Benjamin and I'm unarmed. I would appreciate you don't shoot me.

Might you in fact be the smartass we seen in the bar, he inquired. If you lie, I'll shoot you right now.

I figured a lie in this case would not suit me. I did overstep in the bar and I'm sorry, I told him.

Did you kill my brother Dale, he asked. Is he dead.

I don't know if he's dead, I offered. If he was the person banging on doors at the Menger, somebody knocked him over the head.

Who! he demanded.

I didn't see who, I avowed. I believe the person was angry about him banging so loud on their door. I heard yelling, and opened my door, and seen your brother laid out in the hall and then carried off on a stretcher.

Murry said, You better not be telling a lie. It better not of been you that struck him.

He then fired a shot, and whilst it was not aimed exactly at me, the blast did ring in my ears. Nell! he shouted, that shot is a warning! Next time I'll aim for his head if you won't tell us what happened to Micah and what you might know of Dale! You better come out from behind the nigger!

Up to a point, my concerns had been mostly for you and your mother, but I confess that now they was mainly for me, as Murry appeared to mean business. My legs become wobbly, but pride held me upright. I stood with my hands in the air. Your mother did not make a move. She cared about me, but rightly cared more for you and remained on the ground holding you.

Meantime I wondered where Dickie was, and if he could possibly help us. There didn't seem much of a way. He'd been far off when the riders come in, and I couldn't think how he might reach us without getting seen by the brothers and shot at.

Murry at that time ordered I walk over closer to you two and Horhay. I walked with my arms raised up, whilst he led his horse behind me. I believed he might fire into my back, as he'd gave the appearance he yearned to shoot me and he did not seem a person of much control. Despite he stayed ten paces or so behind me, I heard every noise from back there, the jangling bridle and creak of the saddle and blowing breath of the winded horse. I heard these like they was two inches behind, and kept thinking, at every second, that I'd take a bullet. When we caught up to Horhay and you and your mother, Murry told me to halt and I done so.

Silas meantime was telling Horhay to get his hands in the air. Horhay had raised the one he could lift, but the other laid at his side.

Both hands, Silas ordered, or I'll drop the hammer.

Horhay explained that the arm could not move.

He's telling the truth, I offered. That arm does nothing but swing.

Silas must not of fully believed us, as he told your mother, Stand up. Untie the scarf on the nigger's head and strap his arm to his side with it. Do it now or I'll shoot him, and shoot this fellow as well.

I believed from his voice that he meant it. He was the brother sent cold down my spine, despite it was Murry's gun aimed at my head. I believe there is two kinds of evil, one being stupid and one being smart. Silas possessed the smart kind. I am not sure about

Murry. There was a careful and cagier aspect to how Silas handled his meanness.

Your mother got up, although I could see she was suffering pains. Horhay stood with his good arm raised. Your mother removed his scarf from his head. He looked strangely stripped down and old. She wrapped the scarf fully around him, pinning his lank arm down to his side as Silas instructed.

I want a firm knot, Silas told her.

She pulled it tighter.

Now toss me his rig, Silas said.

She unstrapped the holster and tossed it.

Silas retrieved it along with the pistol Horhay had tossed. Where's your federal army jacket, he inquired of Horhay.

In the wagon, Horhay replied.

Silas commanded him to come forward, and Horhay approached with his good arm raised up and the other strapped down.

I wondered again about Dickie. He was sure to of heard the shots fired and seen us by now. Yet how he might help us when we was now fully outgunned, was a puzzle.

Silas searched Horhay for other weapons and removed a knife out of his trousers. He got close in his face and commenced to state the same question he'd put to him in the bar. He said, So what are you, a Indian, a Mexican, a plain nigger, or a nigger soldier.

Horhay declined to answer.

Silas spat in his face. Are you a nigger, he said.

Horhay again did not answer.

Silas spat in his face a second time. Are you a Indian, he said.

It was plain Horhay had no intention to answer, and Silas was getting madder.

I said, He's a Negro Seminoll Indian who's fought federals in Florida and killed a good many and got the jacket off a dead one. He went down to Mexico and killed a bunch of Comanches.

I figured some of this might be matters Silas would like, given how much he hated the federals and probably hated Comanches as well, on account of most white people did.

Silas did not heed me, however. He did not even look my direction. He spat at Horhay again and strode to your mother. You was afraid and whimpering, Tot, and she held on to you.

Silas said in a serious manner, It seems like you shot a man back on the road near Boerne, Nell. San Antonio newspaper said so. Might that of been my brother Micah. The last we seen him, he was taking off looking for you.

Your mother had trouble speaking, as her pains appeared to be harsh. She said, I don't know who I shot, Silas, but it was not Micah. The stage I was on got robbed, and a stranger run up, and I become startled and shot him.

The newspaper said you shot with a Hammond Bulldog, he told her. I give Micah a Hammond Bulldog some years back. Did you make use of my gift to shoot my brother.

It was not him I shot, she maintained.

Tot, you caught on to what things that your uncle was saying, and stopped your crying and fiercely said, She did not shoot my daddy!

For all you knew, you was telling the truth.

Your mother attempted to hush you, as she did not want you riling Silas against you. She covered your mouth but you tugged her hand off it and repeated that she did not shoot your daddy.

Silas surveyed you and asked you, Did you lay eyes on the man she shot. Did you see the man's face.

It was not my daddy! you hollered.

He chose not to argue with you, but turned to me. Is this your wagon, he said.

I owned as it was.

Did you see the man shot, he said. I can tell from looking at you if you're lying.

I did see him shot, I replied. He was a passenger in my wagon and we come on the stagecoach being held up. Mrs Banes was in the coach and thought him one of the thieves and shot him.

Might he of looked something like me or my brothers, he then pointedly asked.

That would be hard to say, I answered. He had light hair and was clean shaved like you, so if that describes him, then yes.

Might you be lying, he threatened.

I was, Tot, as your father looked nothing like what I had said, but I swore that I did not lie.

Where's the man that spoke to the newspaper, Silas said. Is he traveling with you.

No, I said.

Then what become of him, Silas asked.

I don't know what become of him, I said, that being partly the truth, as where was he.

Why are you traveling with a nigger, Silas then said.

One of my mules went lame, and he offered his horse to help pull the wagon, I told him.

Murry was getting antsy and told Silas, Let's just take the boy, and leave Nell. What do we want with her, anyway. It's the boy we need to get back.

You heard him say that and become distraught, despite Silas told Murry that he intended on hauling all three of you, that being you and your mother and the baby, home to the family. You cried and begged your mother not to let you be taken. This was awful to watch and went on for some time. Your mother tried to assure you that she would not let that happen, but it was plain to you that she held no power against your uncles.

Whilst you cried and clung to her, she asked Silas for water for you and for her, but he withheld it. I have not seen such meanness from a man to a woman, before nor since. I have not felt so helpless neither. I felt wretched to watch him torment your mother when I could do nothing about it. He did not lay hands on her but stood holding the reins of his horse and demanding to know if she killed your father, and what might of happened to Dale. She kept looking to me as if I might give her some hope, but how could I offer that whilst I stood with my arms in the air. It seemed like her fear afflicted her worse than if he had whipped her. She asked could she walk to relieve her pains, and he told her, Not far. She got hold of your hand and the two of you paced in the prairie, making a beaten path in the grass. You sobbed the whole time. Back and forth you went, sobbing. Silas required your mother turn back when she got too far from his range. After a while it seemed like he pulled strings that she was tied to. Stop there, he told her. And turn about. She done as he said. Not so far the next time, he told her. His eyes was partly on her and partly on Horhay. Murry kept watch over me but watched your mother as well, as it seemed to give him some satisfaction to see how she suffered. You was confused, and after a time you pulled free of her and come running for me, but Silas grabbed you and told you he would give you a whipping if you gone to me or to Horhay. He said, Your daddy would want you home with us. Why don't you do what your daddy would want. You owe him respect.

You cried and walked about in circles, your hands over your ears and your shoulders hunched like a very old man's.

Your mother begged that I might be allowed to hold you, but Silas denied her. He told Murry, If he takes up the boy, shoot him.

The day become even hotter. I hoped for help to arrive from the road if not from Dickie, who remained nowhere to be seen. A freighter passed without stopping. A lone rider come by and seen us and hollered to ask if we was broke down and might need help, but Silas and Murry posed like nothing amiss was occurring, and Silas hollered back to him that we was all right, and didn't. Neither Horhay nor myself revealed otherwise. I suspected the brothers would shoot us if we should dispute the matter, and figured they'd shoot the rider as well to keep him from telling. And where would that leave your mother and you. For all I knew, Silas and Murry intended to shoot us regardless, but any chance we might have of helping your mother and you would be greater the later that happened.

Your mother's pains eased at short times, and she sat on the ground and rested. But always the pains took up again. Flies and gnats pestered her badly. The brothers retrieved their canteens from their saddles and drank whilst they watched your mother. Their horses commenced to graze.

Nell, I'm tired of waiting, Murry said after a while. How long till you have that baby.

When your mother didn't answer him, he told Silas, Let's shoot the nigger and this fellow and take the wagon and load up Nell and the boy and head home. She can have the baby along the way.

Silas give him a look of disgust. I'm not going home in a wagon, he said. Do you know how long that would take us. When the baby's born, we'll take Nell and the kids on the horses. We'll take that horse that's pulling the wagon and put Nell on it.

Or maybe leave her behind, said Murry.

That might be a good idea if you plan on nursing the baby yourself on the way, Silas said. You're a idiot, Murry.

It was whilst this discussion went on that I noted the grass rustling about and seen Dickie, prone on his belly, dragging hisself our direction around a large stand of thistles and prickly pear. He must of been at this journey across the prairie for quite a while, on account of he'd covered a good distance from the brush he'd gone off to. Yet how might he even help us. That remained the question. He had his pistol, but he was outnumbered. One of us surely would get ourselves shot before any shootout was over.

About that time, Murry declared he was hungry and went off to look in our wagon for food. Silas took up the watch over me as well as over your mother and Horhay. Whilst Murry was search-ing our wagon he happened upon our stash of peaches that had got sodden during the storm, and he hollered over to Silas that there was peaches but they was rotten. He rifled about in the rest of our things and come across Dickie's small bag that held the cursed necklace.

Tot, by the time you read this account you might or might not take hard stock in curses. You might believe that a madstone saved your life one time, or it didn't. You might or might not rely on Providence generally having a hand in how things might go. Benjamin Franklin hisself was confused on the matter, and changed from believing that God stayed out of our business to claiming that God was fully in charge. My comments on matters like that would be only hunches, so I will just tell you what happened.

The first event that took place is Dickie would not of known of the curse if you had not taken it on yourself to show Horhay the necklace the night before. It might be Providence set that up, or might not.

The second event is Dickie would not of left the necklace there in the wagon, instead of taking it into the brush on his person, if he was not told of the curse by Horhay. Who wants to venture into thick bushes in snake ridden country strapped with a bad luck piece.

The third event is Murry happened upon the necklace, and drew it out of the bag, and exclaimed about it, Whoa! Silas! Look at this! and commenced to carry it to his brother.

The fourth event is whilst tromping over to Silas, Murry tripped on a stony patch in a clump of shrubs and yucca and went down on all fours.

The fifth event is a rattlesnake was resting there in the shrubs, and Murry must of fell on it. It struck him with nary a rattle, not even a meager shake of its tail. After it struck, it rattled so loud we all froze in instinctive alarm. Murry got up, and backed off, and went into a rage, and shot at the snake, but missed it. He screamed, I'm bit by a rattler! I'm bit! and tugged his pants down to look at the marks.

The sixth event is Silas become distracted by this commotion, and Horhay charged at him like a bull and knocked him hard to the ground. I run and jumped him as well, and wrestled his pistol away. Given as Horhay had use of only one arm he made good use of his boots, kicking at Silas's head.

The pistol Silas still had a hold on, after I lifted his, was Horhay's. He drew it out of his belt and pressed the barrel into my neck. But the double trigger confounded him, and he tugged the wrong one of the two. This give me the chance to wrestle the gun from his hands.

Murry come running at us in a hobbled fashion on account of his pants being down from when he'd checked for the fang marks. He could not get a clean shot at us as we rolled about with his brother.

Dickie then rose from the grass and opened fire on Murry. The bullet struck the back of his knee and blew the cap off the front. Murry fell to the ground and commenced loud yelping. Dickie rushed forward and leapt on him and pried his pistol away, and got back mine that Murry had taken from me at the start, as well. We then had the guns and the say so.

Your mother, despite her condition, run to the wagon for rope and brought it to me. We had plenty on hand, thanks to Dickie's belief of keeping out snakes by circling our beds.

Silas shortly give up on struggling when Horhay delivered some blows to his head that rendered him somewhat senseless. I freed up Horhay's bad arm from the scarves that anchored it to his side, despite it was useless regardless, and the two of us bound up Silas. Murry meantime went utterly mute on seeing the state of his kneecap, being that it was entirely gone.

I recall the rattler still rattling then, as this all happened markedly fast. I recall, as well, seeing you out in the grass, standing and watching, as still as a stump and not making a sound. You looked quite small in all that prairie.

*　*　*

So that's how things stood at midafternoon on the ninth day of our travels. Dickie's clothes was muddy and ripped down the front from dragging hisself on his belly. Myself and Horhay was beat up and somewhat bad off from our fight with Silas. Your mother was far toward having the baby. Murry was dumbstruck about his gone knee, and Silas was woozy and limp. I can't even say what you might of thought of the whole ordeal. You did not run to your mother at once, as I guess events had confused you. She went directly to you however, and got hold of you, and you hung on to her.

I drove the wagon near to your uncles so we would not have to hogtie and drag them over to it. Dickie kept a good aim on them the whole time. Then him and myself strapped the brothers each to a wheel where we might keep a eye on them. We did what we could to help them out, despite we did not give a whit about them. Dickie sliced at the snakebite, to let it bleed out what poison it would. He collected the necklace where Murry had dropped it and remarked on if it was cursed, or not, and for who. It had done us a very good turn, but had certainly done poorly by Murry and Silas. Whatever the truth of that question, it did appear like it might hold powers, and Dickie was scared to handle it much. He tossed it back in the wagon.

Meantime Horhay fetched the blanket your mother had left in the prairie and settled her under the post oak, forty or so yards off from where the brothers was strapped to the wheels of the wagon. He got hold of your uncles' canteens and give them to her and you, as you was both badly in need of water.

Your mother's effort at labor become a long, wet, sweaty process and there was no shortage of heat and bugs to pester her. Green stinging flies and plenty of gnats was drawn to our sweat, and chiggers and ticks crawled out of the grass like it was a picnic and we was the feast. I tried to shelter your mother somewhat with another one of our blankets, as I knew she cared for her privacy. But that was a failed battle for sure, considering the labors went on for a while.

You was perplexed of the whole thing and squatted down alongside her. We give up trying to coax you away, and after some time she ceased caring what you was seeing of things, as privacy was but small potatoes compared to her pains.

She tried to withhold her cries, but at times they come forth and you shouted at her, What's the matter, Mama! What's the matter! You had somewhat of a understanding, but appeared like you thought she'd gone hard of hearing. A time or two when she let out a cry, you yelled at the baby, Come out, baby! Come out, baby!

Some moments your mother become so weak from her strenuous

efforts that she thought she might die. She told me her cousin's address in New Orleans so I might consign it to memory. She asked me to see that you got there. She whispered at me that I was to tell you all that she'd told me about herself, if she was to pass. I was to tell you, as well, what had occurred with your father, and why. She feared you might someday go looking for him, not knowing the truth of him being evil as well as of him being dead. She said he had always felt fondly toward you, and you was to know of that too.

Meantime a buzzard come down and perched on the side of the wagon. It situated itself above where your uncles was tied, and appeared curious of them. Dickie was keeping a eye on them and he got amused with the buzzard. Your mother and Horhay and me and you was off under the post oak, but we could hear most of the things he said to your uncles, Dickie's voice being naturally brash. He remarked loudly to them about it being peculiar to have a buzzard alight right over their heads. He said, What might that bird be waiting for.

Silas did not appear wholly vital and made no response to that. Murry, however, cursed at Dickie. His voice come out feeble on account of he'd lost a great deal of blood. His leg laid straight out before him, and it was entirely stiff. The rattler's bite and the cap being gone had swelled it so big it was busted out of the seams of his pants and nearly as fat as a full grown cypress log.

I went over and cut the pant leg off to make room for the swelling, and tied it around the shot knee to stanch some of the blood. He hollered some whilst I done that. Then I went back to your mother.

Another buzzard arrived soon and perched alongside the other.

Dickie said, Whoa, it's two now! There's two of you and there's two of them. Why that might be. I'm scratching my head. What might that mean. What in the world could those birds be after.

Murry then cursed at the buzzards. He thrown up and retched a great deal as well, on account of the rattler's venom. I would of thought most of the venom would of been shed from his knee, there being a pretty good flow of the blood. That wasn't the case, however.

The buzzards appeared like they was remarking to one another about the cursing. Two more soared into view and circled above for some time, then come down and joined the first two, followed by two more again that landed upon the side of the wagon, making a full half dozen gazing down on the brothers.

Dickie stated to Murry, What friendly buzzards you've got there! Close enough you could reach up and grab them but for your arms being bound to the wheels! What might they be awaiting. Buzzards is known to smell death, but neither of you is dead yet. Silas, you might be mistaken for it, but I doubt you stink of it yet. They do look patient, however. It's said they await the will of God.

I went over and asked him if he would stop taunting, there being no reason for it. But he was enjoying hisself and went on.

After a time, Horhay avowed that he seen the crown of the baby's head show from within. Your mother sat with her knees up for Horhay and me to help her. We was trying to do so, when Murry's hollering rose up higher and louder. I looked his direction and seen a buzzard alighted on the ground nearby him and fixedly eyeing his knee.

Murry hollered, Get it away from me! Get it away from me! and swiped at it with the leg but declined to properly kick it, on account of the knee not working without the cap. The buzzard then give a peck to the knee and Murry screamed louder.

Dickie said, Whoa! That buzzard appears to be a impatient son of a bitch! It has forgone the will of God and taken on matters itself!

I hollered at Dickie to shoo it off. Get shed of the buzzards! I yelled and gone back to matters at hand with your mother. She was considerably weak from the strain.

Then of a sudden a loud stirring and uproar broke forth. I turned and beheld the same thing as the rest of us witnessed, apart from your mother, her being fronted the other direction and at that moment bent over her knees and laboring hard.

I should state it was not Dickie's fault what we saw, despite that he had been goading Murry. He meant only to wave his arms and scare the birds off. I suppose the fault mostly was mine, as in my haste to move the wagon close to your uncles and tie them up to the wheels I had not properly set the brake. The bad sister mule and Horhay's mare are blameless as well. Whilst they was accustomed to gunfire and had not been spooked by that, a flock of buzzards taking off from the side of the wagon all at one time, flapping their wings as they flew aloft, was not a disturbance the mule and the mare was trained to withstand. Therefore they bolted. By that I mean they heaved forward and headed across the prairie.

You might be able to guess what this meant for Silas and Murry. It was not good. It was a horror. The weirdest thing was, none of us moved to stop it. I think maybe we was too shocked to move. Or maybe we was too morbid. I mostly believe the reason we none of us moved is there was not time. I remained knelt beside your

mother and watched the wagon roll. Horhay raised up his eyes to
the spectacle and spoke not a word. Dickie still had his arms in the
air from waving them at the buzzards, and had a look of surprise.
You watched and had nothing to say, as what was there. None of us
moved. None of us spoke. The buzzards scattered over the brush.
The mule and the mare strived through the field in a lopsided manner, the weight of Silas and Murry causing a drag to the wheels and
acting as brakes to the progress. The wagon's crooked passage laid
the flowers and grass down flat.

Round and round, Silas and Murry went. Murry managed to
tuck his head. He pulled his good knee up to his chest to spare
that one leg, and stuck the leg that was missing the cap straight
out before him. It must of been hard to hold that leg out, given the
extra poundage it had from the swelling. The leg circled around
like the fat paddle wheel of a sizeable butter churn.

Silas, though, was a gone case, letting his head strike the
ground with each turn of the wheel. Plop it went, with each spin. It
vanished into grass and shrubs on the downward turns, smacked
into the ground, and come up again. I come to believe in the after-
math he might of been dead before the flight started, as who cares
so little about their own life as not even to tip their own head. Plop,
plop it went, round and round. It was grisly, as I have stated. It
was hard to watch, but it was hard not to. I recall needing to gri-
mace and squint, and yet I did watch through the squint. Horhay
looked on, but did not change his face in any way that I noted. You
hunched your shoulders up to your chin, the spectacle being awful.
Nevertheless, you kept your eyes locked on the passage the wagon
made through the field.

The mare and the mule managed to travel quite a distance before the drag on the wheels stopped them. The brothers was left upside down, their legs drooping over their faces. Murry appeared to twitch. Silas was perfectly still. Things become quiet but for the sounds of a hot day in a lone prairie. All of us, excepting your mother, was staring at that grim scene, when occurred a loud and lingering cry from your mother, and of a sudden the baby begun to come forth.

*   *   *

Dickie made haste to the wagon and untied the brothers from off the wheels whilst Horhay and me assisted your mother and she brung forth a girl. Horhay knotted and cut the birth cord, and we cleaned up the baby the best we could for not having much water. I struck up a trifling fire and hastened the flame with gunpowder so Horhay might parch some flour to sprinkle the baby's naval.

Then I went to help Dickie load up your uncles into the bed of the wagon. It was a difficult task. Silas was dead and a terrible sight. Murry mumbled a great deal. He appeared to of chomped off part of his tongue. His snakebit leg and gone knee looked bad and his knuckles was mush, owing to how they'd been tied to the wheels and scraped the ground at each spin. His mind seemed to be slipping. We laid him out in the wagon beside his departed brother. He'd soaked hisself with vomit and smelled of it strongly. Silas smelled strongly of blood and shat.

I then returned to your mother. Horhay had wrapped the baby snug in your mother's serape and you was excited about her and agitated to hold her. Your mother snugged you close and laid the baby in your lap for a time. I kept some distance, knowing the way I smelled from handling the brothers.

Tot, I should of perhaps felt only relief and happiness for your mother but I admit to being disheartened she give birth to a girl. Back at the sulphur springs she'd said she might name the baby for me, as she had expected a boy. I would of very much liked that. However, I come to terms with the facts of the matter in very short order, as your sister seemed a wonder to me, given how hard the birth was, and how sweet she come out, and how thankful your mother was that she'd got her here safe and all right. As well, we was all fortunate even to be alive, so how could I begrudge even one small item in the current state of affairs.

The way things stood at that time was three of the Banes brothers was passed, those being your father and uncles Dale and Silas. The only brother still living was Murry, and he was no longer harmful in any immediate way. Your mother and you and the wee one would soon sail for New Orleans, and live safe thereafter, out of the reach of Banes kin and the vengeful Swamp Fox men. The worry your mother had suffered was mostly eased.

In the time it took to settle the brothers into the wagon and make things ready, mosquitoes come out and the sun sank low amongst stringy clouds along the horizon beyond the road, turning the sky a deep red. The heat dropped and a breeze rolled in. We was in need of water, and set out as quick as we could, and traveled on as dark settled, knowing the town of Victoria was a dozen miles off, or more.

It was a weird, weird ride that night. Your uncles was laid side by side in the far back of the wagon, snugged against the tailgate.

Murry spoke slurred words we could not make out and did not especially try hard to, as what could we do for him anyway. He might of been asking for water, but we had none.

I remained at the reins. Your mother held the baby and sat with you in the wagon bed just back of me, as that was the most comfortable place for her. She had been through a lot, to state what is obvious. Dickie and Horhay rode alongside on the brothers' geldings, those being nice horses, although hard used.

Your mother was mostly intent on getting the baby to nurse right. There was a issue with that, on account of she'd had scant water and I guess her milk had run short. The baby would not take hold, and your mother had a bad time. She was patient, however. At times I looked back from my seat and seen her stroking the baby's head, and seen, as well, the whites of your eyes in the moonlight on occasions you looked my direction. You seemed like you was trying to figure sense out of things on your own, without asking about them. I guess, being wise for your years, you had a inkling that none of us, nor anyone anywhere else for that matter, could spin the events of that day in any reasonable fashion. It had been willy nilly, the bad and the good, the helpless situation we had found ourselves in and the circumstances that rescued us by the good grace of God, or good fortune, or the help of the buzzards, or the curse of the necklace. We none of us knew what to make of those matters.

Dickie spoke of it some, when full dark had set in. He claimed the necklace had played a big hand in the flight of the buzzards and the ride the wagon took those brothers on. He said it had landed Murry on top of the snake, on account of Murry was carrying it when that happened, and this was plainly bad luck in itself, which then led to all the other bad luck that befell the brothers and was, in the end, good luck for the rest of us.

Horhay advised him to toss the necklace and leave it, but Dickie refused to do that. It was the one real treasure he'd found in his lifetime of looking. No matter the curse it carried, tossing it out would mean his life's work amounted to nothing, or so he maintained. He told me to halt, and alighted and fished about in the back of the wagon until he got hold of the necklace and strapped it on Murry's neck so it would curse Murry, not us, if more bad luck was to come.

I myself held that what happened had more to do with my negligence than with a curse, given how I'd forgot to lock the wheels. We spoke of these matters, our mouths thick with thirst, Dickie and Horhay on the horses and me in the wagon hauling my five passengers, two who smelled of blood and vomit and shat, and one who smelled of breast milk and things that was new and fresh to me.

And so on we traveled in that fashion, encountering no one to ask for water in the dark of night, and smelling of birth and death and our own sweat whilst the air around us smelled of spring flowers and the moon crossed over the sky. Coyotes yipped far off in regions we could not see. The land was flat and the road less ragged than those I had traveled back home in the hills, but there was a rough, unevenness to the time, and to my feelings. Despite we had won victories in the passage of that day, I felt profoundly lost in the course of the night. I could not help but wonder what Murry must feel, laid out alongside his dead brother. Despite being evil, they was still brothers, and must of been fond of each other.

*   *   *

After some hours a house showed up beside the road ahead. The land was so flat we made out the line of the roof against the stars from a long way off. Cotton fields around was untended, as I guess at one time there must of been slaves to pick them that now was freed. The fields hosted fresh patches of wheat. A sign by the road stated PRIVATE OWNED LAND. NOT A WAY STOP. KEEP OFF.

Dickie and Horhay and myself decided I was the one should knock at the door, as I would appear more harmless a stranger than Dickie, being younger and not so husky, and might be more welcomed than Horhay, given as how it was hard to know what folks might make of him. We figured he might get shot. We figured as well that I should not mention Silas and Murry. We planned on turning them in to the law in Victoria.

I drawn up in the road and approached the door but was halted by a large dog that run at us from the doorstep and barked fiercely and snarled at me. A rifle barrel emerged from the door and a woman within hollered out, demanding who I was.

I said, My name is Benjamin Shreve and I'm traveling with a lady who give birth down the road and is in need of assistance.

This is not a way stop, the woman said.

She's in a bad state, I said.

Move out or you'll find yourself in a worse one! the woman replied.

Can we have water from your well, I asked her.

No, she said. Move out. I been lied to before about women in need.

Your mother got out of the wagon, holding the baby and moving with some care, given as what she had been through, and come over to stand alongside me and speak to the woman for herself. She told the women that she would appreciate water and might we please help ourselves at the well, as she needed more of her milk to come in for the baby.

The woman then opened the door partway and told the dog to hush. She appeared harsh looking, neither old nor young, and kept the rifle on me. How many of you is out there, she asked.

There's me and two other men traveling, and a boy, I said.

This was but partly false, as Silas and Murry was not traveling but being hauled.

I'll see to this woman and the baby, she replied. The others of you can drink at the well and take up for the night in the shack out back. Any of you come near the house and this dog will alert me.

I believe she lived alone and her husband likely was dead, as so many was, from the war. Probably she was hounded by too many travelers, there being a shortage of way stops along this stretch of the road.

Your mother went with the baby inside the woman's house, whereupon I woke you and led you off to the well, and took water to Murry, although he had trouble getting it down on account of the issue with his tongue. He looked awful, being swelled up and covered with vomit and wearing the cursed necklace. I did what I could, although it weren't much. Horhay and Dickie and you and me drank our fill and splashed ourselves and brought the animals to the trough. The water contained a salt taste that I welcomed, seeing as we had been short of salt. We then left Murry and Silas laid out in the wagon and went to the shack.

It proved to be a laborers' dwelling and did not seem to of been occupied in some time. I suppose the workers was the gone freedmen. The roof was oilcloth, with muslin tacked to the ceiling, and the floor was gunny sacks. A saucer light of old lard sat on a table made of a pine board laid across empty candle boxes. Also there was a three legged stool and a lard tin chamber pot. Antlers was nailed to the walls for hanging things on. One of them sported a pair of old trousers and a tore up woman's shift. There was four narrow beds made of planks alongside the walls, with mattresses that was shuck, not straw, and in my opinion not bad. The home I grew up in was hardly better, so the place did not bother me, but Horhay and Dickie preferred sleeping out. Horhay laid out his blanket nearby the cabin and Dickie laid a blanket off by the wagon to keep watch over his necklace. He feared a passer by in the night might take it. We assured him nobody right minded would come near enough Murry even to see it, but he had determined to keep a eye on it.

Meantime I shook out the gunny sacks and two of the mattresses to make things habitable for you and myself. I brought in the cleanest blankets we had and pushed two beds together and lit the lard light, which was old and smelly. Then I tried to get you to sleep. But you was alert and would not lay down. You sat on the bed and aired a number of questions in a solemn manner.

My Uncle Silas is dead, you remarked.

Yes he is, I agreed.

Why, you wanted to know.

He took quite a few blows to the head, and then didn't last the ordeal on the wheel, I offered.

Was they going to take me, you asked.

Yes, they tried to, I said.

Why, you inquired.

Just them being rotten hearted, I told you. They wanted to take you to live with them so you might grow up and turn rotten hearted like them.

This give you a cause for concern and you questioned how they might make you turn that way, and if you would.

I replied that I didn't know how they might do it, and that you can't tell how folks will turn out, as there's dark roads a person can get on, and it's hard to say how it happens. But you wasn't on one currently, I assured you.

You're good hearted now, I said. That's all that counts at any one time. Just keep yourself on the right road. If you get on a wrong one, you'll know it. You'll feel it. Just get off it quick. You can do that.

You thought on that matter and asked, Was the buzzard going to eat Uncle Murry's knee.

Yes, I think it intended to, I replied.

My uncles was hanging upside down, you remarked.

I agreed and posed how this was due to bad luck, as sometimes things was, but how your uncles might of been right side up or sideways or upside down when the wagon stopped, and their luck would of been poor no matter which way they was landed.

I have a sister, you said. She come out a girl.

Yes she did, I said. And you're going to have to look after her.

How, you wanted to know.

By helping your mother, I told you. Sisters can be a lot of trouble.

Why, you asked.

They get into mischief, I told you. They get headstrong about it. You got to be patient with them. It's hard work, but they're worth it. You just got to be up to it.

I'm up to it! you declared with a great deal of enthusiasm.

I know you are, I said.

I've got to look after my mama, too, you offered.

No, you have to help her look after you, I said.

You snugged against me and said, I was scared my uncles was going to take me.

I was too, I owned. I was very scared about that.

Are we glad Uncle Silas is dead, you inquired.

I believe I am, Tot, and you can be too, if you want to, I offered. Your uncle Silas was mean, don't you think. He was scary. Bad things happen to everybody, but sometimes they happen especially to people like him who go about stirring up trouble, and that's fair.

Uncle Murry is scary too, you said.

Not anymore, I said. He can't hurt you any longer. He's got no cap on his knee and he's snakebit, so he can't even run. Can't even get out of that wagon and walk. He's got not much left of his tongue, neither, so he can't even call you names or say things you don't want to hear. He's whipped. We're giving him up to the law and they'll see that he can't hurt you, nor any other person. Does that sound like a good idea.

You agreed that it did, and said, We're not sorry he's beat up, are we.

No, we're not, I assured you. We're sorry he's such a bad person, is all. If he'd behaved better, he would of fared better.

I think these items made sense to you, as you become more at ease and went to sleep. I laid there awhile alongside you looking at how the muslin sagged from the ceiling. Old water leaks from the roof made stains that bore shapes of clouds and trees and livestock of various sorts. There was a lot going through my head. When I could no longer stomach the smell of the lard light I snuffed it and fell sound out beside you.

* * *

I knew nothing more of my own existence until the woman who owned the place shook me awake and I sat up at once. She held a lantern. Your mother stood alongside her, holding the baby.

The woman said in a gruff manner, Your wife prefers being out here with you, to being in my house with me.

Tot, the idea she'd called your mother my wife got me fully awake, and I sat up.

She said, I've cleaned her up and wrapped her belly and give her a dress. Her birth place is washed. It aught to be washed again tomorrow with milk and water. She's dosed with castor oil and she'll empty herself tonight or tomorrow. I give the baby some nappies. I'm leaving a bucket of corn for the two of you and the boy. Is that a freed nigger that's out there, sleeping on the ground.

I said, No ma'am, he's a Indian.

She appeared to mull that over. She said, You be on your way by daylight. You're but a hour out of Victoria.

Yes ma'am, I told her.

She left whilst I was still trying to grasp how she'd called your mother my wife. I couldn't figure if she had just thought it, or if your mother had said it to her. I didn't care to know for sure, as I wished it to be the latter.

Your mother was worn down and got into the bed with us. The baby fussed, so I got up and lit the lamp to help however I might. This become my favorite night of my life to now, despite how poorly it had started on the long thirsty drive, and how little of it was left, and despite we was in a sorry shed of a place, in two spindly plank beds shoved together, and on shuck mattresses, with a stinking lard lamp on a half rotten table being our only light. The baby was cross, and you was restless and kicked in your sleep. Yet it was a very nice night.

I will not forget helping the baby latch on with a proper suck, and how tiny she was, and changing the nappie, and playing like this was our place and you three was my family. I was, as I have before now owned, far, far, far around that bend which Dickie had spoke of, stuck on a ledge too narrow for turning, knowing the drop was sure to be rough. Yet if I'd been given a choice that night of undoing the time back to when Dickie first showed me his coins and asked that I take him to Boerne, I would of said yes all over again and played things the same, and not been sorry about it.

*   *   *

Murry and Silas remained laid out in the back of the wagon as we rolled out early and traveled steadily until we come on the Guadalupe where two ferries was running passage across to Victoria. Carts and wagons was lined up to go over and we awaited our turn. You and me passed some time planning our sand forts we would build, drawing them out with our fingers on the wagon seat. There was a boy about twelve years old riding a shaggy mule with a shuck collar and driving a half dozen beeves over to market. He was having a bad time keeping his herd rounded whilst we waited, as they seemed to understand he was young and might be pushed about. Horhay and me lent him a hand whilst Dickie took charge of the wagon.

At that time, Murry become more alert than before. He did not sit up nor attempt to speak much, but requested water, which we give him. We offered shares of what food we had, but he could eat nothing. I said I'd untie the part of his pant leg I'd used to bandage his knee, but he made clear he did not want me near it. The blood was drying and crusted, and I guess he figured that messing with it would hurt a great deal. You climbed out of the wagon and eyed him from the tailgate and appeared to take pity on him, as he had not always been bad to you in your younger years. He give you somewhat of a smile, but your mother seen it and called you back to her and said not to get near him. She mostly stayed in the wagon and nursed the baby and did not look at Murry.

When the ferryman dropped the ramp and told us to board it was midmorning. Dickie paid up the two dollar cost, although he was cranky about it on account of his coins was dwindling.

The mule balked about boarding, so I give the reins over to Dickie and got out to sweet talk her on. The boy and his beeves come on behind, and a Mexican pushing a cart of goat skins come on behind him. It was a sturdy ferry, fortified with end ramps and good cleats and treads and kept on course with a cable pulley. We locked our wheels and secured the mule and the horses and found ourselves well situated with room for you to get out of the wagon and move about and drag your hands in the water.

On reaching the east side of the river we seen it was tricky to disembark, as there was a steep hill to pull up. As well, we foresaw trouble due to a man driving a large freight wagon drawn by three teams of oxen. He drove down through the crowd, causing confusion and irritation by pulling in front of folks who was waiting to board. They shouted at him but he was not dissuaded. He yelled that it was his rightful turn to board, as he'd waited a hour in line at the other ferry and then been told his load was too large. He shoved his way onto our ferry even before we had time to get off it.

The boy's cattle was mostly thereby blocked from departing by way of the ramp and took it upon theirselves to depart from the sides of the ferry, rocking it and nearly tumping us over. They splashed their way through the shallows and charged up the bank untended, further disrupting the folks awaiting their turn to board. Folks on the hill there whacked at them and yelled at the poor boy until Horhay and Dickie and myself helped him round up the herd.

Tot, there's a reason I am telling you all this that took place at the ferry, which you will soon understand.

We then moved on into town, Dickie and Horhay riding out front on the horses belonging to Silas and Murry. You and your mother, with the baby, was up on the seat with me. This was a Friday morning and there was heavy commerce, Victoria being a hub for a railroad laid between it and Lavaca, which is nearly to Indianola, and Indianola being second only to Galveston in the business of imports and exports.

I had not seen a railroad before. The depot was under repairs, as the Confederate rebels had tore up the track in the war to stop federals from using it when they come in by sea and invaded. Now the federals was building it back. It was of interest to me but does not pertain to matters at hand, so I will not dwell on it.

We come on the sheriff's office alongside the depot. I went to the porch and told the man guarding the place that we wanted to see the sheriff and was he in.

He is, but he's busy, the man said.

I asked was there another person in charge that we might see.

The man said the sheriff's deputy was out hunting fugitives of the Huntsville prison who was spotted in town. He asked what it was that we needed.

I replied that we had a criminal to turn over to him, and remains of another to turn in, both laid out in the wagon, the one dead and the other in need of care.

He asked who they was and what crimes had they done, and I explained they was brothers by the name Banes and their crimes was too many to state. I said, The woman you see there in the wagon just give birth to the baby yesterday and we're trying to get her and her kids to Indianola and on a ship to New Orleans. I'd like to turn these men over to the sheriff as soon as we can.

The guard then strode out to the wagon to have a look at the brothers whilst I remained on the porch, hoping we might be admitted to the sheriff's office. He went up to the wagon and peered in the back and called to me, There's but one man in here.

Dickie meantime was allowing his horse a drink at the trough. Horhay's horse was done at the trough, and Horhay was leading him back to the wagon. At the guard's statement Dickie turned and acquired a look of alarm. He dropped the reins and run straightaway to the wagon. I figured the guard was mistaken, but Dickie glanced in the back and hollered, He's gone! Murry's gone! He's made a escape with my necklace on him!

Horhay made haste to see for hisself, and nodded to me it was true. Your mother half rose from the wagon seat and turned to look in the back. She was holding the baby against her, and you stood up alongside her, and the two of you gazed over the gear piled in the center. The bewilderment in your faces caused me to hurry over and see for myself, Silas, dead and covered as we had left him, and the blanket that Murry had laid on, bloody and bare.

Dickie become wild. He yelled again how Murry was gone, and where had he gone to, and how had he done it, and how might we find him. He commenced a frantic search amongst our travel provisions, tossing things out of the wagon as if he might find a grown man hid under a two pound sack of beans. He looked under the wagon itself as well. He run out in the street, hollering at folks had they seen a man who was badly bloodied and missing a tongue and part of a knee. People appeared to think him senseless, and give him only scant glances.

His commotion brought the sheriff out of the office. I suppose a escape is never good news to a sheriff, no matter if he knows nothing of who it was that run off, or why. He rushed to the wagon to gaze at the sight of Silas, stone dead, alongside the blanket Murry had laid on. Plainly he thought Dickie out of his mind, as Dickie was yelling about the necklace and acted about to bust into tears, proclaiming how it was gone forever and it was his fortune, no matter that it was cursed.

The guard tried to explain to the sheriff what he knew of the matter, that being not much, and the baby awoke and begun to yowl on account of all the disturbance.

I might of stepped in and done some explaining if not for my eyes being fixed on you, Tot. You took a firm hold of your mother's dress there on the wagon seat, and I recalled the pledges I'd made to you on the night before, of how Murry could do you no harm and would soon be in the hands of the law. These was now lies. Your uncle was somewhere we didn't know of, possibly up to mischief we hadn't guessed at, and having a future before him in which he might carry on all breeds of evils, not even to mention revenge.

The question become, How had he made the escape. He could not of climbed out of the wagon and walked. He probably could not of climbed out of the wagon and even stood. His snakebit leg with the gone cap was swelled as big as a log. He could not of bent it, and could hardly of dragged it behind him. Crawling would of been painful, to say the least about that. Had he fashioned a crutch he might of been able to go in a crippled manner, but somebody would of let on if they'd seen such a man, clotted with blood, hoist hisself out of the wagon and drop to the ground in the middle of town.

It was Dickie who then come up with the only sensible tale we could tell ourselves at that time. It involved how the hefty wagon of freight that caused so much trouble back at the crossing, pulled by three yoke of oxen, had come alongside our wagon whilst driving aboard the ferry, before we could even get off. We had all of us been distracted by cattle rocking the ferry and plunging off into the shallows, and the confusion they caused thereafter when the boy could not get them trailed up. None of us had then thought to check if Murry remained in the wagon. Whilst we was still aboard the ferry he could of pulled hisself over the side of our wagon and dropped hisself into the nearby bed of the freight wagon, amongst all the freight. If that was what he had done, he was by now back on the other side of the river, a good distance gone and widening the gap by the minute.

When Dickie had this idea, he paused from his yelling and stated it plainly. Then he went to the horse that Horhay had rode, it being the one belonging to Silas and being the fittest, and likely the fastest. He snatched the reins from Horhay and mounted, and wheeled about, and took off at a rapid pace for the ferry crossing.

None of us even called after him, as none of us thought it would do any good.

* * *

Thereby Murry was fled and Dickie was in pursuit of him. Horhay and me and your mother and yourself was dumbfounded. The sheriff, who was quite young, took us into his office. He was kind to your mother, and thoughtful. Myself and Horhay explained the encounter we'd had with Silas and Murry, and give our sworn statements of it. Your mother told of her situation and why she was trying to get out of Texas. She showed her ticket money for passage and made clear who Silas and Murry was.

The sheriff remarked that he knew somewhat of the likes of the Banes brothers already, as he'd been appointed as sheriff to replace one suspected of having Confederate leanings and hindering the

progress of reconstruction. He'd heard a earful about the gangs up
in the three state corner and the growing numbers of Clue Cluck-
ers up there. He said if Silas Banes was one of that ilk, we was thoroughly justified killing him off, as these kinds was murdering more
freed Negroes and good Union folks in the northeast part of the
state than Indians was killing settlers out west.

Yet further knowledge of crimes done by these Banes brothers
was needed, he said, before matters could be resolved. He therefore
told the guard to fetch a agent of the Freedmen's Bureau, and the
guard made off in haste to do so.

The bureau agent was prompt to arrive. He walked with a limp
on a wooden leg, and he was quite handsome. I figured he'd lost
his actual leg in the war, on account of so many did and the federal
government granted a number of false legs to them that was Union
soldiers.

The sheriff asked the agent if he would take charge of our situation, and then he rode off to gather a posse to hunt for Murry.

The agent commenced to question us, but when he seen the
strain the questions had on your mother he asked that we leave him
to speak with her alone.

So you and Horhay and myself went outside whilst your mother
remained inside with the agent and the baby. Horhay offered to take
you to a bake shop across the way to pass the time, and you went
off with him. I sat in a chair on the porch and heard through the
window the conversation within, although it come to me muted,
as I positioned myself so as not to be seen. I strained to make out
what was said.

Here is some of what I heard.

Your mother told of the Swamp Fox gang attacking the home of a white man named Smith on a Christmas night, on account of some freedmen and freedwomen was living with Mr Smith and the gang thought this not right. They beat him senseless and stabbed his young daughters for trying to aid him. They killed some of the freedmen living with him. Silas and Murry Banes, she said, and the other Banes brothers, there being two, those being her husband, now dead, and the brother named Dale, now dead as well, had all taken part in the murders.

The agent noted, So there is but one brother still living, named Murry, and he is wounded and on the loose.

Yes, your mother replied.

The baby then become cross and your mother asked if she could feed her. The agent offered to give her privacy, or perhaps bring her a cover. She told him a cover would do, and I heard the thump of his false leg as he went to another room and returned. Forthwith the baby got quiet and I made out sounds of her suckling.

The agent remarked how she was a pretty baby.

Your mother inquired if he had children at home.

Two, he replied.

After a time of quiet, your mother spoke up and recounted further crimes of your father and uncles as if in one breath. She told of a number of murders, and of the Swamp Fox gang having their way with the young black girl no more than a child. She spoke of a massacre of freed people by fifty or more white men at a place called Whitakers, and the burning of that place, on account of it was owned and run by freedmen and was making good money. She could not state for sure if the Swamp Fox and his gang took part in that occurrence, although she had reasons to think so. She talked of them making a target of Mr Kirkman, on account of his efforts to stop their crimes. She spoke of Cul Baker, the Swamp Fox hisself, boasting whilst in her kitchen of a Negro he shot with so many bullets the man come to look like a pincushion. The gang shot holes in the man's head whilst jumping their horses over his body.

There was more of such tales she reported. It was when she come to the one of the small girl with the penny whistler that your mother faltered and was unable to say the full story. Her telling become slower, her words not properly strung together but halted between and very quiet.

She fell silent for a moment then, and I heard neither of them speak. The baby must of ceased nursing and fallen asleep, as there was no more sounds of her suckling. And then in a voice so low I strained to hear it, your mother said, I waited too long to report the crimes when I knew of them, sir. I might of stopped some if I hadn't acted a coward. It wasn't about me taking a beating. I had stood those and could last another. But what would I do if they took my son.

The agent told her she'd done what she needed, but she refused to agree with that.

No, she replied. There's crimes I might of halted had I gone sooner to Mr Kirkman. Now they're laid at my door. Nothing can take them away from my door.

I can't say how the agent answered, as the sheriff rode into the yard at that time. He did not alight, but hailed me, so I went out to speak with him. He told me he'd gathered up men from the bar and about the town to search throughout for Murry. Some of these men was heading off to the ferry and he intended to join them. Meantime he had arranged our passage to Indianola. We was to take the U.S. daily mail stage, which would carry us through the port of Lavaca and on. The stage would depart at noon, that being less than a hour away. It would have us to Indianola by six o'clock in the evening, in time for you and your mother and Horhay to board the ship for New Orleans.

This all come as a shock to me, Tot. I had not thought of parting from you and your mother so soon. By wagon, we would of had this day of travel and half of the next. We would of had another night together. By stage we had only six hours.

The sheriff stated the stage would go to a hotel in Indianola called the Casimir House nearby where a ship of the Morgan line would be docked. Passage could be purchased at the hotel. The ship would leave at six in the evening, as soon as the mail from the stage was loaded. As it was Friday, missing that ship would cost a delay of three days until the next one, and we should not linger in Indianola, with yellow fever on the rise. Infants did not fare well with that, he advised. He had arranged a ride for me to return on the mail stage the following morning. I could leave the mule in his stable until then. The horse that had belonged to Murry would now become federal property. The saddle and bridle as well. The bureau agent would see to these things, the sheriff said, and I was to pass that word on to him. As well, the agent would write up reward papers for us having brought in Silas Banes.

Having finished with his instructions the sheriff said, Do you have any questions I can answer for you in short order.

I will tell you, Tot, I had a number of questions tearing through my mind, yet none of them was for him, and none of them could be answered in short order. They involved what my life would be like without you and your mother, and how I might even get through saying goodbye. Also how I might possibly gather my wits and do it so soon. I recalled the promise I'd made to you about building sand forts and how we would walk on the shore together and pick up shells. None of this now would happen. And once I no longer had use of Horhay's horse, how would I get from here in Victoria all the way back to Ecleto with the double harness and but one mule. All the while the sheriff was giving me further orders, and I could hardly listen to what he said.

He rode away and I pulled myself together, there being times a person has to. Things had to be done for you and your mother, and my dread didn't make them less urgent. If you was to miss the boat out, your mother would lack the money to pay for board, and yellow fever might creep in, and all manner of evils could happen. I had no money myself to pay into the situation. How could I care for you and her and the baby, even for just three days. And where was Murry. If he was strong enough to get out of the wagon, what else might he do. I recalled a rat snake I stoned nearly to death when I was a child. I caught it eating our chicks, and smashed its head in and knocked a eye out, but the snake crawled off. I had never fully got past the feeling that it was wait-ing for me somewhere.

I knocked at the door of the office and entered and recounted the sheriff's instructions to the agent and your mother. Your mother appeared fairly done in by her talk with the agent. Her dress was wet with milk stains. She did not rise out of the chair, but asked if you was with Horhay. I assured her you was, and that you was only across the street in the bake shop and he was looking after you.

I waited with her whilst the agent went off to bring his wife to help her. We could of made promises to each other during that time, but they would of been false ones. I could not foresee my future, and she could not foresee hers. We said nearly nothing.

The agent's wife come and invited your mother to stay at her home and recover from having the baby. But your mother was scared of Murry showing back up. So the woman took her into a room to help her get clean. You and Horhay finally returned, bringing gingerbread. I tried to appear hungry, and ate some, as you was proud to of brought it.

In swift measure, our plans was resolved. Horhay sold his horse and his tack to the federals for one hundred and thirty dollars, as he would not need them if he was to go with us by stage to Indianola and travel from there by boat to New Orleans and from there on to Florida and Las Bahamas. Him and myself both thought the price low, but the bureau agent did not have leave to offer more.

The question arose as to who should receive the certificate of reward for killing Silas and bringing him in. Horhay and me agreed Dickie deserved the money the most, as he had scared off the buzzards and sent the wagon rolling, although it was me who had failed to set the brakes. Dickie was gone, however, and we did not know where to, and he'd already got his certificate for the likewise amount of four hundred dollars for killing the brother named Dale at the Menger. Horhay therefore urged that I take the certificate, saying he'd earned enough bounties during his lifetime and he would be leaving Texas and the United States and would not return to claim a bounty.

So I took what was offered, thinking but little about it. It was a written note signed by the agent. I was uncertain if I had earned it, nor was I sure if I wanted to of earned it, nor did I think it ever would be redeemed. There was procedures for that to happen, as verifications had to be sought and Victoria had no telegraph service even to send word to the bureau agent Mr Kirkman, up in the three corner region, of how Silas Banes was dead and brought in. Also, it was Governor Pease who had offered rewards, and he was not thought to last in the seat, so who knew if the state would even make good on the promise.

The truth is, I didn't much care at that time if the paper might be redeemed. My hopes for the future, past six o'clock in the evening when you was to leave on the boat, seemed nothing but pipe dreams that was over.

I left my change of clothes in the wagon, those being no cleaner than what I had on, and carried the baby whilst you and your mother and Horhay and me walked down to the post office and boarded the stage. Your mother had on a plain dress of a pale color that the agent's wife had brought her to change for the soiled one. It hung large, and made her look paler than ever, but it was clean, with plenty of buttons to help in the nursing, and your mother was grateful to have it.

*　*　*

It was a strange event for me to be carried along at a good pace on a well fitted coach drawn by a team of four horses, as I am accustomed to making my own way, in my wagon. It's not often in my life I am not in charge of the reins. Therefore on this last leg of the journey I felt entirely under the jurisdiction of fate.

Horhay sat by a window, with you alongside him, and your mother alongside you, and myself alongside her and next to the other window. Mail bags and parcels was piled at our feet and stacked on the seats about and behind us. We sped through the day. The sky was gray and the land flat. Tall weeds and grasses covered the prairies. At times we spied the tracks of the railroad laid alongside us some distance out. Patches of water flooded the road in places and pooled in marshy hog wallows. We halted at a swing stop for a change of horses, and there your mother nursed the baby and we ate biscuits hard as brickbats. Then we continued on.

Your mother laid her head on my shoulder and slept at times. She sought out my hand under a mail bag lodged between us, and I took hold of hers and did not let go for whole hours of travel. We was lost to ourselves, and in some ways we was lost to each other as well. I strove to find some distance from her in my mind, knowing how I should need it, and yet my hand declined to let go, and her fingers kept holding to mine, and I could think of nothing but how to hold up, and how your mother and you might fare in New Orleans, and if I might ever be happy again without you two. I questioned if my duty to Sam and the promise I'd made to my father was worth what it was costing me of my happiness.

Meantime Horhay had opposite kinds of feelings. He got a whiff of salt in the air and appeared like he become younger and delighted with life. He asked of you if you smelled the salt, and you sniffed and replied that you couldn't, but then sniffed harder and shouted, I do! I do! although I think that you didn't. Horhay took you into his lap, and you put your head out the window. Then I believe you did smell it, as you become lively and urged him to tell you all he recalled of the sea. I tried to forewarn you it was unlikely we would have time to build sand forts, or splash about in the waves like we'd planned, as I did not want you unprepared to be disappointed. You would not hear me, however. You was caught up in Horhay's excitement, and peered from the window, and sniffed of the air, and paid no attention to what I was trying to tell you.

A few miles out of the port of Lavaca I got a whiff of the salt myself. It come to me faint at first, and whilst I had dreamed of seeing the gulf, the smell of it now seemed a damp odor that carried a feeling of dread.

We arrived in Lavaca and found it a port that sat on a bluff overlooking a bay, that being the largest region of water I had yet seen in my lifetime. Building was going on everywhere, on account of Union gunboats had bombarded the town in the war and repairs was still underway. We pulled up at the post office and the driver got down from his seat and come to the window and told us to stretch our legs, as this would be our last chance at that before reaching Indianola. The mail would have to arrive to Indianola on time, he said, as most of it was to go on the boat to New Orleans that you and your mother and Horhay was planning to be on as well.

Your mother went into the office to find a private room where she might nurse the baby. I stood at the edge of the bluff and looked out over the bay. A pier extended over the water below, and men was fishing from it. Small boats sailed and steamed about. The water was gray, the same as the sky. Across the way laid a stretch of land.

After a spell your mother come with the baby and stood next to me on the bluff, watching the boats. She asked what I might be thinking.

I guess I'm thinking the water's grayer than I expected, as I had imagined it blue, I said.

She took that in, and said, But what are you mostly thinking.

I'm thinking how I'm going to miss you, I owned.

We kept on looking out at the water and not at each other. I guess I felt embarrassed about my feelings for her, and I think she tended to keep herself inward, no matter what her feelings for me. I recall the wind blowing over the water was at our faces.

Can I wait for you when I'm settled there, she asked.

I will tell you, Tot, for such a cause I could ride out a long wait. I could ride out a lifetime wait to be with the two of you and the baby. But how could I make that promise to your mother when my future was yet uncertain and my obligations was plain. I had swore to my father I would look after my sister, no matter what might befall. He asked it of me and I give him that vow. How could I up and leave to New Orleans when my sister was yet lost. It was her own doing to get herself lost, that much is true, but most everything else in her life aforehand was set for her by occasions beyond her choosing. I am obligated to care for such a girl, and be in her reach, wherever she might of run off to in years after, as nobody else is sworn to, and nobody else would.

I said, Nell, I can't ask you to wait for me. There might be a time I can go, if my sister comes home and goes along, or if I find she won't ever come home. But how can I make a promise that I can't be sure I can keep.

There was no good answer to that, but after a while she said, I'll be waiting for you regardless.

She seemed to mean it, yet there was a sadness to how she said it. We both knew how things stood and how people can lose each other in this world, it being large and time being long. So it was a stout reckoning we had, and a hard one. Up until then I'd been hoping some turn of events would change the way things was headed. But if Murry Banes was to make it home, he would be all that his mother had left of her sons. And if Nell was right about Mrs Banes, which I figured she was, then revenge would eventually come.

You was already back in the coach with Horhay, and the driver hollered at Nell and myself to hurry. We boarded and seen three men crowded into the seat behind us amongst the mail parcels. They was complaining to one another about the train from Victoria that had brought them along in the morning but bogged on occasions, it being small with a feeble engine. They had been called on to get out and push. It appeared they had all been strangers to one another upon boarding the train, but now was well acquainted.

One of them wore a felt top hat and nice button up boots, worse off for some mud, and bragged of hisself in a manner the other two seemed to of tired of. He paid ready made compliments to your mother, saying how nice it was to find hisself in the company of a lovely lady with such pretty eyes. As well, he boasted to us and the two other men whilst we traveled, saying he come from humble beginnings and even to midlife had earned his way by measly means like skinning of deer found dead of black tongue in dry seasons, and yet had risen beyond these labors to own a gainful freighting business that hauled goods west from Indianola and down south to Mexico. He had brought along stewed apples and fresh bread with tinned butter, but offered none to anyone else, and spoke whilst he ate, talking of things that had took place in the war. He had several times run the blockade through Horse Pass on a fleet little ship, he said, carrying upwards of forty bales of cotton out and returning with such prizes as arms and tools and medicines. He said at one time a Yankee warship chased him hotly and run him aground on the beach. Despite how much I disliked him, I found myself thinking my own life too ordinary by comparison, same as it was with Dickie's, and I was glad your mother paid him only polite attention, and none otherwise. Listening to the man made me miss Dickie, who talked as much but wasn't a braggart, and I wondered if Dickie was having luck in tracking down Murry.

The road we traveled was mostly along the shores of Lavaca and Matagorda bays. The land was marshy and covered in stalk grasses colonized by flocks of storks and other long legged birds that walked in stately manners, some of them a color of pink that surprised me. Our braggart passenger said the pink birds was called spoonbills on account of their bills was like spoons. Small birds scuttled about in the water as well, and overhead soared numerous gulls. The air was damp and cool and unnaturally heavy under the gray shroud of clouds, and it seemed to me that the state of the world as I knew it had changed entirely, with all these strange shrubs and creatures to one side, and the long stretch of water off to the other. I thought of my mare waiting for me in Boerne, and of people and places I knew back home in the hills, and

I wondered how I would find things there now, and what I might say to the widow if she was to knock on my bedroom door. I questioned if I could find the same comfort from her that she had tried to find from me. It seemed like we was both of us lost causes.

At times on this leg of the way the baby become fussy and your mother covered herself with the poncho and nursed her beneath it. The braggart traveling with us talked of the pirate Lafeet burying a stash of treasure at a place called Blackjack on the bay, and yammered on about Indianola and how it was banged up less by the Yankees than by Confederates when they found out that the Yankees was coming. They had tore up the wharves and warehouses and set off a bunch of gunpowder within the lighthouse over on Matagorda Island, leaving it but a hollowed shell that listed off to the side and was at risk of falling over, the bank of sand under it being washed out by the tides. They had taken the light out and hid it from Yankees, he said, but it was back now, and sat atop a wobbly wooden structure until the lighthouse might be fixed.

Shortly before six in the evening we rolled into Indianola past a blacksmith shop and a gas lamp depot advertising safety gas lamps warranted not to explode. Also a meat market and dry goods emporium. The air smelled strongly of salt and fish. Roads was jammed with commerce coming and going. Signs pointed the way to a bathhouse off near the wharves, and we passed by a ice cream saloon and shops of millinery and toilet items and what appeared houses of ill fame. Taverns was crowded, as it was that time of the day.

Our stage pulled up at the Casimir House on a street near the wharves. The braggart departed to his home, whilst you and your mother and Horhay, along with the other two passengers riding with us, went into the Casimir House to buy your tickets for passage to New Orleans.

Being unclean and shabbily dressed I did not go in but assisted the driver unloading mail parcels and piling them into a large pushcart. From where I stood I could see the wharves and a long pier that reached out over the water. A large ship was docked at the end of the pier, and I figured it was the one that would take you. The water was only a bay, and not the gulf, although it spread to the horizon.

The name on the ship was Harlan. It was a steamer with a smokestack rising out of the center and large paddle wheels on the sides. There was two tall masts but no sails I could see. Folks milled about on the deck and others was on the pier and appeared to be waiting in line to board. I would of liked a closer look at that time, but wanted to keep a eye on my satchel with the madstone in it, as well as Horhay's hide bag and your mother's duffel that she had purchased in San Antonio to replace the one stole from the stagecoach. The duffel held all that your mother owned, including her Hammond Bulldog pistol and the blue dress, also the poorly fitted dress given to her in Boerne, and the scanty one bought by Dickie. It held as well the white shift imparted to her in Ecleto, that had no sleeves to it, and toiletries. As well, it held a few items you had been given, including the creatures I'd carved for you.

Tot, here I am going on about such things as the town, and the braggart, and your mother's bag, on account of wanting to play for time. It seems like time is ticking now as I write you this account the same as if we just now stopped at the Casimir House and your mother and Horhay and you was inside buying the tickets. I'm inclined to go on about Indianola and the wharves and piers, and schooners and sloops out on the bay, the sorts of which I had read of in Moby Dick, and mostly the steamship Harlan secured at the end of the pier, awaiting for you to board it. I'm inclined to go on about Moby Dick hisself. Also about a freight wagon that rolled past loaded with barrels reeking of tallow, and how noisy things was, and a long parade of French sheep just landed from somewhere and coming up the street with half a dozen large shepherd dogs. The sheep was bleating for food, or water, or maybe just missing their fields in France, and a herd of beeves was moaning on a wharf down the way, headed off to somewhere I felt sure they didn't want to be going.

But I have promised to stick to the point and not go on about other things, and these is all other things. The point is that you and your mother was leaving. When you come out of the Casimir House she had a firm grip on your hand. You had got wind of the fact that there was not time to build sand forts with me, and you was complaining about it. Horhay walked out behind you. Him and your mother was urging for you to hurry.

You seen me waiting for you, and run to me, and asked was we going to make sand forts. You nagged I had promised that we could do that.

I told you we was now out of time, and how sorry I felt about it.

But you become upset in a way I had not before seen. You had withstood the stagecoach thieves acting to be Comanches taking your things, and you had been all right seeing your mother shoot somebody you did not know was your father, and seeing one of your uncles laid out in a stupor whilst you was hiding under the bed, and watching another get killed whilst tied to the wheel of a wagon, going round and round, and a third nearly done in as well. And all of that is not even to mention the fear you must of felt on hearing the threats your terrible uncles made of hauling you off from your mother, and what you must of felt at bearing witness to all of your mother's pains when she give birth to the baby.

You had held up. You had kept your wits through what was doled out, taking the days as they come and the facts as they stood.

But now at the moment of your departure, things was too much for you of a sudden and you begun pitching a fit about building forts in the sand. You hollered at me that I'd promised you. You yelled at your mother that nothing she said ever turned out right. You waved your arms about, and wailed and cried, and was deeply aggrieved at what you figured was my deception. People was looking at you. I felt a dog to of made the promise and talked it up to such a degree. You worked yourself into such a fit of frustration that you laid down in the dirt and kicked your legs and become dead weight.

I knelt alongside you and did what I could to explain the situation to you, about how I wanted to build the forts as bad as you did and was equally disappointed that we was now out of time. However, nothing I said made you feel any better. There was a great deal of noise and confusion, and you was cheated and understandably felt betrayed, and it was myself who had done it.

I wanted to fall to pieces in the same manner, and cry about the unfairness of life and how I was brokenhearted. The baby, as well, took up the terrible feeling that things was amiss, and maybe that life was hard, and no good, for she commenced to yowl, and your mother was at a loss to comfort her.

The stage driver informed your mother she better get moving if she was to get on the ship, and he started off down to the pier with his pushcart of mail. Another man come along at that same time and hurried your mother, saying the ship was about to depart. Horhay hoisted you off the ground with his one good arm whilst you was thrashing and yelling. You was still screeching at me to take you to build the sand forts, whilst he carried you down the pier.

By that time your mother was crying as well. She might of been crying for leaving me, or for the way you was acting, or for leaving her mother and father and kin in Texas when she didn't know if she'd ever see them again. She hardly looked in my eyes. She was trying to deal with the screaming baby.

I picked up her bag and walked down to the wharf and out to the end of the pier with her. Both her and Horhay tried to give me some money, as they knew I had only a dollar or two to get all the way home on. But how could I take a cent from them. Your mother had nearly nothing to spare, and how could I take from a woman regardless. Horhay was short of money hisself, and he had a long way to travel. How could I take the five dollars he kept trying to give me.

Him and your mother was both still trying to hand me money, and I was declining and telling your mother I would write to her, when a sailor grabbed hold of the bags and carried them up the plank, and the ship blasted a whistle so loud we all covered our ears. The lingering passengers on the dock hurried to board, and you and your mother and the baby and Horhay boarded along with them.

I lost sight of you at that time, but seen you again when the ship took off and gained some distance from the dock and headed out to the pass. You was standing behind the rail of the deck and looking at me. You appeared to of stopped crying. Your mother and Horhay stood either side of you, your mother holding the baby. Your face had a look of puzzlement and forlornness, there being a great deal happening too fast for you, or me either, I own, to make sense of. Soon you was too far off for me to make out how you looked, and then you was too far off for me to make out who you was, and then you was too far out for me to see you at all.

* * *

I stood a long time watching the Harlan become small in the stretch of water. The sun must of been low by then, but the clouds was too heavy and dark for me to tell. Folks about me walked back to the wharf, and things become quiet, and after a while there was nothing more than the sounds of water slapping at beams below the pier, and fish jumping every so often.

When I could no longer see the ship nor the smoke that trailed from the stack, I figured you must be nearly out to the pass, or even gone through it already. I was sorry how your departure had proved messy and quick and disheartening, and sorry I couldn't do any better by you and your mother.

But it is the nature of folks, in general, to get on with things, I guess, and mosquitoes was buzzing about me. I was hungry and had to figure a way to earn my supper. I returned to the wharf and dug in my pocket to see what I had in the way of money, and what do you think I should find, but the five dollar bill Horhay had tried to give me. I guess he had stuffed it in there when I wasn't looking. Something about that kindness broke loose my sadness, and I sat on the wharf and soaked the toes of my boots with tears for quite some while. Then I went up the street to find dinner.

I come to a tavern called the Green Tree and for twenty-five cents was served a meal of crabs called blue ones and stone ones, the flesh being hard to dig out of the shells. Also I had some boiled shrimp. I tried eating the tails, so that was a issue and I had to be told better. I ate a fish called a flounder as well. I declined the oysters sealed in a can, as those didn't appear enticing. I offered the keeper I'd clean the tables and sweep the floor and wash dishes if I might earn a hearty breakfast for in the morning, as I had to spare what was left of my five for the journey home. He agreed, and I did the work, and he was happy with how I done it, and I inquired if I might sleep in the tavern, but he declined that I could.

It was muggy outside when I left, and the town was dark. Hordes of mosquitoes flocked about me. I went down to the bathhouse to see if it might be open for use and cheap, but found it locked for the night. I walked the streets at a fast pace to out smart the mosquitoes, but they found me wherever I went. I'd heard they could feast on a person until his blood would not clot, so I begun to feel desperate. There might be fewer of them where there's fewer people to feast on, I figured, and walked a ways out of the town and along the shore on a grassy and beaten trail. Trees alongside grew bent to the wind and there was no sandhills, the actual shoreline being far out on the long barrier lands of the island and peninsula that shielded the bay. You and myself could not of made much of a sand fort, Tot, even had there been the time. There was shells, however, and I picked up a few, thinking to send them to you.

After a while of trying to outpace mosquitoes I stripped off my trousers and got in the water, but mosquitoes still pestered my face. The water was muddy and chilly. Pretty soon I enjoyed all the fun I could stand of slapping my face and headed back to the pier where I figured the breeze might confound the creatures.

Along the way there, a curious shape in the water got my attention. I thought it a devilfish of some sort. It drifted to shore and revealed itself as a sheet of oilcloth, so I fished it out and carried it back to the wharf and out to the end of the pier, and hung my wet shirt on a post, and sat and covered myself with the oilcloth up to my eyeballs.

For a long time I sat thus, half naked, under the wet oilcloth, watching the blinking light of the makeshift lighthouse out on Matagorda Island and trying to picture it out there, all those miles away, atop its wobbly wooden base amongst the sandhills on a island too far off to make out. It seemed to blink out of nowhere, atop nothing. Time and again I counted the seconds between the flashes.

It was a lonely night without you and your mother. I missed Dickie and Horhay as well. The gap between the end of that pier and my home back in the hills in Comfort seemed a world to cross, and I dreaded making the journey alone, passing by all those places where we had traveled together. The sound of water knocking against the beams under the pier disheartened me further. I tried to encourage myself into a better humor by thinking how I might someday go on a cattle drive like I'd dreamed about doing. But pushing cattle up north had started to seem a dull trudge of a outing, nothing but tick fever and cramp colic and dry watering holes. A lot of mornings of heading out, and a lot of nights of rounding up and making coffee of used up grounds over weed fires. Calves born on the trail would need to be shot to keep their mothers from lagging, and the mothers would moan and bellow for them for miles along the way. It felt a grim business of a sudden, and no fun at all.

After a time, a fog come in and I had to squint to make out the blink of the lighthouse. Pretty soon there was nothing around me but fog. I recalled how Benjamin Franklin said a person who thinks hisself in possession of all truths, and believes those who differ are far in the wrong, compares to a man walking in foggy weather. Those at some distance ahead on the road appear to him wrapped in the fog, and those behind him, wrapped in the fog as well, and those in the fields either side, all wrapped in the fog. Yet nearby and about him, things appear clear, despite he is just as much in the fog as any of them.

For my own part, it was plain to me then, and I think in other ways always had been, how thick of a fog I was in. I couldn't make out the blink of the light at all after a while, nor even the region where it had been. It seemed like I sat in the middle of nowhere, just some gray place, and there I was, shirtless and cold and wet, hunched under a soaked shred of oilcloth and trying to see something.

After a time I give up, and laid down, and went sound out asleep.

*   *   *

I roused to the loud sound of gulls screaming overhead. The fog had somewhat lifted but daylight was yet murky. I retrieved my shirt from the post and made my way to the bathhouse and there paid twenty cents and extra for soap, and come out clean but for my clothes.

The tavern keeper proved good for his word and fed me a solid breakfast of buttermilk, eggs, honey, and a good portion of a mutton leg. I sat by the window whilst I ate, and kept my eye on the mail stage outside the Casimir House across the way so it wouldn't depart without me. But my thoughts was with you and your mother and Horhay. I wondered how you was faring out on the ship, and if the waters was rough, and if the baby had learned to nurse better.

When I seen two passengers place their luggage into the stage boot and the driver load mail, I went over and boarded.

I probably should of felt grateful to be clean and not hungry on the way back to Lavaca and then on to Victoria, but traveling alongside two passengers who appeared nearly as gloomy as me, I sank into a melancholy and begun to pity myself. I thought how you and your mother was gone, and how I could never forget you. I had nothing I cared to look forward to, and not much I cared to look back on, as my life from that vantage felt to me like a waste of my time. My hope of a cattle drive had turned dark. As well, my desire to set eyes on the ocean had come to just about nothing, as I had seen only the bay, and not even the gulf, and certainly not the ocean, and nothing of waves nor white sandhills nor broad stretches of sandy shoreline. This was a disappointment.

I went round and round in my mind on the way things stood.

I had mules to return in Boerne, one of them lame and laid up in Ecleto, payments owed for their let, a mare to retrieve, and a widow waiting in Comfort who did not love me, with chickens to feed. My wagon, along with the double rig I'd borrowed from Mr Reed of the Reed House in Boerne, awaited me in Victoria. I had but one mule to hitch until I should reach Ecleto and hitch up the lame one as well, and how could I harness one mule to a double rig. I would need to purchase a single rig, but I had no money. I could trade in the double rig in Victoria, but I'd need it when I arrived in Ecleto. As well, Mr Reed would be looking to have it back. I could sell my wagon and ride the mule home, but I'd have to pick up the lame mule and lead her behind me most of the way, and would need to spend what I made for the wagon to pay for the rig and for rent on the mules when I should arrive in Boerne. And where would that leave me when I got home.

Without a wagon, that's where. I might as well of been strapped with the cursed necklace, for all the misfortunes laid in my path. I wished to be on the ship with you and your mother, and felt cross with my father for having me promise to care for my sister despite that he knew how hardheaded she was. I felt cross with my sister as well, for taking off like she'd done, and for leaving me by myself to search for her as long as I had, and to miss her and wait around for her to come back, if she ever should even choose to. Her general selfishness, and not even to mention her thoughtlessness toward me, even before she took off, and even in spite of I think she did care about me, seemed harder than ever to tolerate. I tried to remind myself to feel pity for her and the lot in life she'd got handed, but mostly now I felt anger and disappointment at how her running off had left me tied down to her, despite she was nowhere to be found.

These was my morbid and bitter thoughts when our stage rolled into Victoria six hours later and I got my miserable self out, and there stood Dickie. He was holding the reins of Silas Banes' horse that he had rode off on. I could hardly believe it was him. My spirits lifted. I had thought not to see him again. I nearly run and embraced him.

What are you doing here, I asked.

Waiting for you, he said. How else did you think to get home with one mule and a double rig and no money.

It's the oddest thing in the world, Tot, the friends you make in a lifetime. The first I'd seen Dickie he was a stranger shatting alongside the Ficklin privy in Comfort and hollering at the sheriff within. And now here he was, waiting for me in Victoria when there was plenty of things more beneficial to him that he could be doing.

But what of the necklace, I inquired.

Gone, he replied. Gone with that son of a bitch Murry.

He explained he'd spent twenty-four hours trying to track down Murry, and not found even a lead. He'd seen the sheriff's posse out scouring the region, empty handed as well.

Nobody in this town nor twenty miles down any road seen hide nor hair of a snakebit devil dragging a leg with no cap on the knee, he said. He's a ghost. He's gone. It's like the curse swallowed him whole.

Myself and Dickie then had a good talk. He explained he intended to give up the search for the necklace, or else it would draw him into its power and he might spend his whole life trying to track it down. He said it was like a callous woman, hard to let go of on account of you happen to love her. He'd loved one of them for a time, and finally said so long to her, and never been gladder.

Thankful though I was to see Dickie, my conscience knew there was things he would rather do with his time than to help me get home. I advised he could hunt for riches washed up from old shipwrecks, as there was known to be those along these shores. I relayed how the braggart I'd met on the stage from Lavaca to Indianola had said that the pirate Lafeet had buried a bunch of treasures at a place called Blackjack, in a point somewhere on the bay.

You should search for that, I told Dickie. I can get home on my own.

But he wouldn't allow as I could. He said I looked badly hunched up and worn down, having gone around the bend like he'd warned me not to, and I appeared rudely chewed up by mosquitoes. Besides, he hated mosquitoes and didn't like sodden sand and salt water and vastly preferred dry air and dry land. He planned to travel with me as far as Ecleto, where I could retrieve the lame sister mule. If she'd healed enough to do her share of the pulling, he would depart from me there and ride north to Austin, and present his paper for slaying Dale Banes and see if the governor might square up. For my part, I could continue west from Ecleto and stop in San Antonio to collect the fee Mr Pate of the Ficklin had promised, and which I had not been paid. I could then go on to Boerne, and return the mules and retrieve my mare there, and make my way home to Comfort no more impoverished than when I had started.

That being Dickie's determination, and my being grateful for it, we went to the sheriff so I might retrieve my wagon. He was kind to us, and agreed how Dickie had earned the right to Silas Banes' horse, on account of his part in the death of the man and our needing the horse to get home. We said our goodbyes to the sheriff, and hitched the horse alongside the mule, despite neither of them was keen about that, and rolled out by late afternoon.

*   *   *

Tot, I've learned that there's human traits which prove bothersome in some situations yet are unexpectedly welcome in others. This was the case with Dickie's habit of telling more stories than people in general would like to hear. He talked the entire way to Ecleto, a journey of three days and two nights, and I was glad about that, on account of it kept me from drowning myself in longings for you and your mother. He remarked on a range of subjects and spoke of his many digestive issues and told of a time a intolerable bowel stoppage led to the station keeper at Pegleg Crossing on the San Saba providing relief for him by shoving a gallon of mineral oil up his rear end with a horse plunger and nozzle. He talked of a pack of greyhound dogs the Ficklin kept at the Concho station for hunting down antelope, and of bear baitings and dog fights and cock fights and a man he once met whose whiskers was scalped while the hairs on his head was untouched. He told of the warrior named Crazy Horse acting as decoy and tricking a hundred U.S. soldiers into a ambush where they was all killed, although I already knew about him. Also attacks on stagemen and burning of stations. He said he was passing through Central City in Colorado last year when the town raised up five thousand dollars and offered twenty-five dollars apiece for Indian scalps if the ears was attached. These folks was quite tired of the Indians, he said, and the Indians was quite tired of them.

It was all gruesome stories he told, as I guess he knew they would get my attention and keep me afloat somewhat from my thoughts. No doubt he was figuring, like I was, how it can be rude to pity yourself for lost love when you've still hung onto your scalp.

We arrived to Ecleto of a evening after bad weather again and dined at the station with Mr Sandler. The good sister mule had fared well and seemed able to pull. Her sister and her seemed glad to be back together. I think they was fonder of one another than either of them had let on.

Dickie departed early the following morning, his farewell being the only brief thing he'd said the whole time since I'd met him. I think he was sorry to part with me, as I was with him, not knowing if I would see him again. Neither of us saw any use in prolonging what was unpleasant.

It was a long, long slog on my own after that. I arrived to San Antonio several days later with the mules and collected the twelve dollars Mr Pate had beforehand promised the Ficklin would pay me for bringing the mail from Boerne. I stopped in at the photographer's shop and asked if he still had the faulty tintype he'd taken of you and myself. He dug it out of a stack of other such faulty tintypes and give it to me. Your face was blurred on account of you turned it to look up at me, but I can remember your face with no trouble and I'm grateful of having the tintype.

I went on to Boerne and returned the mules where I had let them, and found my mare in Mr Reed's pen. She appeared fat and rested, and nickered and trotted over when she seen me walking in her direction. I was so happy to see her I nearly cried. She is the best of mares, and my longest friend, and the only remaining gift that my father once give me, other than his nice razor, as I might of afore stated.

The following morning I give back Mr Reed's double harness, and took back my single one, and hitched up my mare, and rolled out for home, where I found things mostly as I had left them. I had been gone sixteen days, those being ten for the journey, with all the excitement and mishaps, and but six to travel back home. I stood in the widow's kitchen and explained to her, hat in hand, the best way I could, that I'd found a woman I loved and I might not be much of a comfort to her anymore. She was kind about this, and did not seem greatly to care, on account of she missed her passed husband and I was not him.

Therefore I settled back into her home, and into my work. But my heart and my thoughts was uneasy. I commenced to doubt myself and to wonder if maybe I should of gone off on that boat with you and your mother after all. I asked myself if I might, even yet, find my way to New Orleans, and if I could live with myself if I should forsake my sister as trade for my pleasure and happiness. I thought of Samantha returning home and learning that I had left the state and left her with nothing and no one she trusted to turn to. I tried to recall, by the word, my father's request of me in regards to her, and what, by the word, I had promised him. Was it even that promise that tied me to her, or just that I loved that little girl. Every day, I thought of writing your mother and vowing that I would come, but I was uncertain as yet, and what good would a false promise do her.

At the end of June, when I had been home just more than a month, a letter arrived addressed to my name at the Comfort post office, which, as I stated before, is housed in the store across the street from my work shed. The postmaster, Mr Hildebrand, give it to me when I stopped in the store to purchase a piece of cloth to patch up a shirt I had tore. I pretty well knew the letter must be from your mother, as who else would write to me. I carried it over into the shed and opened it there and read it about a dozen times, and have read it so often since then that I know it by heart.

Dear Benjamin, it said. I have got here to New Orleans safe with Tot and the baby. I miss seeing you and hope you will come and bring your sister if she might ever show up. Horhay said on the boat he believes you will come. He told me you have a powerful conscience but maybe a stronger heart. I was sad to part with him at the dock. I wonder if he has made it to Las Bahamas. We was all sick on the boat, even him. Benjamin, I will wait for you no matter if you say you are coming or not. I have told my cousin about you. Although, I have not told her about that night we had in the wagon, and all we said to each other and did with each other at that time. She might not like to hear about that, although she is not awfully prim. At any case, these recollections is private. Also how you helped with the baby. I think on them more than I ought to. Tot asks about you every day. He sometimes asks for his daddy, but mostly he talks about you. We have named the baby Bernice. I hope you will come. Nell.

Tot, you might think such a letter would cause me to pack up my things and start for the boat. Yet my conscience continued to drain me of conviction. I wrote your mother as such, and explained again my hesitations and obligations. Seeing them laid out on the page, they did make good sense to me. But it was plain to me as I wrote, and likely plain to her as she read, that I was up at the edge of giving in, and forgiving myself already, and going to her. I suppose I hadn't expected I'd miss her as much as I did, or rather I hadn't expected the missing to be so stubborn.

She wrote me another time, and said how well you was doing and how you got on with the kids in the house, those being your second cousins and somewhat older, and how they doted on you and the baby. She said she was happy, and thankful to me every day for saving your life with the madstone, and whilst I would like to think that I did, I know it was Horhay who had the stone, and luck or God that put him there in our path. But I won't forget that ride on the ornery mule with you asleep before me. Your head was laid back on my shoulder, and my mind was full of worry for you, and the mist was lifting and the sun was in my eyes. Getting you there to the madstone was the worthiest charge I have carried out in my lifetime. I value the stone as much for that memory as for the chance it might prove useful to someone again, at some other time.

I can't even tell you how often I've read those letters your mother wrote to me.

But in August a letter arrived from your mother's cousin. You might guess of the news it told. It said typhoid fevers come over the house you was in. It come over everyone in the house, and your mother did not last it. She had not been entirely well since she got there, it said, having not regained much of her strength after the journey and birth of Bernice. She had borne her dying with forti-tude and was glad that her children was safe with family, and she give me the credit for that, on account of I hauled them so many miles, through so many troubles, and seen them onto the boat. You and the baby was now recovered, the letter said. It said you had bravely stood the loss of your mother and seemed, since then, to feel a need to care for your sister, encouraging her with the rubber teat on the bottle. The letter said you looked to your cousins as family, and was greatly loved by all, and you and your sister would be educated and well seen to. Your mother had asked, before passing, that I be advised of what had took place.

Tot, of the many things I thought the future might hold after our parting at Indianola, this was not one. Your mother had lived through bad times and grave troubles, and I had not thought that death would take her so quietly. She had lasted the hardships during her time with your father, and give birth to the baby out in a prairie under hard circumstances, and survived threats and dangers, and avoided the yellow fever in Indianola. I believed she was healthy and safe in New Orleans. It seemed to me worse than injustice that the typhoid then took her. It seemed a mistake in the history of how her life should of played, and even a broader, more general mistake in history altogether.

Upon reading the letter with that news, I dropped down into a hole of sadness I have not yet found my way out of these months later. My visions on our long journey, of having a life with you and your mother, was so clamped into my mind that they have become like memories despite that they never happened. I think back to the night in Ecleto when you left your mother to be with me, and I returned you back across the street to be with her. When I got you into that house and looked in the window to see you was settled, the light from the moon broke through clouds and shone in. And there you was, in full light, for that short time, the two of you there in the bed. And there was the room about you, a small rug alongside the bed, a chair in the corner, and a chest of drawers, nicely carved, a washbowl atop it. And for the first time in my life I felt I knew my future. I felt I was already living it, like I was there in the room with you. And yet I wasn't there in the room, and the clouds come over, and that vision was over, and now it become like a memory of a time that never happened, in a place that never was.

Actual occasions happen in actual places, and a person can go to those places, and stand in them and recall the occasions. Yet my visions posing as memories took place in my thoughts and nowhere else, leaving me no place to stand but in my own mind. I suppose the closest we had to a home was my wagon, and there's times when I care to do nothing but lay on the ground under it and stare at the place where I carved your name, and mine alongside it, into the underside of the floorboards. It was the day out in the prairie whilst your mother was pacing with labor pains that I put those names there. You and me had gone under the wagon for shade, the day being hot, and I told you the tale of Moby Dick and whittled a cat and a hog for you, to go with the dog I had made you, so you might have something to play with. The smell of weeds and flowers comes back to me when I'm under there now, and it's like ghosts of us, of a sort, live there, and I visit them, time to time. I've carved your mother's name beside ours, as I think of her laying her head on my shoulder the night of the hail when we sheltered there, and how I wanted to keep you two warm. So she's under the wagon with us. I can feel of the names with my fingers, as proof to myself that we was once there.

But that is no longer your story, Tot. It becomes mine. I vowed at the start to keep to the point and not go on about other things, so I will return to matters pertaining to you.

When I learned of your mother's passing, I wished I could fetch you to live with me, but how would that ever help you. Any future that I might give you was nothing but small potatoes compared to what you would have. As well, I would not be much able to care for your sister, and you should never be parted from her.

The only manner by which I could benefit you, it seemed to me, was to write this account. You might recall from earlier pages how your mother had feared she might pass away in those weeds and grasses out on the prairie whilst laboring with your sister. She had asked would I tell you all that I knew about her if that should happen. She said you should know of your father as well and be told he was cruel but had loved you regardless, and be told why he was dead.

So I have written these things for you. I hope you will read this account and that it might settle some things in your mind as to how things actually was. I know it can't settle what might of been and never will come to be, on account of you've lost your mother, who was so stanchly devoted to you.

Now, Tot, on what is known as a lighter note, you might find it of interest that Dickie showed up here in town again, a couple of weeks ago, and there is a story to tell. He had with him the four hundred dollars owed him for killing your uncle Dale, and was stopping by on his way back out west. He had on new boots and a nice hat, and carried plenty of cash, but allowed how the money was not a real treasure, as he had not found it but rather received it, and it did not make him happy. His plan was to tread back over his tracks and search out the place at the Horsehead Crossing near Castle Gap where he'd dug up Carlota's riches. If Horhay's tale was correct, then he'd overlooked a good many of those, which was silver platters and gold vessels and whatnot, and they was not cursed like the necklace.

And speaking of that item, he showed me a page he'd tore out of a newspaper in Austin. I believe what it said will interest you. It told how a Mrs Banes out of Grayson county had got arrested for attempting to sell a necklace known to belong to the Empress Carlota of Mexico and thought to be stolen. She took it over the border into Louisiana and tried to extract a good amount from a jewelry expert who, it turned out, knew of the necklace, having recalled a likeness he'd seen of the empress sketched in the New Orleans Picayune newspaper before the time she departed from Mexico. He reported Mrs Banes to the law and the necklace was taken from her. The government shipped it off to the empress, who is currently shut away at a palace in Belgium and thought to of gone insane, but still might like having it back. Mrs Banes was arrested for trying to peddle a stolen item, yet released on saying her son was the one that give it to her. Her son was therefore arrested and discovered to be a member of the Swamp Fox gang known to be murderers of freedmen. He had been living of late with his parents, the paper said, in a decrepit condition, a part cripple and currently mute on account of his tongue appeared to of partly gone missing in one of his bloody encounters. He was arrested for dealing in stolen goods and jailed at the prison in Huntsville. His mother, who already had suffered the loss of two sons by the names of Silas and Dale, and presumably also a third son, named Micah, although no one was sure what happened to him, had shortly afterwards discovered her husband dead as well, kicked in the head by his horse.

The newspaper noted it seemed as if the family was cursed. This give Dickie a great deal of pleasure. It also give him false confidence in what he claims is his natural good luck for having got shed of the necklace, such that he plans to trust his luck until the string should run out. I believe his thinking to be wrongheaded, as how many lucky people dig up a cursed necklace to start with.

I told him of my concerns, but nevertheless he took off for the west. When he was gone, I got the bug to fetch my own bounty in Austin. I intend to go soon. The journey will cost me a couple of weeks of no work, but if the governor squares with me, I'll come back with four hundred dollars. I'll set that money aside and might go on a cattle drive in a year, or maybe in three, and add to my savings further that way. Then maybe someday I'll build up a ranch like I've thought about doing, and maybe my sister will come back home and I'll give her a life of leisure to do as pleases, that being her nature regardless.

The hard truth I face sometimes is that she might never come back and I might as well of gone off to New Orleans with you and your mother when we was in Indianola. Things might of turned out different for her.

But thinking of how things might of been is never a help to what is. And who can guess of the future. Dickie once stated that buried treasure always gets found. It never stays lost nor buried.

And despite how my sister run off in pursuit of a pipe dream, she is a treasure to me, and if Dickie is right about what he said, she'll turn up sooner or later. I think if a person should talk as much as Dickie, there's bound to be words of wisdom come out at some point.

I am hopeful, as well, of seeing you someday again. I can always be found through the post office in Comfort if you would care to write to me, or if you should need me for any cause whatsoever. If I move away in the future, I'll always leave word where I am. I fully believe that things will be well with me, and that years from now, when you read this, they will have been well with me for some time.

I'll send this account care of your mother's cousin with a note asking for you to receive it when you are nineteen. I hope you will read it and find that it answers some questions. Otherwise you might tinker too much in your mind about how things might of been different, when you won't even know how they actually was, or wonder how things was set on the paths they went on, and who fixed them that way for better or worse. Ceaseless wondering of that sort could be bothersome to you. Reckoning offers more peace to the heart, as it has a end.

Therefore I'm heading across the street to the store with the post office, nearby the Ficklin station where I first seen you and your mother seated within the stagecoach. I will send the pages inside a package, along with my highest hopes for your future, and these few shells I picked up from the shore at Indianola on that sad night, and a very large share of respect.

Your friend evermore and no matter what,
Benjamin Shreve

NOTES ON THE HISTORY

In telling this story, I've taken a few minor liberties, moving several historical events to a year later or earlier than they actually happened. For example, the hunt for silver ore in El Paso, which Dickie describes in the initial pages as "a bust," took place in 1869, not 1868, and the Christmas massacre at the Smith home occurred on Christmas of 1868, several months after Nell mentions it in her conversation with the Freedmen's Bureau agent in Victoria. Aside from this type of small and intentional discrepancy, I've kept the story within the confines of recorded history. Cullen Montgomery Baker, known as the Swamp Fox of the Sulphur, was an actual outlaw whose gang terrorized Blacks in the tristate area of Texas, Louisiana, and Arkansas just as depicted. I should add that William G. Kirkman, the agent of the Freedmen's Bureau stationed in that area and mentioned as the agent to whom Nell reported the gang's crimes and locations, was shot dead by Cullen Baker and his gang while leaving his office late one night in October of 1868, which would be shortly after the end of this story. The biography *Cullen Montgomery Baker: Reconstruction Desperado,* by Barry A. Crouch and Donaly E. Brice, gives a thorough account of this murder and other crimes of the Swamp Fox gang.

The towns and way stations mentioned in the book all existed as described. The lighthouse on Matagorda Island, damaged during the Civil War and dismantled in 1867, as stated, was moved and reconstructed two miles to the southwest in 1873, where it now stands. Indianola itself, once a thriving Texas port second in size only to Galveston, was demolished by a hurricane in 1875. The captain of the steamer *Harlan* carried word of the devastation in a letter to the editor of the Galveston *News*: "We are destitute. The town is gone...Dead bodies are strewn for twenty miles along the bay. Nine-tenths of the houses are destroyed. Send us help, for God's sake. D. W. Crain, District Attorney." Indianola was rebuilt but struck by a second hurricane in 1886, followed by a fire that completed the ruin. Most of the area once occupied by the town is now under seawater. A marker on the shoreline designates the place where the courthouse once stood. For readers drawn to the story of Indianola's rise and fall, I recommend Brownson Malsch's extensive history of the place, titled *Indianola: The Mother of Western Texas*, and Linda Wolff's compact guide: *Indianola and Matagorda Island, 1837–1887.*

Matagorda Bay and Pass Cavallo (often called Horse Pass), through which Benjamin lost sight of the steamer *Harlan* as it headed into the Gulf of Mexico, are known to archaeologists and treasure hunters for the many ships wrecked there, most of the remains of which are still lost deep underwater. Not mentioned in the story but of interest is the history of the ship *La Belle*. It was part of Robert de La Salle's expedition and was wrecked in Matagorda Bay in 1686 but has been excavated and is on display at the Bullock Texas State History Museum, in Austin.

Like any writer who deals with the past, I relied on numerous scholarly histories such as the ones I've mentioned above—too many to list them all. I'm especially beholden to historians whose books enlightened me about the hazardous days of reconstructing our nation—or attempting to—after the Civil War. I would refer those interested in the subject to *The Army in Texas During Reconstruction, 1865–1870*, by William L Richter; *The Dance of Freedom: Texas African Americans During Reconstruction*, by Barry A. Crouch; *Grass-Roots Reconstruction in Texas, 1865–1880*, by Randolph B. Campbell; and *Murder and Mayhem: The War of Reconstruction in Texas*, by James M. Smallwood, Barry A. Crouch, and Larry Peacock. Readers with specific interest in the fictional character "Horhay" might refer to *The Black Seminoles: History of a Freedom-Seeking People*, by Kenneth W. Porter; *Our Land Before We Die: The Proud Story of the Seminole Negro*, by Jeff Guinn; *Black Seminoles in the Bahamas*, by Rosalyn Howard; *Florida's Negro War: Black Seminoles and the Second Seminole War 1835–1842*, by Anthony E. Dixon; and *Black Indians: A Hidden Heritage*, by William Loren Katz.

As a last point, I should admit that madstones are, of course, ineffective in drawing the rabies virus out of wounds. However, in historical times, when the animal bite failed to fully penetrate—or when the animal didn't, in fact, carry the rabies virus—the stones were thought to provide cures and became valued possessions, passed down in families through generations. They are essentially gallstones made of concretions of mineral salts mixed with hairs and fibers that accumulate in the bellies of cattle, horses, deer, and other animals. Those found in albino deer were thought to have the most curative powers.

ACKNOWLEDGMENTS

As always, I'm deeply thankful to Stephen (Steve) Harrigan, a profoundly great writer and my longtime friend, for his candid and thoughtful commentary on this story while I was making it up.

I'm thankful as well to my late friend Kenneth Groesbeck, who answered an endless stream of questions about subjects such as the anatomy of old wagons and the distance an aging horse or a pair of mules can pull a wagon on a rocky road in a single day. He also forgave me when I drove the fictional sister mules a little farther on a few days, in the service of timing, than they might actually have been able to go. Kenneth passed away before the publication of this book, but even when he was severely ill he volunteered to read the final draft in case I had made any mistakes in that sort of detail.

Lawrence T. (Larry) Jones III alerted me to the existence of Henry A. Doerr's photography studio in San Antonio in the 1860s and shared his passionate explanation of how tintypes were made.

It's impossible to state the extent of my appreciation for my agent and cherished friend, Gail Hochman, and for my friend James D. (Jim) Landis for introducing me to Gail long ago. Gail placed this book, and my last, with the incomparable editor Ben George and the extraordinary team at Little, Brown—a stroke of good fortune for me. My hat stays off to Gail, always, and I offer a heartfelt thanks to the publisher and deputy publisher of Little, Brown—Bruce Nichols and Craig Young, respectively—for accepting the book for publication.

Ben George's unflagging editorial attention to even the smallest details, as well as his occasionally relentless counsel in the face of my resistance—such as "I am suggesting (coming close to insisting?) that here we do need to have a few sentences about…"—have improved this book in too many ways even to keep track of. Ben is a real champion for his writers and has nurtured this story and these characters in the most personal way. Thank you, Ben!

I'm also grateful to Barbara Clark for her careful copyediting and her willingness to overlook Benjamin Shreve's misspellings and haphazard use of punctuation, and to Pat Jalbert-Levine for managing the book's production.

Gregg Kulick created a stunning jacket design and generously allowed me, with my two cents, into the process. My niece Amy, her son Trip, and my nephew-in-law, Joe, rode around in circles on horses named Dollar and Rock while my niece Christine snapped photos that Gregg then skillfully integrated into the jacket art. Those were some very fun days, and I love seeing family there on the jacket, riding into the story.

Alyssa Persons, Danielle Finnegan, Bryan Christian, Maya Guthrie, and Sarah Maymi at Little, Brown have been thoroughly helpful with getting this book out of the house and into the world. I couldn't have wished for a better team.

Paul Bogaards and Stephanie Kloss of Bogaards Public Relations also went to bat for this story. Paul's singular enthusiasm and long-standing knowledge of the industry is a boon to any author fortunate enough to have a book in his hands.

I would be negligent not to acknowledge the many chroniclers in the past whose writings showed me a period of time that otherwise would have been unknowable to me. The most helpful of these accounts were Nathaniel Alston Taylor's *Two Thousand Miles in Texas on Horseback* and Mark Twain's *Roughing It*, which Twain described as "a personal narrative...a record of several years of variegated vagabondizing" and which offers uncountable intriguing observations, some of which have found their way, in various forms, into Dickie Bell's experiences while searching for treasure out West. If not for Mark Twain, I would never have known of the flies at Mona Lake.

Most of all, as always, I'm grateful to my husband, Marc Lewis, my son, Joseph, my daughter, Lizzie, and my entire extended family for beautifully and generously giving me the kind of love and companionship that my character Benjamin Shreve is lacking at the end of this story but that we know, from a glimpse of him at the end of my novel *The Which Way Tree*, he will eventually find.

ABOUT THE AUTHOR

Elizabeth Crook has published five previous novels, including *The Which Way Tree*; *The Night Journal*, which received the Spur Award from Western Writers of America; and *Monday, Monday*, a Kirkus Reviews Best Book of the Year and winner of the Jesse H. Jones Award from the Texas Institute of Letters. She lives in Austin, Texas, with her family.

About the Author

Elizabeth Crook has published five previous novels, including *The Which Way Tree*; *The Night Journal*, which received the Spur Award from Western Writers of America; and *Monday, Monday*, a Kirkus Reviews Best Book of the Year and winner of the Jesse H. Jones Award from the Texas Institute of Letters. She lives in Austin, Texas, with her family.